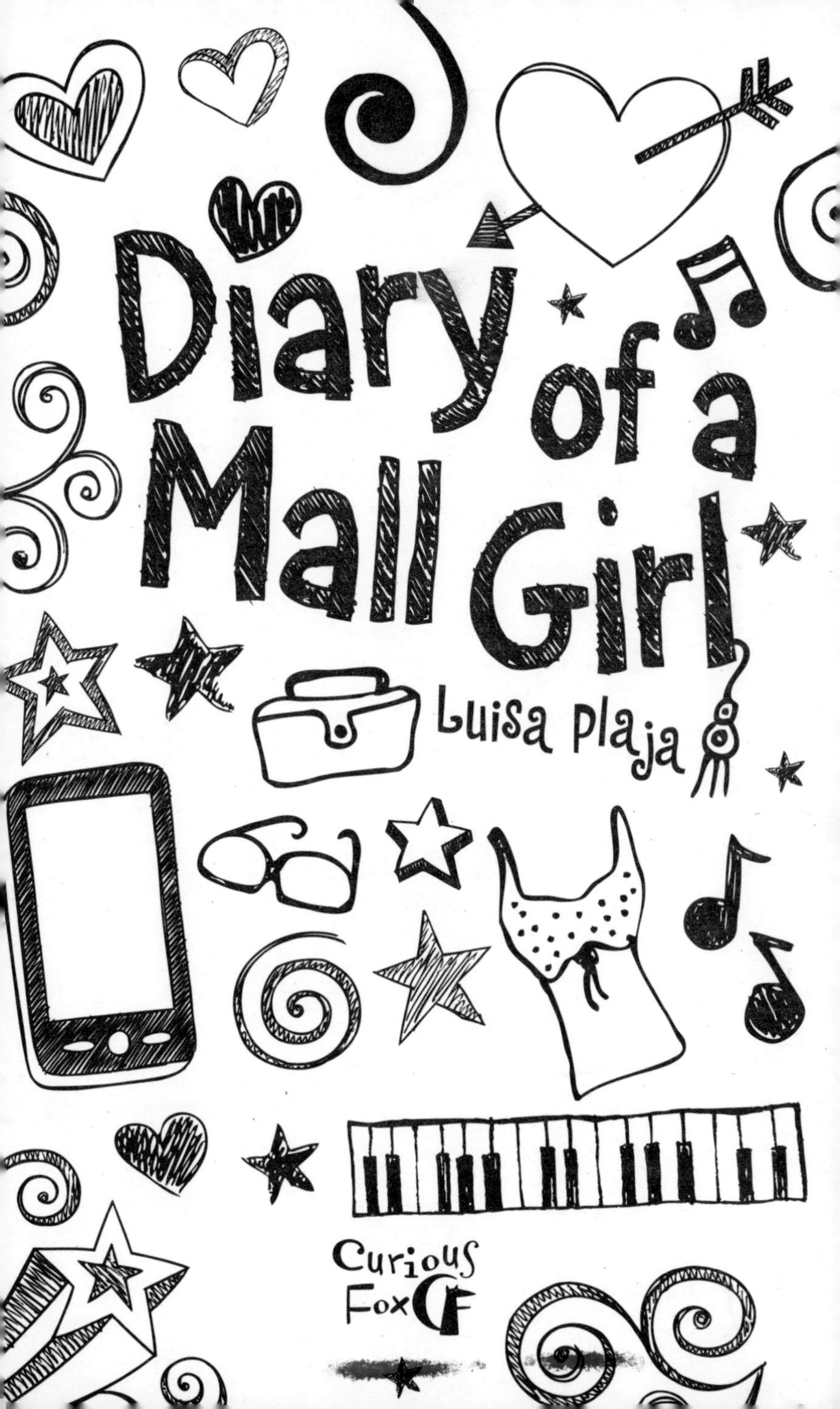
Diary of a Mall Girl
Luisa Plaja
Curious Fox

First published in 2013 by Curious Fox,
an imprint of Capstone Global Library Limited,
7 Pilgrim Street, London, EC4V 6LB – Registered company
number: 6695582

www.curious-fox.com

First published in 2011 as a serialised ebook by Fiction
Express (www.fictionexpress.co.uk)

Cover design by Victoria Allen

Cover images:
Shutterstock – © Maaike Boot; © Anastasiya Zalevska;
© blue67design

All characters in this publication are fictitious and any
resemblance to real persons, living or dead, is purely
coincidental.

ISBN 978 1 782 02012 7
17 16 15 14 13
10 9 8 7 6 5 4 3 2 1

A CIP catalogue for this book is available from the
British Library.

Typeset in Palatino 10pt

To all the readers whose votes and messages helped to shake up Molly's life, with special thanks to Zoe Crook, Alexandra Fouracres, Andie Frogley, Emily Gale, Caroline Green, Amber Kirk-Ford, Daisy Lovick, Jenni Nock and Kip Wilson Rechea, and extra thanks to Laura Durman and Laura Knowles.

Friday, 6th May

Tales of woe from the Hart residence, 5th floor, The Lilies eco-mall, Lilyford

My life is OVER!!!

When I told Mum this FACT almost an hour ago, she waved a giant gloop-covered spoon at me and said, "Don't be so melodramatic, Molly. And can you get your brother for me? Tell him dinner's ready."

"JAMIE!!! I'm not even exaggerating, Mum. I swear. JAMIE!!! My life is absolutely over. It's official. JAMIE!!!"

Mum clutched her head and staggered about, still holding the dripping spoon. "Ow. Molly! My ears! We do have neighbours, you know. In fact, never mind our block of flats. They can probably hear you at the other side of the shopping centre!"

So who was being melodramatic *now,* eh, Mum? The Lilies, where we live, is the third largest shopping complex in Europe. Well, it was when it was first opened, at least – this factoid seems to change every two minutes as new malls pop up in random cities. But anyway, as far as I know it's still one of the biggest for miles around, and one of the first in the world to boast being "ecologically sound" and featuring "adjacent affordable residential units". *Adjacent,* see? We don't actually live *in* the mall, despite what people at school seem to think. "You're so lucky you live right in the middle of the shopping centre!" they often sigh.

And now my mum was at it too. OK, it's true that my local shops include huge branches of every major chain store you can think of and I can easily be at the back of the queue in Primark within five minutes of leaving my house. But even so, it was highly unlikely that Jamie's Saturday job colleagues in the giant food court could hear a word we were saying, whatever my volume.

Clearly this was another of those situations where *I'd* have to be the adult.

My voice was ever so calm and mature as I explained. "You asked me to get Jamie. I called him three times!" Really, what more could she possibly have wanted? "Surely I had to be a *bit* loud, Mum. You know he's probably plugged into his iPod."

A blob of liquid detached itself from Mum's spoon and plopped onto the side of her shirt. Her *work* shirt. She would *so* have told me off if I'd done that to my school shirt. I live in a house of total double standards.

Mum grabbed a cloth and wiped at it frenziedly, pausing only to glare at me like it was my fault. Like I *asked* her to get hysterical. Then she sighed and said, "I meant that you should leave the kitchen, walk down the corridor, knock at the door of his room –"

"His stinking den?" I held my nose. Childish but effective, like so many things in life.

"– and tell him politely, at normal volume, to come and eat." She gave me a despairing look. "Is it really that hard? You know, if it was shouting I wanted, Molly, I could have done it myself."

See what I mean? I'd bent over backwards to help out my mother with her trivial errands, despite being in the midst of a dire crisis, and I even got criticized for *that*.

My life is not, in fact, merely over. It is also, as they say on

Nickelodeon HD, "A GIANT BOWL OF SUCK".

Whatever Mum was cooking looked like a giant pan of... something else.

"What's for dinner, then?" I asked her.

Mum sighed for about two years. I aged right in front of her. It was excruciating. "Molly, I'm a busy single parent. I've heated up some soup for you. Eat it, don't eat it. I don't care. Now, go and get your brother, then come back and tell me why your friends aren't talking to you and your life is supposedly over."

"It's not *supposedly* over. It *is* over." I stood up and puffed indignantly. This was all adding to its basic over-ness. "And I never said anything bad about the dinner. I just asked what it was." Though my thoughts about it might have shown on my face, I suppose. Trust Mum to pay attention to all the wrong things about me.

Jamie appeared in the doorway then, which at least saved me a journey. He sloped about and leaned on all available furniture in his typical Jamie way. My brother thinks he's actually too cool to support his own body weight.

"What's for dinner?" he croaked in that deep voice that he developed a couple of years ago, suddenly making the entire female population of our school go all giggly and silly for some utterly inexplicable reason. There are loads of girls at West Lilyford Community College who can't believe I'm his sister. This girl called Tasha – who left school last year and now works full-time in a kiosk at the mall – even said to me once, "Were you, like, separated at birth? Because you're *nothing* like Jamie Hart."

I didn't like to point out how little sense that made, as Tasha and her friend studied my non-Jamie-like face for a few seconds before she added, "Even though obviously you're a girl and stuff. And he's a boy. So..."

Her friend – who now works full-time in New Look – chimed in helpfully, "I reckon Jamie got all the looks and she got all the brains!"

Which was actually quite nice of her – I mean, it could have been a lot worse – but my (then) friend Wendy wasn't having any of it.

"Molly is a genetic anomaly," Wendy said. Her brother is training to be a doctor so sentences like that are the equivalent of "pass the ketchup" in her family. "She gains her superior intelligence by sapping brain cells from girls who find her brother attractive. Though it doesn't make much of a difference in your case."

My (then) other friend Ameera added triumphantly, "Yeah! What she said!" and we marched off, leaving the Jamie-fans frowning in bewilderment. They probably stood there all lunch break, trying to work out whether or not we'd actually insulted Tasha.

Life used to be good, back in the olden days, when I had friends.

Now I was in friendless misery in the kitchen and Mum was sweetly answering Jamie's question, even though it was the exact thing I'd asked her ten seconds earlier. *Nowhere* are standards more double than in the way Mum treats me and Jamie.

"Vegetable soup from the Snack Box on Level 1," Mum said, eyes shining with motherly love. "And fresh rolls from the bakery."

Jamie smiled his lazy smile and actually Mum might have been right before, because I was sure I heard the sound of female hearts sighing all across the mall.

I scowled at him as he said, "The kiosk on Level 2 next to the doughnut maker?"

Mum nodded.

"Cool. Tasha works there. I'm seeing her."

"You're *seeing* Tasha?" I asked. The girl whose brains couldn't sustain me?

"Yeah." He actually went a bit red then. "We're meeting at the rink tomorrow after work."

I decided to challenge him. "Aren't you still going out with Ellie?"

"Ellie?" Jamie frowned with the effort of remembering the name of the Year 11 girl I knew he was with last night. Mostly because I saw them snogging in the stairwell of Service Entrance B when I popped out to get some crisps from the 24-hour mini-market. And I forgot to mention this to Wendy, who developed a massive, tragic crush on Jamie a couple of weeks ago. Yes, Wendy too! I've lost her. I knew it couldn't last. At least Ameera would still rather date a trendy boutique than my big brother, but that's no use to me if she's going to bow to Wendy's command.

Anyway, Wendy overheard Ellie herself talking about the snog at lunch break, and I happened to let slip that I'd known about it. Wendy gave me the full lecture about "hiding information" when I should "understand how she feels", and the next thing I knew, Wendy and Ameera weren't talking to me anymore. And I am friendless and my life is over.

Wendy's sudden crush might be tragic but, believe me, the true tragedy is all mine.

"Oh... yeah." The girl-related cogs in Jamie's brain were turning slowly. "No, Ellie was yesterday. Tasha's tomorrow. Tasha's amazing." Jamie paused, giving me a brief moment to feel a bit sorry for Ellie. "Hey, want to come along, Measly? There's a whole group of us going."

Despite what my (ex)BFF Wendy expects from me, I don't even *try* to keep up with Jamie's love life. But I was supposed to be going to Wendy's boring brother's boring birthday party tomorrow night, and now that was obviously off the cards for me. Plus I am secretly in love with Jamie's mate Liam and the chances of him being at the rink are extremely high. If I can stop Jamie from calling me "Measly" in front of him, I might even be able to make Liam notice that I'm not twelve years old anymore.

So I said, "OK."

Mum beamed at her son, having conveniently ignored the Jamie-is-a-total-player portion of our conversation. "There you go, Molly. Your life can begin again. Oh, and don't forget that you're coming to my work thing tonight, too. Your new life is pretty full already!"

And she dished out our soup and continued smiling all through dinner, truly believing that harmony had been restored to her broken family by one generous invitation from her son and one dull "thing" at her work tonight.

She is SO wrong, on SO many levels.

Excuse me. I need to scream over some loud music now.

Seven minutes and two Adele tracks later

Dear Future Me, like say when I'm about twenty and living in my own place in a big city with a job in television, a cute actor boyfriend and matching designer shoes and handbag (I mean shoes and handbag that match each other, not the boyfriend, though either would do)...

You are so lucky!!! I wish I was you!!! I mean, I know I *will* be you, obviously, as you are me in the future. But do I really have to go through *five more years* of torture to get there? I want to be you NOW!!!

Do you even remember how tragic your life was all those years ago? Of course you don't – why would you? Well, luckily I'm here to remind you.

"One day you'll look back on it and laugh," Nan tells me a lot, when I have a good old rant at her and she listens like no one else in my family ever does. "You'll forget the bad times and wish you were a teenager again."

Dear Future Me: NO. Just no. OK?

I called Nan after dinner tonight, after all the Jamie-beaming and not-listening I got from Mum, and she was brilliant, as ever. The only problem with Nan is that she comes out with advice that's based on her own youth, when there was no internet and if you missed your favourite programme on TV that was it, you had to wait for something Nan calls a "repeat". The dark ages. In Nan's day, people of my age even sometimes wrote *letters* to their friends and *posted* them through *letterboxes*! So the stuff Nan comes out with can be pretty quaint.

Tonight was a prime example. First Nan did her supreme listening thing and then she announced, "Molly, you should keep a diary."

"A what?" I asked, though obviously I do know what a diary is. I was just worried about what Nan meant at that particular point in our conversation. "You mean, like, write down who Jamie's seeing and when, and show it to Wendy every day? Like a love-life log?"

Nan laughed. "No! Don't give that side of things another thought. Much as I love my grandson, I don't think he's quite ready for the kind of relationship your friend is after, and she'll realize it soon enough. No, darling, I mean you should keep a diary for yourself, to work out your feelings."

I might have pouted a bit. OK, a lot. Not that Nan could see, but I'm pretty sure she could hear my pout when I pouted, "But I have *you* for that!"

"That's very flattering, Molly, but we're both getting older. There might be feelings you don't want to share with your grandmother."

I cringed a lot then, because of course there are already plenty of feelings I don't want to share with my grandmother. Feelings about Liam, for a start, and how hot he looks in his burger-serving outfit in the food court. But that wasn't the point. "Nan, no one keeps a diary nowadays. A blog, maybe, but not a diary."

"A *what*?"

"It's like a public diary," I explained, even though Nan is totally a silver surfer and I'm sure she was humouring me. "You write it online. People leave comments."

"Well, you don't want *that*," Nan said. "You need to write it down on paper and work things out yourself. Trust me, it helps. I used to write reams when I was your age."

"Wait, you mean *hand*write it?" I was horrified. As if I don't get enough homework already!

She laughed again. She was finding my pain pretty amusing, all things considered. "Just do whatever suits you, Molly Munchkin. Consider it a letter to your future self, if you like. As long as it's private. Now. Shall I get your dad for you? Don't mention Jamie's girls to him, though – I can't stand any more comments about boys being boys!"

I love my Nan, I really do. I'm secretly glad she usually answers the phone instead of Dad, who moved back in with her after the divorce. Not that I don't love Dad, but there's no way I could tell him half of what I tell Nan.

So, OK, Future Me. I hope you're enjoying this. I'm giving Nan's crazy diary thing a go. I'm typing it, though – I'm maintaining a milligram of sanity here. Besides, if I didn't use the laptop, how could I paste in priceless gems like this Facebook exchange between my two ex-BFFs, from two minutes ago:

Wendy Bo: Just found two meanings for "Mall Girl" in Urban Dictionary! One is SHEEP, other is FASHION VICTIM! HA HA HA

Comments

Ameera ***coooool*Hassan:** aw mate, u mean Molz???

Wendy Bo: who else? Molly "Mall Girl" Hart. lollll. baaaaaa

Ameera ***coooool* Hassan:** aw come on W, give up, wot if Molz sees this? Delete now???! Pleeeeez. u no she is a gr8 m8

Wendy Bo: DON'T CARE!

Ameera ***coooool* Hassan:** go on chat now?

Wendy Bo: oki

And then the two girls who were my BFFs yesterday went on chat WITHOUT ME! Probably to talk ABOUT ME!
Nice, huh, Future Me?

Ten minutes later
I couldn't resist it. I changed my login and took a minute's worth of deep breaths before I sent Wendy a chat request. I typed:

Molly MALL GIRL Hart: Ha ha Wendy. u r a TOXIC FRIEND and I don't care!!! U can totally GET LOST! And I'm not coming to your brother's party thing tomorrow night either and you can JUST BE BORED without me!

I thought she'd ignore me like she did all afternoon at school, but after about five minutes I got:

Wendy Bo: Sorry, Molz. I was out of order, wasn't I?

I checked the screen three times but the words didn't change.

Molly MALL GIRL Hart: Wendy, is that really you?

Wendy Bo: Course. lol. Luv u babe. Sorry I got crazy.

Molly MALL GIRL Hart: U called me a sheep! And a fashion victim! 5 mins ago! On the wall that everyone from school can see!

Wendy Bo: I'll delete it right now.

Molly MALL GIRL Hart: Wendy, is this about your brother's party?

Wendy Bo: No! Yes. You have to come! You're right – I'll be so bored without you. I need you! Molly, I'm sorry, I swear! Plus Ameera says I was being way harsh before.

Molly MALL GIRL Hart: U were.

Wendy Bo: I'm sorry!!!!!!!!!! Please come tomorrow. I won't even ask you to bring your brother. :P

Molly MALL GIRL Hart: I'll think about it.

Wendy Bo: What's Jamie doing tomorrow, anyway? NO, don't tell me! I need to learn my lesson, right?!!!

Molly MALL GIRL Hart: gtg Wenz x

Wendy Bo: I luv you 4eva Molly babe! xxxxxxxxxxxxxx

I closed the chat box but ten seconds later Ameera was messaging me about going round the mall tomorrow before the party. I said yes as long as we could spend several hours afterwards walking up and down the Bedford Road, the busy dual carriageway where she lives. She LOL-ed. We always have this conversation. I'm not completely joking, though. The mall feels about as exciting to me as the road anyone else lives on, most of the time.

Anyway, Future Molly, what do you think of all that? I bet your cool television friends don't get at you all day and then insult you on Facebook but still expect you to go to their boring brother's boring family birthday party. Especially when the aforementioned brother has had a crush on you forever and your friend Wendy actually seems quite freakishly keen on the idea and makes jokes about double-dating and – cringe to end all cringes – "double sisters-in-law", i.e. her and Jamie and you and Harry? (In case you have forgotten, Wendy's brother William is nicknamed Harry because he's so sweet. Harry Bo – *sweet* – get it? Or are you too sophisticated for Tangfastics, Future Molly? If so, I'm not even sure I know who you *are* anymore!)

So my life isn't *completely* over and I still have friends after all.

But do I *want* to go to that party tomorrow instead of hanging round with Jamie's easy-going mates... including Liam?

But if I don't go to that party, will Wendy ever forgive me?

Hey, Future Molly, what should I do?

I suppose I'd better get ready. I'll have plenty of time to think about it at Mum's work thing, won't I?

Snoooooooze.

Saturday, 7th May (only just), early early morning
Work thing – wow

Did I really write "snooze"? Because NOT SNOOZE AT ALL! Mum's work thing was FANTASTIC!!! In fact, I might never sleep again!

Though my eyelids are pretty droopy.

So here are the highlights.

First Mum got mega dressed up and me and Jamie chucked on any old thing and dragged our heels behind Mum as we walked through the mall to Mum's legal firm, which is tucked away in a side lane together with a wool shop and a sweet shop that everyone mostly forgets about.

I love the mall at night – it's all security guards and eerily bright lighting that clashes with the hushed silence. That is, apart from where gaggles of my schoolfriends are hanging around in loud groups or in quiet snogging couples, and also near the cinema, the restaurants and the rink. Half my school is here and if I fancy people-watching or gossip-gathering, there's no better place to be.

Mum's work thing was the launch of some project involving art students from the local college. The legal firm were sponsoring them to create some works of art to dot around the mall, with big plaques underneath advertising legal services or something. You can see why I thought "snooze", really. But that was before I got there.

When I got there, I changed my mind instantly.

Well, *almost* instantly. The first thing I saw when I walked in, apart from tables full of tall glasses of white wine and piles of canapés, was a girl from my year. She started at our school a few weeks ago, just after half term. She seems nice enough but a bit boring and quiet, and I've had my own dramas to deal with, really, so I haven't actually had much to do with her.

But now she was standing by a large splashy abstract painting and talking to a guy. And so I looked at him and... wow. Just wow. He was *amazing*. Scruffy and cool and intriguing. He looked a bit like the painting, actually, but obviously in guy form. *Hot* art-student guy form.

I shook off my mum and Jamie, which wasn't hard seeing as Mum was already talking to a colleague and Jamie was already talking to a girl. I walked over to New Girl and Art Boy and I said, "Hi."

They stopped talking.

"Oh, hi," said the girl. She was wearing a long grey cardigan over black leggings and it looked like she'd made even less of an effort than I had, which I respected, really.

Art Boy said, "Oh, is this your friend?"

I started to mumble, but the girl jumped in, casual as anything, "From school," she said, as if we spoke to each other every day and even, you know, knew each other's names.

The girl said, "Molly, right?"

I nodded, feeling a bit sheepish that I had no idea what her name was.

Art Boy said, "Hello, Molly."

His accent was really unusual – sort of mega-posh and foreign at the same time. And hot. I died and went to heaven. Then I came back and remembered to mumble, "Hello." If he'd told me his name, though, I'd totally missed it while I was up there.

He was talking again, anyway. He was in full flow, in fact. I only understood about every tenth word of what he was saying, and most of these were "the". Wow. He was clever as well as hot. "So Jewel and I were just discussing Nimbyism, as represented in my painting," he finished.

There was a pause. I thought, *so her name's Jewel. Doesn't really suit her*. Then I thought, *wait – Nim-what? I've vaguely heard of Impressionism and Symbolism, but Nimbyism? And it's represented in his painting? And I'm supposed to say something about that now?*

Jewel and Art Boy looked at me expectantly.

I said, "Oh."

Art Boy's lips twitched. "You do know what a Nimby is?"

I did not. "Yes, of course."

"It stands for 'not in my back yard'," Jewel explained brightly. "It's people who have this attitude that certain unpleasant things shouldn't be near them. You know, in their back yards."

"I don't have a back yard," I said. "I live in the mall." This was not going well. "Well, next to the mall."

Jewel smiled. "I know. So do I. I live upstairs from you. That's how I know your name. It's on your door buzzer."

Oh yes. Mum let me and Jamie write that when we first moved in. Wow, though, who knew I wasn't the only mall girl in school?

"That's nice," said Art Boy, smiling at both of us. "You live in the same building and go to the same school. You're connected."

"Yes, and you've done art work for the firm my mother works for," I said, trying to establish a connection with him, too.

Jewel looked at me. "Hey, talking of school, do you know a Wendy there?"

A Wendy? My brain was still trying to figure out the Nimby. "What's one of those?" I asked.

Art Boy looked like he was trying not to laugh. I perhaps wasn't impressing him as much as I'd have liked. Or, in fact, at all.

"It's a person. Called Wendy," Jewel said. "Only she wrote on the wall of our school's Facebook page earlier, being really rude about people who live in the mall. I thought she was getting at me, but then I realized she might be one of your friends."

"Oh right!" I said. "Oh yes. Wendy Bo. Yes, she's my friend. I don't think she even knows who you are. Don't worry, it was definitely me she was having a go at. Not you."

"Some friend," said Jewel, and she smirked. She was actually pretty bold, for a quiet new girl.

"So is this your mother's firm?" Art Boy said, obviously wanting to bring the subject back to mature, college-aged levels.

"Yes," came my intelligent response. Then, "No. I mean, she works here. It's not her firm exactly. Like, she doesn't own it."

He nodded. "Is she a Fiona?" he asked.

"What?"

"Is she a Fiona? You know, one of the Fionas in the legal practice. I heard there were quite a few Fionas here."

Really? Mum hadn't mentioned *anyone* called Fiona, ever. How weird. "Oh, no. Mum's an Amanda. I don't know any –"

Jewel said, "Is it a big legal firm then, Molly? Are there lots and lots of..." she paused and pronounced the next two words very, very carefully, as if to an idiot, "*fee earners* here? Fee-earners? Bringing in the money for the firm?" She stifled a small, but kindly, laugh.

My cheeks burst into flames. Or that's what it felt like, anyway. "Oh," I said. "Oh. I'm not sure."

"Right," said Art Boy. He didn't look fazed. "So anyway, I should mingle. Listen, just in case I don't get to speak to you two again, how would you like to come to my private view tomorrow night? It's at the college."

I didn't want to ask what that was. I didn't want to talk ever again. I did, however, want to spend more time with Art Boy.

Anytime. As long as it didn't involve talking.

I nodded, due to the never-speaking-again thing.

"Sure," said Jewel. "Just text me the details and I'll be there. I can pop down and get you on the way, Molly, can't I?"

I nodded again.

I spent the rest of the evening in a bit of a daze, snaffling canapés and watching Art Boy continuously explain the Nimbyism Symbolism, or whatever, of his painting. I wondered whether anyone else understood him. I wondered whether I could go out with someone I couldn't understand, and I decided it would actually be quite good fun. I fancy Liam loads but I occasionally get slightly put off him when I hear some of the things he says to his mates.

Oh no.

Where should I go tomorrow night?

Because there's Liam. Who I have liked forever. Plus a nice, easy-going night out with Jamie at the rink.

Then there's Wendy. And the party of the brother who fancies me. But is boring. Except that Wendy might never speak to me again if I don't go, and she *is* a mate, despite what Jewel implied. And shouldn't mates come before boys?

And lastly, Jewel. Intriguing and maybe not-so-boring new girl. Plus Art Boy. Art Boy!!! Swoooooon!!! As long as I keep my mouth shut.

My life might not be over after all, but instead it is WAY COMPLICATED!!!!!!!!!!!

Friday, 13th May

After-school oh noes

Dear Future Molly, O Glamorous and Sorted One,

Look at *you*! I'm so glad you finally figured out how not to mess everything up! I mean, seriously. It had to stop *sometime*. Now please tell me it happened exactly on Friday 13th May, unlucky for some but not for you, eh, Future Molly? Because that was the day you finally made your whole life perfect, forevermore? Am I right? It had better be, that's all I'm saying.

And while I'm on the subject, here's a quick note for Past Molly, i.e. myself just one short week ago:

Molly Hart, what WERE you thinking when you decided to dump your long-term BFFs and even your brother – your kith and kin, as Nan would say – to spend an evening with some girl you only met last week and a mysterious arty boy you barely understand, and whose name you *still* don't know, despite everything????!!!

Seriously, WHAT? And WHY?

Also: WHEN, WHERE, and possibly even HOW?

In fact, think of any question word and it probably applies to this tragedy. Howl each one, Present Molly, and howl it loudly. Channel your inner Adele. Only way less tuneful, unfortunately.

Hmm, actually, "when" and "where" are not all that satisfying, as howled words go. They definitely lack the dramatic passion of "why". And "how" goes a bit too far down the werewolf route.

Never mind. For today's diary-writing purposes I'll focus on: WHAAAAAAAAAAAAT?

As used in the following sentence:

WHAT. A. WEEK!!!

Here is my retro-diary: a full week in the life of a mall girl, aka "What a Mess".

Last Saturday, 7th May, morning
Normality is underrated

So, apart from getting back from Mum's work party on Friday and stressing for half the night about what to do the following evening, Saturday started out normal. It was like any Saturday at one of Europe's busiest eco-malls, or any Saturday outside my front door, which is about the same thing.

Living practically inside the mall has its downsides – like upsetting my BFF Wendy after being exposed to more gossip than I'd like, for example. I would never have seen her crush – my brother Jamie – snogging some random girl if I lived somewhere with fewer service entrances, stairwells and other fertile snogging grounds. (*Fertile*? Ugh. Did I really just write that? I'm starting to see what Nan means about writing my thoughts down in private. My thoughts are clearly not fit for human consumption. I'm not even sure *I* want to read them. In a minute I will wash my typing fingers with soap and water. Which I realize doesn't seem all that dramatic, but believe me, it will do. There's enough *other* drama in my life right now.)

Anyway. Living by a huge shopping centre also has wonderful upsides, and Saturday at The Lilies is one of them. It starts out peaceful with the natural light shimmering through the glass roof, away from the mall's solar panelling and wind turbine. It's so quiet that you imagine you can hear the clicking heels (or squidging trainers) of the staff arriving for work. The security guards hang about joking to each other as the first, non-trouble-maker customers arrive. It's all leisurely pensioners and calm-looking mums with pushchairs containing sleeping toddlers.

But not for long. The toddlers wake and scream and the mums stress and shout and the pensioners tut and shove. Then everyone else floods in: shoppers of all ages, including half of my school. (The half that doesn't work there.) And after that, it's a free-for-all – a mob, circulating in increasingly irritated waves for hours and hours. There's always something (or someone) interesting to look at. I love it!

I don't even have to leave our flat to watch this spectacular weekly phenomenon unfold. Our kitchen has a balcony, and with the right light and a careful angle, I can see part of the entrance to the food court. Who needs a panorama of rolling hills and lakes when you can lean over and see a patchwork of shopping bags and clutched lattes? This is why I always take my laptop, phone and homework onto the balcony on Saturday mornings.

Last Saturday, though, I was too hyper to enjoy watching the mall-filling process. Mum was asleep – weekends involve sacred lie-ins for her – and Jamie was off filling baguettes already, in the stall next to the gorgeous Liam who I wouldn't be seeing that night. Earlier I'd told Jamie my decision not to go out with him and his friends, and he took it well.

"Huh?" he said, adjusting his disgusting uniform. It looks

like it's made of white school-issue toilet paper, but wearing it for eight hours every Saturday still doesn't put any girls off him. "Who said you were even invited, Measly?"

Then he beamed to himself to show he was teasing. I think. Anyway, his expression was enough to stop me throwing something at him and screeching out the "*You* did!" that was on the tip of my tongue. Just about.

He headed for the door, pausing for a second to press buttons on his smartphone and shake his head. He muttered, "Liam, mate, I tried. You're on your own now." And then he left.

"Jamie! Come back here! *What* did you say?" I yelled, but it was too late. A few minutes afterwards I saw a crowd of people spill out from the direction of the glass lift that connects our flats, the mall and the underground car park, and Jamie's unmistakeable swagger was among them.

Well. I decided I'd have to interrogate him later. Possibly I'd visit him at the food court and torture him for information by changing my order every two seconds or embarrassing him in front of whoever he was currently trying to impress – Tasha from the kiosk, I suppose.

That's if I had time to catch him there alone in between shopping with Ameera, who texted me at some ridiculously early time this morning to say that she needed to start shopping ASAP, and going out with Jewel and Art Boy tonight to whatever a "private view" was. I was still hopeful that it would be worth it, though, even if it meant giving up a night with Liam (*what did Jamie mean?!!!*) and breaking it to Ameera that I wouldn't be going to Wendy's boring brother's boring party. (I chickened out of telling her earlier when I texted her back. It would surely be easier to tell her to her face.)

Later
Easy as a waterfall in the Sahara Desert

It was not easier. It was a thousand times harder, especially with Ameera going on and on about the party and what we should wear and how she'd style my hair and shouldn't we get our nails done right now? Though Wendy's mum's cousin worked in the nail bar on the high street, so if we went there instead and talked about it tonight then Wendy's mum might actually *like* me for a change! (Wendy's mum is weird with my whole family, mostly because of our connection to the mall which she says is *"killing the high street"*. Wendy's mum runs the Chinese restaurant there which *"shouldn't have to compete with your plastic food court"*. Wendy normally enjoys the fact that her mum isn't keen on me – it appeals to her rebellious side. Also, lately it's given her the chance to make tons of Romeo and Juliet references in relation to her and Jamie's non-existent relationship. Ugh.)

I followed Ameera as we flitted from shop to shop, with her picking things up and cooing at them and me agreeing with everything she said, all the while thinking: *I have to tell her I'm not going tonight! How hard can it be? I'll tell her about the hotness of Art Boy! She'll understand!*

"Ameera..." I started when she was happily raking through rails in her favourite and most scarily expensive boutique.

"Yeah?" she said, holding up a short silver tunic dress with little mirrors all over it that I knew for a fact would look gorgeous on her and hideous on me. "How about this? Perfect for you, don't you think? Let's see if we can find you a cheap copy of it for tonight."

"Yeah, all right," I mumbled. "Ameera..."

She pouted. "See, this is no fun. You're just agreeing with everything I say!" She put the dress down and scrutinized me with her dark kohl-lined eyes. Then she sighed and said, "Are you trying to make a point? Wendy told me you saw what she wrote yesterday. About how you're a mall girl and that means you're a sheep and a follower with no mind of your own?"

It sort of hurt to hear her say that, even though I knew she didn't agree with Wendy's mean Facebook comments. Or right then I didn't think she did, anyway.

"I backed you up, you know, Molz. But right now you're kind of... sounding a bit like that, to be honest. You've been doing it all morning."

She moved to another rail and I followed her. I thought she meant well. Ameera often tried to protect me from Wendy's sharp-tongued tendencies. "Yeah, you're right. Sorry, Ameera. It's just..."

"See, you even agreed with *that*!" She brandished a woolly white top at me. "Is this what Wendy means, then?"

"What?" I bit my lip because I was on the brink of telling Ameera that *she's* the one who's sheep-like! She totally sided with Wendy when she stopped speaking to me, for a start, when I hadn't really done anything wrong! But I reminded myself not to lose my cool. Ameera and Wendy have been my friends forever. It would be crazy to fall out over a misunderstanding and a party that neither of *them* want to go to either! I just had to find the right way of breaking the news. They had to understand.

Ameera shook her head, smiled and nudged me. "You're all right, Molz. Only joking. I'm glad Wendy apologized to you for what she wrote," she added. "I know she didn't mean it. She's just a bit crazy in love, isn't she? I think you two should talk it over tonight, sort things out a bit more. Maybe even develop a proper strategy for her and Jamie to get together. You have insider knowledge!" She laughed. "There won't be much else to do, anyway. Most of the guests will be over 60. Us three can have a proper girlie bonding session. I think it's what we need right now, don't you?"

"Uh, Ameera..."

She pointed into the distance. "Hey, there's that new girl from school! Julie, or whatever her name is. I've heard she doesn't talk to anyone, ever." She squinted. "Though she seems to be waving at us. Wee-erd!"

I followed her gaze, and sure enough Jewel was waving. And walking towards us.

"She's called Jewel," I mumbled.

"No, I definitely heard Mr Hall call her Julie in PE."

"Well, he's wrong, it's Jewel," I said, resisting the temptation to point out that – *see!* – I was now disagreeing with Ameera. "She was at my mum's work thing last night and I found out she lives in my building and... Jewel! Hi! My friend says you're called Julie."

Jewel stopped in front of us and smiled a bit awkwardly. "Hi. Yeah, it's Julie." She avoided my eyes and looked right at

Ameera when she said that.

I blurted, "But Art Boy called you –"

Ameera frowned. "Who's Art Boy?"

I thought Jewel/Julie might say, "Yeah, who IS Art Boy?" but she just gave a nervous laugh. "Speaking of which, I'm glad I bumped into you, Molly," she said. "I got that text about tonight. It starts about seven, so if I stop by at –"

Ameera's eyes narrowed. "Tonight?"

Uh-oh.

"Yeah, we're going to a private view at the college," Jewel/Julie said, seemingly unaware of the effect her words were having on my friend. "You want to come too? I'm sure it'll be OK with..."

"Tonight?" Ameera repeated. She glared at me. "Molly?"

"Yeah..." I mumbled. "Listen, it's not that... But I kind of arranged this thing with Jewel – Julie..."

"Wait, does Wendy know about this? Even though she's been telling you for weeks that she desperately needs you at hers tonight, right from the start of the night?" Ameera didn't leave me a space to answer before she continued. "Were you even planning on *telling* either of your *best friends*?"

My temper flared. "Ameera, come on! Yesterday at school you weren't even *talking* to me! Some friends!"

"Yeah, whatever." She narrowed her eyes even more until they were just smudges of kohl. "Maybe Wendy was right after all. You *mall girls* should stick together!"

And then my friend Ameera – who's normally the calm, patcher-upper out of the three of us – flung the woolly top at me and stormed out of the boutique.

The shop assistant stared at me for a second before going back to untangling a mass of bikini straps.

"Oh, well," Jewel/Julie shrugged. She peeled the top away from me and hung it back on the rail, making it blend in and disappear among its clones. She seemed way more relaxed now that Ameera was gone. "They shouldn't have badmouthed you on Facebook."

"That was Wendy, not Ameera," I explained through my shock. "And she had a reason... kind of."

"Bet it wasn't a good one."

"I dunno, Julie," I mumbled miserably.

"Jewel." She grinned. "To my friends. I'm only Julie at school. I'm glad you decided to come to that thing tonight. Want to hit the food court?"

Saturday 7th May, evening

Back from private view weirdness at Lilyford College of Higher Education

I ended up spending the rest of the day with Jewel, having such a laugh that I almost forgot to worry about my (ex?) friends, and I mostly concentrated on not snorting any fruit smoothie out of my nostrils as we talked.

There was no sign of Liam at the burger bar, and Jamie was too rushed off his feet to torture – not that I wanted to ask him about Liam in front of Jewel anyway. But we hung around the food court for ages, people-watching and making up silly stories about why exactly they were at the mall, where they came from and what they'd had for breakfast.

In my head, I was making stories up for Jewel too, because she seemed to avoid all the questions about herself that I directed at her. She did tell me she'd had chocolate breakfast cereal wheels, though, which didn't seem nearly sophisticated enough for someone like her. She must have had a pretty colourful life before she landed in Lilyford – she was coming out with all kinds of far-fetched scenarios for other people. Either that or she'd watched a lot of films, I suppose. 18-rated ones, with subtitles.

The mystery of Jewel deepened when we took the lift back to the residential block and she got suddenly shifty. She pressed the button for my floor and practically shoved me out of the lift when we got there, calling, "See you later! Don't come up – I'll come down, OK?" The lift doors closed before I could even reply. Hmm. Intriguing – or maybe her parents were particularly embarrassing? I made a mental note to ask Mum if she knew anything about them.

Then there was the private view. *That* was weirdness itself.

It was kind of like Mum's work thing, with the trays of canapés and tall wine glasses, except that the surroundings were a lot more school-like (well, college-like, I suppose) and the whole place smelled of earthy paint.

Another difference was that there was some kind of camera crew hanging around. I noticed them and nudged Jewel, and that was when her strange behaviour began.

"Looks like we're going to be on TV," I chirped at her, giggling a bit at the thought. That would show Ameera and Wendy how right my decision was, despite the trouble it had caused.

Jewel didn't laugh. "He didn't warn me about this!" she hissed. She kind of shrunk back as the cameras swept the room. Then she straightened, bracing herself. "Can I get you a drink, Molly? Or something to eat?"

The table with the food and drink was in the corridor outside, and Art Boy was walking towards us. After not understanding a word he'd said last night, I didn't really want to talk to him without Jewel around. Not at first, anyway. But Jewel seemed desperate so I said, "Yeah, OK. Orange juice or something, and whatever snacks look least suspect." She'd gone before I even finished talking.

"Hello, Molly," said Art Boy, taking her place. "Thank you for coming."

Great! I was fully understanding him tonight! I was obviously getting more in tune with him. It had to be a good sign.

Or maybe it was easier when he wasn't talking about art. I'd prepared a bit for the possible arty nature of conversation tonight by looking up "art words" on Google when I was getting ready earlier. I'd found an A–Z list and tried to cram some of it into my head while I was choosing what to wear. Despite this, it was good to start on safer ground.

"Thank you for having me," I said politely. Mum would be so proud. "Congratulations on the... er... exhibition thingie." Mum might be less proud now. "So which one's your... thingie bit? Arty... stuff?" Total lack of pride.

I craned my neck as he pointed towards a side room. I had an ulterior motive here: his work would probably have his name near it somewhere, and I really wanted to know what that was. I kicked myself for not having asked Jewel before, but we were really too busy laughing about other things.

I couldn't see into Art Boy's exhibition room at all from where we were standing. I'd have to have a good look later.

"Where's Jewel?" Art Boy asked.

I told him and he nodded. Then he talked a bit about how important this evening was to all the students on his course, and how happy he was to share his work with his friends. He looked right at me when he said that, too. Wow! Then he added some question about what types of art I liked best, and I understood nearly every word he said, despite the subject matter. This was really going *way* better than the night before!

It was definitely time to wheel out the artistic vocabulary I'd studied online, now that Art Boy and I were clearly on the same wavelength.

"Well," I began solemnly, "I particularly like achromatic... acrylics." I tried to stop my face from showing that I was pulling these words from the depths of my brain. "Also batik... bisque. Yeah, that's good stuff right there. And I *love* a full chroma. Preferably in charcoal." I'd stopped to do my hair before I reached "D", but I was confident that I was already impressing him. He was frowning hard, considering my words carefully. Or possibly not understanding a word I'd said. Had I outwitted Art Boy himself with my artistic knowledge? Google is great!

"That's interesting," he said at last. And then he said something long and complicated that contained three uses of the word "the", two of "and" and one "a". Oh no! My Art Boy signal was scrambling again!

"So very true," I mumbled. "I couldn't have put it better myself," I added more confidently.

He laughed. "Listen, Molly, it's great that you're into art. I heard tonight that I'm being commissioned –"

"Ooh, you mean you've got a job?" I gushed with relief at my comprehension returning. Besides, I knew that getting any kind of work was a big deal for a student. Jamie once told me that his boss prefers to employ schoolkids because she thinks college students are "less reliable". Imagine being turned down for a job at the *food court*!

Art Boy nodded. "Yes, in a manner of speaking."

"That's fab, Art Boy!" I caught myself. "I mean, fab for an artist. Boy. Or girl. Either, really. Er, well done!"

Art Boy gave me another strange, but kind of smouldering, look. He certainly hadn't got any less gorgeous in the last twenty-four hours. "Thank you, Molly," he said in his funny foreign/posh accent. I couldn't help thinking he was taunting me with the way he knew my name and I didn't have a clue about his. "Yes, thanks to some people I met at your mother's firm and a college contact, I've been commissioned to paint a mural in your mall. It's a huge privilege, and really exciting."

"Ooh, fantastic!" I was off again. I wondered about literally holding my tongue – like sticking it out and gripping it between my thumb and forefinger to stop myself talking. Would it look weird?

Yes, probably, I concluded. I tried simply shutting up instead.

"And there's a production company who want to make a

documentary about my art and myself as an artist," he added with a modest eyebrow-raise.

"That's just AWESOME!" I practically screamed in his face. Hmm. My fingers inched towards my tongue.

"I'll need some volunteer assistants for the main project."

Did he mean *me*? He looked at me meaningfully. He *did* mean me! Woo HOO! I thought I'd better not sound too keen or it might scare him off. "When can I start?" I shrieked. Oops.

He laughed. "Around 6pm next Friday, at service entrance D. That's when we first meet to survey the location and discuss plans. The television crew are covering the meeting too, of course. Thank you, Molly. And bring your friends – we'll need as many hands as possible. Ah, here's the lovely Jewel now!"

Jewel didn't smile as she handed me a fancy-looking pastry stick and a glass of orange juice. "Hello," she said frostily to Art Boy. I waited for her to say his name – at last I would know it! – but she didn't.

Art Boy said something to her but I stopped listening and started daydreaming. I was on telly painting a work of art with my gorgeous Art Boyfriend, and Wendy and Ameera were watching, telling each other how wrong they'd been and how sorry they were that they'd ever called me a Mall Girl, when clearly I was an individual and a highly successful one at that. As I dreamed, I bit happily into one end of my canapé...

...and released a shower of gloopy spattered globs. Of what can only be described as... cheese.

Within a blink, they'd hit Jewel and Art Boy, making interesting patterns on their clothes and shoes.

"Molly!" Jewel said, recovering first as she brushed specks of cheese off her shoulder. "You've just squirted the entire contents of your canapé all over us!"

I glanced at my pastry. She was right. It was empty. What a waste of good cheese. I was hungry, too.

"Argh!" Art Boy yelled, tugging at his clothes in alarm. Wuss. Beautiful, talented wuss. He was in a right flap. He'd failed to notice the artistic potential of what I'd done.

The cameras suddenly swept nearer to us – towards the action, I suppose – and I changed my mental image of Wendy and Ameera's viewing. It went from a scene of Mall Girl redemption to one of cheese-related humiliation.

But before the crew reached us, Jewel pulled at my arm and the next thing I knew we were out of the college and she'd flagged down a taxi and told the driver to take us to the mall. She was so grown-up! She was also clearly not in the mood for talking, her mouth set in a grim line all the way home.

"Thanks for saving me from the cameras," I mumbled after she'd paid for the taxi – *where did she get that kind of money?* – and she was striding towards the lifts with me scurrying after her.

"Maybe *you* saved *me*," she said, and then she laughed for ages before she said, "Sorry I've been moody, Molly," and promptly clammed up again. I decided not to ask her what she meant, seeing as she clearly didn't want to talk. We walked in silence past the rink where Jamie was supposed to be, and where I could have been right now on a night out with Liam. But there was no sign of my brother or any of his friends. Weird.

Also, after Jewel waved me out of the lift at my floor and

I turned the key to our flat, I could have sworn I heard Jamie moving about in his room. But I must have been imagining it. The last time Jamie was in before midnight on a Saturday was years ago, and even then it was only because he'd decided to nurture my belief in the Easter Bunny by hiding eggs for me. He hid them so well that Mum found one when she was dusting last week.

I hesitated outside Jamie's room but then I went to my room instead and collapsed on my comfy bed. When I saw how early it was, I realized I could go to Wendy's brother's party after all – right then and there. I could patch things up with Wendy and Ameera. But I didn't think I'd be very welcome – well, even less than Mei-Lin Bo, Wendy's mum, usually made me feel.

I took ages to get to sleep, wondering who I could persuade to come with me on Friday evening. *"Bring your friends,"* Art Boy had said. I didn't want to let him down, but unless I made up with my ex-BFFs, did I actually even *have* any friends? There was Jewel, but she hadn't exactly seemed keen on Art Boy or the cameras just now. What was up with her leaving in such a rush, even with the whole cheese thing? Maybe she was super camera-shy? Or maybe she and Art Boy had been *more* than friends and they had unresolved issues? Or cheese allergies? In any case, I should tread carefully. I didn't want to risk losing what was possibly now my only friendship in the world.

I fell asleep and dreamed about painting the mall with cheese, watched by hot boys, camera crews and sneering ex-friends.

Sunday 8th May

Bizarre happenings chez Dad and Nan

Sunday was a typical day at Dad's, chatting to Nan and doing my homework while she made me tea and muttered about "maths nowadays" and "whatever happened to simple arithmetic".

Dad made his usual effort to chat to me for about half an hour, and then had his obligatory "boys will be boys" chat with Jamie, during which I slunk off with Nan so that we could eat biscuits and roll our eyes. Actually, that part went a tiny bit differently this week.

Normally Dad asks Jamie about "that hectic love-life of yours" and Jamie laughs and croaks, "Shut up, Dad," but then complains about something like the fact that he had to turn his phone off because of a flood of messages from five hundred different girls. Which then leads to Dad going, "I was just like you in my day, ho ho ho," like a deluded Santa. (I happen to know that when Dad was young he didn't even *have* the kind of phone that could receive texts or be turned off.) Then they both stop talking out of their egos and shout abuse at the football instead. I don't think Mum's ever for one minute regretted the divorce.

"How's it going with all the girls?" Dad nudge-nudge wink-winked at his son this week, right on cue.

"Dad, shut up," said Jamie – *but he didn't laugh*!

Instead, his face went completely red and his mouth wobbled in a downward curve, and then he took out his phone and looked at it... well, I'd have to say *mournfully*. And he sighed, and there was a huge silence.

Nan raised her eyebrows at me, pausing mid-biscuit.

I held my breath and my hand froze over the selection box. *Weirdness!*

Eventually, Dad said, "Oh."

"Ref-er-EEEE!" Jamie shouted, and everyone breathed again.

I wondered what had happened with Tasha. I'd asked Jamie about his night out on the way here – though obviously with more of a Liam-focus at the time – but he'd just grunted and given me non-answers, which was nothing unusual. He insisted he hadn't said anything at all about Liam when he left for work. Mostly there's no real point in talking to my brother. I considered trying another interrogation at half-time, but I got caught up in explaining quadratic equations to Nan instead. Surprisingly fun.

All day, on and off, I thought about messaging Ameera and/or Wendy, and maybe even telling them I was sorry. But I couldn't decide whether I actually had anything to apologize for, or not unless they apologized first. So I didn't write to them at all.

Friday 13th May

After a week of being Molly No-Mates at West Lilyford Community College

Let's just say my week at school was torture. Wendy and Ameera were cold and hostile, and a few of the girls in my class noticed but stayed out of it. Or – worse – they *sided with my ex-friends*! I heard one or two of them whisper *"mall girl"* and laugh when I came near! I can't believe I've gone through nearly four years of secondary school trying to be nice to these people (mostly) and this is the thanks I get! I might never forgive Wendy and Ameera for this. Wish they'd talk to me again so that I could tell them this FACT.

I'm also now thinking I really messed up. How badly did I handle the Ameera thing at the mall? And I should at least have told Wendy I wasn't going to her brother's party! Not to mention the fact that I could have made a different decision and not fallen out with them in the first place. Or would it have happened anyway?

At least I have Art Boy. Hope he's got over the cheese-splash.

So I made it through the week with thoughts of televised mural-painting, even though these thoughts were slightly worrying and put knots of near-panic in my stomach. Here's a full breakdown of my terrible school week:

I spent Monday lunchtime alone, after trying and failing to track down Jewel. I did some homework in school time. Happy Monday to me!

On Tuesday, Jamie saw me hanging around by myself and he sneaked me into the sixth form room where I read magazines and felt super small, young and uniformed. It was nice of him, though, especially since he'd carried on being utterly miserable for most of the week. Everyone except Jamie mostly ignored my presence among Years 12 and 13, though Liam did say an awkward hello. Twice. Interesting.

On Wednesday and Thursday I got called into various offices to see assorted teachers about my work experience placement for after the exams. I'm supposed to be going to Mum's law firm but there's some paperwork problem that would be too boring to mention if it wasn't for the fact that it kept me occupied between lessons for two whole days. Score! Mid-week admin mix-up joy!

Then today, at last, there was Jewel. Or rather, Julie, when she's at school. I was very happy when I finally found her at first break. But Julie is SO different from Jewel! No wonder I'd never really noticed her before last week. Julie kind of shrinks into her scarily neat school uniform and is so quiet that she makes a mouse sound like a Rihanna album on maximum volume. And apparently her usual hang-out is the *library*! I thought she was joking when she told me that's why I hadn't seen her, but it turned out she wasn't. So I went there with her and we sat and read *books*! Which was all right, really. Though we're a strange kind of friends, and I still haven't asked her anything about Art Boy, plus I've just realized I don't even have her phone number.

So this is how I survived a full week of school without Wendy and Ameera.

Grr, why do I miss them so much? I wonder if they miss me too? They have to! We've gone around together for years and years! It's weird, us not being three BFFs at school... and out of school. It's just wrong, no matter how childish I think they're being. Or what they think of me!

And now there's only about an hour to go before Art Boy's meeting, and it's time to sort things out.

Future Molly, your perfect life begins NOW, with this perfect opportunity...! Go, YOU! GO!!!

Friday, 13th May, later

****fingers in ears* La-la-la, I can't hear me!***

OK, so that didn't quite go as planned. And I'm using "quite" here to mean "at ALL, even in YOUR FREAKIEST NIGHTMARES!"

Still. Let's just pretend none of it ever happened, eh?

No use in dwelling.

It is, as Nan says, probably for the best.

Saturday, 14th May, morning

OK, here's the truth...

I think I'll write down some of the things that I'm pretending didn't happen.

They're not playing on my mind at all. This is merely a way to keep my writing fingers exercised, seeing as I currently have no friends to message or Facebook, and not even any proper homework. (It's all revision for the next few weeks, i.e. sitting around posing with a pile of study guides and looking pained until Mum brings me drinks and sandwiches and feels deeply sorry for me because she "remembers exam hell all too well". Must not let on that I'm not all that bothered – I can't possibly have forgotten any of the stuff we've done since the last lot of exams, which seems like yesterday. And I'm not doing any actual GCSEs this year, unlike Wendy, who has been revising for her single early GCSE for the past 15 years. She'll be dying of nerves – must wish her luck.) (Oh. Can't.) (Life. Sucks.)

Anyway. I strongly pretend-deny the occurrence of the following chain of events...

Firstly and most importantly, seeing as that's where it all

began, there was my decision to go to Jewel's flat and persuade her to come to Art Boy's mural meeting.

Now, at first glance, doing this makes a lot of sense. Did not the hotness that is Art Boy himself say, *"Ah, here's the lovely Jewel now!"* immediately after he asked me to bring my friends? Putting aside the fact that saying *"the lovely Jewel"* makes him sound about ninety or a bit smarmy, and remembering instead that English is probably not his first language so it's unfair to judge, it is clear that by "friends" he actually meant Jewel. So dragging Jewel along was *entirely* what Art Boy intended, and therefore the greatest decision I could possibly have made.

There's also the fact that I'm dying of curiosity about Jewel's life, and I desperately wanted to see the inside of her flat and possibly comb it for clues when her back was turned.

On the other hand, there was all of Jewel's secretiveness last week, not to mention her frostiness with Art Boy at the private view, and our sudden exit. I'm not at all convinced it was cheese-related – there has to be something going on between those two that I don't know about. So maybe I should have considered that inviting her wasn't a wise move for those reasons.

On the *third* hand (this is *my* diary – I can have as many hands as I want!), there's the absolute truth: Jewel is the closest thing I have to an actual friend right now, and I wanted her to come with me for that simple reason.

Also, who better to confront the aftermath of the cheese incident with than another of the victims? If Art Boy was still annoyed with me about covering him in gooey dairy by-products last Saturday, maybe Jewel could help defuse the situation by demonstrating her own speedy recovery.

So, with no hesitation at all (except all of the hesitation above), I decided to go up to Jewel's flat. It was one floor up from mine, after all. What could possibly go wrong?

It was a bit early but I'd already got ready for the meeting, in the hope that I could maybe sit around in Jewel's place for a while, gathering lifestyle evidence before it was time to leave. I'd dressed for "being on TV" rather than "working on a mural", but I figured that would be OK. Art Boy had implied there wouldn't be any actual painting to start with.

However, this meant that I was wearing what Nan calls "unsuitable shoes", so I pressed the button for the lift even though the stairs in our block of flats are quite nice, really. They're opposite the lifts and have a great glass-fronted view of the mall, without the squinting required from my kitchen balcony.

The lift was taking ages. As I waited (and waited, and waited), a boy huffed past me up the stairs, hauling a large rectangular box with a music shop logo on the side. He was good-looking in a roadie-at-the-gig, effortless kind of way; he was wearing black jeans and a faded band t-shirt and he seemed pretty strong. A few minutes later, the same boy walked by in the other direction, slightly red in the face but with his hands free now and taking the stairs two at a time. And a few minutes after *that*, I saw him walking up again with another huge box.

Curiosity got the better of me. "Is the lift out of order?" I asked as he neared me.

He jumped and dropped the box on his foot. "Ow," he said,

quite casually, considering.

"Er, are you OK?"

He looked down, frowning. "If I've broken it, Mum will kill me."

I felt embarrassed then, not to mention worried that I was intruding on his domestic misery. "Oh no! Sorry if I had anything to do with you breaking your foot. And, er, any resulting murder."

He picked up the box and wiggled his Converses at me. "No, I'm fine. I meant the keyboard." He slapped the cardboard side. "I think the packaging's pretty sturdy, though. And Mum won't really kill me, of course. She needs me as her hard-working slave. I'm bringing this up to our flat for her now."

"Oh. Good." I was starting to regret having said anything at all, to be honest. I was also wondering why I'd never seen this boy before if he lived in my block of flats. I hadn't known that Jewel lived there either. Either my fellow mall girls and boys had been hiding themselves away, or I was spectacularly unobservant. "I mean, not about the slavery, but good about the staying alive."

"Yeah, jury's out on that one," he deadpanned.

Weird. His tone of voice really reminded me of someone. But who?

"Though that's generally why I don't use elevators," the boy continued. "Because I think they're death traps, and mostly I quite like my life." He reconsidered. "Or I like *hating* it, anyway. That's always fun."

"So, wait, you're carrying that box up... how many?... several flights of stairs because you're scared of lifts?"

He shook his head. "Six flights. And I was kidding about the slavery. I volunteered to do this for Mum because I wanted the exercise. Also, I'm not scared. I'm rational. I *know* they're death traps. Why would you get in a small box that's liable to break down any minute, plummeting hundreds of feet at high velocity? Besides, I overheard someone earlier saying it's been behaving strangely today – opening at the wrong floor, that kind of thing. I'm not taking any chances. It's Friday the 13th, you know."

My brain was ticking slowly. "Six flights? You live on the same floor as my friend Jewel..." I meant to add her surname there, but I suddenly realized I didn't know it. I hardly knew *anything* about her. We were *such* strange friends.

As soon as I said Jewel's name, the boy's whole demeanour changed. His face closed off and he said coldly, "I live in the same flat as her. I'm her brother. What do you want from her?"

What was going on here?! Well, clearly he was Jewel's brother, which explained why there was something familiar about him. And *that* was weird because I had no idea she had a brother, let alone one who seemed so close in age to us. Why wasn't he at our school? But, more importantly, what was he *talking* about?

"Hey, hang on. I just told you I'm her friend. From her new school. Why would you think I *wanted* anything from her?" Except a bit of an evening out at Art Boy's mural meeting, of course. It seemed a bit too complicated, and this boy seemed a lot too hostile, for me to add that.

"Because you called her Jewel," he said. "And I know she's

changed her name to something she thought sounded more ordinary. Even though I did warn her it would never work, especially when there are people like that art guy around who know the truth. But my sister is really, *really* stubborn." He picked up his box and frowned. "And when she gets it in her head to do something, there's no talking to her. Even if I'm warning her about people who want to take advantage of her." He narrowed his eyes then, as if he meant *me*.

I felt myself snap. First my best friends fall out with me and now total strangers who happen to be related to my new friend think they can have a go at me for some bizarre reason? I was in *no* mood for this.

"I seriously don't know what you're talking about," I told the boy. "And I am *so* your sister's proper friend. Also, I'm not someone who *ever* takes advantage of people, whatever you mean by that. I'll have you know I'm *lovely*." Well, my ex-BFFs might have disagreed, but his sister shouldn't, at least. Plus my Mum, Dad and Nan loved me, and Jamie enjoyed having me around for teasing purposes. And Wendy's brother had a crush on me. I was all right! Wasn't I?

There was a ping! sound. The lift had arrived – finally.

We both stared at it for a moment and then a wave of pure crazy came over me. That's the only way I can rationalize what I did next...

...which was to grab the boy's cardboard box – surprisingly light – and jump into the lift with it.

"And I'll prove it by taking this up to your flat for you!" I called to him. "You can take the stairs and meet me there, and then you can *ask* Jewel and she'll *tell* you what a great friend I am!"

"What are you doing? Give that back!" The boy jumped into the lift as the doors started closing. He said a few words which, because this diary was Nan's idea, I probably shouldn't write down.

The doors clunked tightly together. "You're rude," I informed him.

"You're a thief," he replied. "Even if you really *are* Jewel's friend."

The lift started moving. "Of course I am! What *else* would I be? I keep telling you I don't know what you're... Wow, are you OK?"

The boy had slammed himself into a corner of the lift with his eyes tightly shut. He didn't reply, but he went so pale that he practically blended into the transparent wall. Plus he seemed to be shaking.

"You're *not* OK, are you?" I can be very astute sometimes. "You're *terrified*!"

The boy muttered something I couldn't make out, but the message was clear. He wasn't at all happy – and he wasn't at all happy that I'd noticed it. In fact, he was sort of waving me away, but it wasn't like there was anywhere I could go.

I propped the box against one side of the glass lift and walked over to him, unsure of what to do. I sort of patted him on the shoulder and he opened his eyes a tiny bit. His mouth wobbled as he mumbled something. "Please leave me alone," I think it was. Ungrateful.

"Nearly there," I said in what I hoped was a soothing voice.

Then I realized that neither of us had pressed a button when we got in and that the lift was travelling way past his floor and up and up, to the very top of the residential wing. The lift's made of glass and the view from it is awesome, but I can sort of see how it would be much less awesome if you were scared of heights, or lifts. Or probably both, judging by the boy's reaction as we climbed.

I left his side and quickly pressed the button for Jewel's floor. It didn't light up but the lift started to descend. Phew. Down, down... to the sixth floor...

...and beyond. Without stopping.

I pressed the button furiously again and again, casting glances at the quivering boy while waves of guilt washed over me. Then again, no one *asked* him to start a row with me *or* to follow me into the lift.

I pressed three buttons at once, as a test. They lit up. All of them. There was a creaking sound and the lift stopped.

Between two floors. The ground floor and first floor of the mall, to be precise.

We were stuck, suspended in a glass box, in full view of all the shoppers, and the workers around Service Entrance D.

I heard a whimper.

"It's OK," I said. "Don't panic. I'm sure we'll be moving soon."

"I'm not panicking," the boy managed to say in a really panicky way. "I'm good. I'm just going to... shut my eyes a bit more. OK?" His voice trembled.

I pressed the alarm button. A bored voice came on the intercom, going, "What – *again*?! Hold on, we'll sort this out. It's been playing up all day!"

The boy shifted slightly. He didn't talk but his body language seemed to say, *"See, I told you!"*

"Er... sorry," I said.

He nodded slightly.

"I used it earlier and it was fine! I use it all the time! I love lifts! I..." I thought I'd better stop speaking, as I wasn't getting any signals that my words were helping. The opposite, maybe.

We waited and waited and the boy was silent. I would have thought he'd gone to sleep if it hadn't been for the slight shaking of his shoulders.

Minutes went by. Then more minutes. Enough of them to make it Meeting Time.

I watched as the unmistakeable arty hotness of Art Boy himself arrived at Service Entrance D, accompanied by a gaggle of girls. He positioned himself to greet hoards of fellow studenty-looking people as they arrived. The side lane filled with happily chatting groups. In the middle of it all I spotted an older woman who was beaming at everyone from the depths of her dark blue suit and corporate hairstyle.

I watched as the television cameras homed in on her, manned by a group of bored-looking people who didn't look entirely unlike Art Boy's student gang, only with more denim and less poise.

No one looked up. I thought about waving or jumping around to get their attention, but that probably wouldn't have been a nice thing to do to my lift-mate.

I ogled as Art Boy addressed his crowd and people seemed to hang on his every word, some of them even making notes.

While all this was going on, the boy stuck silently against the wall, his eyes screwed tightly shut.

The television team left quite quickly and then the arty gang gradually started to drift away. I'd totally missed the meeting, and I'd been literally metres away from it the whole way through. How frustrating was this? And would Art Boy ever forgive me for the cheese thing now?

Eventually a voice crackled through the intercom. "Sorry for the delay! You should be moving soon," it said, way too chirpily for the prevailing mood. Another voice in the background said, "No, not that one! That's the lift cable!"

My poor, poor lift-mate. Even *I* felt a quiver in my stomach then, and I've been using this lift for years.

There was a loud creaking sound like the one that had started this nightmare. The lift shuddered and started to move.

Finally – *finally* – the doors opened at the sixth floor.

"We're, um, here," I said to the boy, resisting the temptation to add something like, *"There, that wasn't so bad now, was it?"*

He stood up very slowly, as if he was worried that his legs had turned to jelly. His fingers clung to the glass sides.

Jewel was standing in the doorway of the nearest flat, looking worried.

"I just got home and found the door open!" she said. "Oh my God, Jasper, were you in the elevator? Are you all right?"

"Yeah," the boy – Jasper – said in a shaky voice. "I was in

the middle of transporting keyboards for Mum. I, er, got stuck. With... her." He trailed off, like talking was too much effort.

"That's my friend Molly," Jewel said, looking backwards and forwards between us. "Molly, I see you've met Jasper, my long-lost twin."

"I hate my life," Jasper muttered. He took a deep breath, picked up the box and marched with new-found strength into his flat.

"But at least you *like* hating it," I mumbled, mostly to myself. I followed him because I thought Jewel was right behind me, but when I turned around she was still standing by the front door, clearly looking a bit shocked that I'd just walked in. Oops.

A door slammed from about where Jamie's room is in our place. The layout of Jewel's flat was identical to mine. But that was where the similarities stopped. Our decor wouldn't stand out in a discount sofa advert – in fact, I think Mum actually modelled it on a furniture showroom. Jewel's looked all colourful and funky and the walls were covered in pictures of bands and stills from various gigs. It looked awesome. I couldn't get near enough to see whether I knew any of the artists in the photos but I did recognize an ageing rock star whose name I couldn't quite remember, and there seemed to be loads of shots of him.

"Are you a fan?" I asked Jewel, pointing at one of the larger photos as I edged back towards her and tried not to seem rude for having just walked into her place uninvited.

"My mum is," she replied, after a pause. "I guess I used to be. My brother definitely isn't."

"Right," I said. *Huh?*

"Listen, Molly, I know Jasper can be a pain but he's also really, *really* claustrophobic. I don't know how you persuaded him to use the elevator, but if I know him, he's extremely embarrassed about getting scared in front of you. I'd better go and check on him." She gripped the door as I stepped out. "See you, OK? Sorry!"

She shut the door – a bit apologetically, maybe, but the result was the same.

I'd tortured Jewel's brother, stood up the mysterious Art Boy, and my evening had come to an end. I took the stairs down to my flat, ignoring my unsuitable shoes.

So that's what happened. I admit it now. But please let the record show that it's not at *all* what I planned when I decided to see if Jewel would come with me to Art Boy's mural meeting.

My life is freakier than a freaky nightmare.

Saturday, 14th May, late afternoon

After a trip to The Kitchen, Hart residence, 5th floor, The Lilies eco-mall, Lilyford

My week seems to be developing a bit of a brotherly theme. Jamie and I have reached a new level in our relationship. We just had an actual conversation, and it wasn't even prompted by Mum standing with her hands on her hips and yelling, "Apologize and explain yourself to him/her NOW", as has happened historically.

A few minutes ago I popped to the kitchen for comfort food and encountered Jamie, still in his work uniform, rooting through food cupboards and looking miserable. He didn't seem to notice me as he shoved aside several tins of beans and tuna before settling on a pack of chocolate breakfast cereal wheels. He opened it and tipped it straight into his mouth, in typical disgusting Jamie fashion.

"You pig! Are you comfort eating?" I bellowed, starting on a bit of a mean (and hypocritical) note, I admit. Habits are hard to break. Besides, at that point I didn't yet know that he'd matured a bit from his usual overgrown toddler behaviour.

He jumped, not half looking guilty, but he recovered quickly. "Ha ha, Measly," he said. Then he sighed. "Actually, I think I might be." He put the cereal box down.

"So what's up?" I asked kindly, though I automatically added, "And stop calling me Measly."

Then I winced, because I know full well that saying this is normally a cue for him to tease me even *more*, possibly chasing me around the flat going, "Measly! Spotty spotty Measly!" and throwing sofa cushions at me until I do something worse to him.

But he said, "Sorry." And then added, with what was clearly a monumental effort, "Molly."

"Wow," I couldn't help gasping. "Jamie, seriously, you're scaring me now."

He laughed. "I'm not *that* bad, am I?" He sat at the kitchen table, tracing patterns in the crumbs I'd left after eating some crackers earlier. Mum would be having a go at me about them as soon as she came back from her spa treatments and noticed, but I'd been planning to blame them on Jamie. He usually deserved it.

"Actually, you are. You're *horrible*!" Possibly a little far-fetched, but basically true. "I can never understand what all those girls see in you! I can't believe even *Wendy* has a crush on you!" Oops. I'd accidentally broken the Number One BFF Law – Thou Shalt Not Reveal Crushes Without Authorization In Triplicate. Though with Wendy not talking to me already, how much worse could things be? And she'd never find out, anyway.

"Is Wendy the gorgeous stylish one with the huge eyes and the long dark hair, or the other one?"

"Jamie!" I stamped my feet indignantly, despite my previous lapse in loyalty to Wendy. "*This* is what I mean! My friends are *all* gorgeous and stylish and... stuff!"

He grinned. "I'm only joking. I know who Wendy is, and you're right, your friends are great. A bit young for me, maybe..."

I rattled off a list of girls in our year that Jamie has been "connected to" at one time or another.

"Yeah, or not," he admitted. "Seems different when I've seen them hang around with my baby sister half my life. Anyway, that's not the point. I've given up on all that." He sighed. "From now on, I'm all work and study."

My laugh bordered on a guffaw.

"I'm serious, Measl – Molly. If I can't have..." He gave me a look before he decided to continue. "...Tasha, I'm not interested."

Wow, was he really not kidding? Was my brother properly in love? With someone who didn't even like him back? What alternate universe was this?

"So why can't you have Tasha?"

"I don't know," he said, misery spilling over his face and into his crumb-drawing, which now resembled a squiffy rainbow, or a series of interlocking unhappy mouths. "Because she doesn't want me. She stood me up last Saturday. She didn't even call, or reply to any of my texts."

I got a cloth and cleaned up some of the crumbs. There would be no Jamie-blaming today.

"Are you sure she doesn't have a good reason, Jamie?" I said as I wiped. "Have you tried actually speaking to her in person, like going up to her at the mall or something? What if she's lost her phone?"

He shook his head. "I haven't got the guts. Can't take the rejection, I suppose. I, er, thought of sending Liam to speak to her at the kiosk for me."

My heart did a little flutter at his name. I am a hopeless case. "And?"

"He's gone away. He left last Saturday on some last-minute family holiday. His parents couldn't resist the cheapie term-time offers, and Liam's first exam isn't till June. I don't trust any of my other mates to talk to her, or even to tell them about any of this. They'd just use it as a chance to have a good laugh at my expense."

I thought about Jamie's friends, and realized he was right. None of them are bad-looking by any stretch, but there's a reason Liam's the only one I've ever fancied.

"After Tasha stood me up," Jamie continued with a grimace, "I told the guys I'd remembered something I had to do at home, and they all went off to the cinema instead. None of them are really into skating anyway. I'd only dragged them there because Tasha suggested it."

"Oh. Well, would you... like me to try speaking to..." I couldn't quite bring myself to offer. Tasha was never exactly nice to me when she was still at school, if she even bothered to acknowledge my existence.

Jamie seemed grateful anyway. A look of doubt crossed his face, together with a flicker of a smile. "Nah, you're all right, Molly. Thanks, though. Liam's back on Friday anyway, but I've decided not to ask him. I've got this new theory about why Tasha didn't show. And it's pretty gutting."

"Really? Why? What?"

He sighed. "Well, in a chat I had with her last Saturday lunch break, I mentioned that Liam wouldn't be there, that he'd gone away. And she went a bit funny then, though I can't exactly put my finger on how. But then after that she doesn't turn up. Makes me think it's Liam she was after all along. Not me." He grimaced again. "Least I know she probably doesn't stand a chance because Liam's totally crazy about someone else."

My brain went, *"Who? Who?"* but I knew how unlikely it was that Jamie would say, "*You*, of course, my wonderful, angelic sister Molly." Even without the "wonderful, angelic" part, which, let's face it, Jamie would *never* say, even in the most alternate of alternate universes. And I didn't particularly want to hear any *other* answer, so I didn't ask.

I hinted instead. "I wish someone was totally crazy about me," I said. Talk about mega-super-hint with cherries on top. My heart sped up a bit as I waited for Jamie's answer.

He looked a bit surprised. "Someone is," he said.

"Oh?" Boom boom BOOM!

Jamie smiled. "Your friend's trainee doctor brother, of course. Harry Bo, isn't it? I served him at my sandwich stand that Saturday morning and he was asking after you, going on about his birthday party and how he hoped to see you there. He even invited *me*! He definitely has a thing for you!"

"Jamie! Shut up!" To think I was almost starting to *like* my brother, and he was just mocking me as usual!

Then I realized he wasn't teasing. He didn't have that glint in his eye. In fact, he seemed genuine when he said, "What? It's true! I thought you knew."

"I *do* know, Jamie, but I don't care." Oops. That sounded a bit heartless. I had nothing against Harry, after all. Though I did wonder whether Wendy talked him into inviting Jamie. "What I mean is –"

"Yeah, I get it. Wish I didn't care about Tasha, but I do." He gave a mega-sigh. "I can't help it. She's just so..." He shrugged to sum up her total so-ness. "Anyway, thanks for letting me go on at you, Molly. Guess you're OK sometimes."

"Oh. You're, er, welcome. I think."

He nodded at me and went off to his room, probably to wallow on iTunes. I cleared up the rest of the crumbs and marvelled at the way that people you thought you knew inside-out could surprise you. As could people you didn't know at all – i.e. Jewel. And Jasper. And who knew what Harry was like, really? I'd never really got to know him – and never thought of that before!

A couple of very tiny thoughts about Liam might also have crossed my mind.

Saturday, 14th May, late

After a Molly No-Mates family fun night in

Spent Saturday night watching the Eurovision Song Contest with Mum and Jamie. What has become of the Hart family? And what is *with* those Moldovan hats? Though maybe I should get one to make myself look arty and interesting, in case Art Boy ever forgives me for missing his mural meeting and not bringing my friends. It seems unlikely, but how can anyone outright dismiss a girl in a tall pointy hat? It should at least encourage him to approach me, even if it's solely for jeering and laughing purposes.

Will scour the mall's side-lane outlets for pointy hats on my way home from school on Monday because it's worth a try and can't possibly make things any worse.

Me, Mum and Jamie had a laugh watching TV together, anyway. Never thought I'd say this, but it was nice to see my brother smile after the way he's been lately. I think I've gone soft.

When Mum went to get us a drink, I suggested to Jamie that we should emigrate to Azerbaijan together, leaving our problems far behind. He was surprisingly keen, despite neither of us having much of a clue where it is. It's got to be in Europe, anyway, so it can't be *that* hard to get to. I'd miss Mum and the mall, but I'm sure she can visit and they probably have shopping centres there to help with homesickness. Dad and Nan are expecting us tomorrow and I don't want to let them down, so we can think about leaving on Monday.

The Eurovision Song Contest was obviously having a strange

effect on Mum, too, because she came back from the kitchen and said thoughtfully, "You know, I think I might need to re-evaluate my life a bit. Try to get out more, as they say." Then she went very quiet for ages.

She'd probably welcome our departure, then.

Sunday, 15th May
Just back from Dad's

I held my breath a bit at the appropriate time but Dad *didn't even ask Jamie about his love life*! No remarks were uttered about boys being boys and no attempts were made by Dad to imply his own teenhood studliness. Last week's reaction must have put him right off the subject.

Instead, Dad asked Jamie about revision and exams, and when Jamie grunted something vague in reply, Dad actually *gave him a lecture on the importance of qualifications*. He sounded like a... well, like a *dad*!!!

It is the end of an era.

It's clearly the right time to go.

Monday, 16th May
Back from school and disappointed

Jamie changed his mind about our Azerbaijan exile after remembering that the whole of Years 12 and 13 have officially been on study leave since last Friday at 3.35pm, so he can lounge around at home and prowl the mall all day while Mum's at work and I'm at school, which is way better than running away to some place he can't even find on his smartphone's SatNav feature. (Probably because he can't spell it.)

I take it back about Jamie. My brother can be *incredibly* selfish!

Wendy had her GCSE exam today. When I got up this morning, I prepared a "good luck" message without thinking. Then I hesitated for so long over the "send" that my finger got fed up and pressed it for me before I could protest.

I got a reply a few minutes later. It said: "Thx M".

I looked for Jewel at lunchtime but she wasn't in her usual spot in the library. I sat there by myself instead, studying an atlas and locating Eurovision finalist countries.

Later

Must-see TV (?!)

Switched on the TV too early for Eastenders and saw the tail end of a local news report about Art Boy and his mural meeting. The reporter didn't say much – and if she'd said Art Boy's name, I'd missed it. Argh! But I just caught Art Boy himself say to camera, *"There's still time to join in and we're meeting every Friday evening at The Lilies. You can't miss us!"*

There followed a great shot of Service Entrance D last Friday night, filled with arty types. The Moldovan hat would so have blended in. Luckily the cameras didn't pan up to the glass lift to show me with a terrified Jasper in all our trapped glory.

Tuesday, 17th May

Back from school and indignant

Wendy smiled at me today in the corridor. Ameera saw and went extra-huffy. Strange – they're usually the other way around. Is it Jamie-related, or has Wendy actually forgiven me before Ameera? Wait – have I actually done anything wrong? I need to focus on this. They need to apologize to *me*. I think. It's all getting a bit hazy already, and it didn't happen that long ago. With a memory this bad, perhaps I should revise for end-of-year exams after all.

I didn't see Jewel all day. Again. Has the whole family upped and left as secretly as they originally arrived, after Jasper's lift trauma and brush with a crazy mall-girl neighbour? Will I ever know the truth?

Life is one great mystery.

Wednesday, 18th May
Back from school and not nosy at all

I could go up there. Just check everyone's OK. I could maybe offer to pick up homework for Jewel if she's ill. That would prove how friendly and non-crazy I am. Or something. I'm dying to get another look at those pictures all over their wall. I'm so sure they hold some answers.

Hang on – Mum's calling me. She's shouting something about how she's going out and will I heat up dinner for myself and Jamie?

I need to speak to her right this second. She'd better not be asking that just because I'm a girl! Jamie might be heartbroken all of a sudden, but he's still perfectly capable of lighting a cooker ring and heating up a carton of soup for me.

Not much later

Unfairness

Mum had already gone out! I don't even know where she's gone. And the whole double-standard argument I was about to have was irrelevant anyway, because *Jamie's* gone out too.

I thought he was supposed to be all about the work and study from now on?

Why does everyone I know have a better (and more mysterious) social life than I do?

The world is so unfair.

Thursday, 19th May

Back from school and scary

Just saw Jasper on the stairs. Unfortunately, I was in the (totally fixed) glass lift myself, otherwise I would have asked him about where Jewel has got to. Maybe. He sort of caught my eye and looked away quickly, so he might have run a mile if I'd actually spoken to him. Perhaps he associates me with fear.

Great. I'm like some kind of Ninja Mall Girl.

Friday, 20th May

Back from school and cringing

The strangest thing just happened. Our doorbell rang after Mum had disappeared into the bathroom with a pile of freebie skin treatment sachets from department store promotions. I knew she was in it for the long haul. She called out, "Can you get that, Molly? Only if you know who it is, though! Use the chain and the peephole!"

Well, so far so normal. Mum has been saying that ever since we moved here and she realized that the security to stop mall-goers entering the residential wing is virtually non-existent. (There's a code you're supposed to enter on the lift for residential floors and a special lock on the doors to the stairwell above the food court, but our dodgy lift never actually asks for the code and the stairwell door often gets left unlocked by hurried residents.)

I was quite far from the front door at the time so I yelled "WHO IS IT?!!!" as loudly as I could, which I'm sure made Mum roll her eyes and crack her facepack, or otherwise ruin whatever beauty treatment she was getting up to in there. Even though, let the records show, she'd just called to me at a similar volume.

I sort of wondered for a minute whether it might be Jewel, come to tell me where she'd been all week. Or Ameera or Wendy, or both, come to apologize in person and make up by going for a food-court latte? That would be so cool. I really did miss them.

But no. It was a boy's voice, muffled through our solid front door. And it was saying, "Molly, is that you? Look, sorry, I know this seems weird but can I talk to you a minute...?"

I recognized who it was straight away but I confirmed it through the peephole before I opened the door, thinking he was right – it *did* seem weird, even before he said any more.

What was he doing turning up like this?!

OK, I can't bring myself to write about this yet. I need another moment to recover.

A few deep breaths and cringey thoughts later

"What are you doing here?" I blared at Jasper as he stood there in his faded band t-shirt.

I didn't mean to be rude to Jewel's "long-lost twin brother". Then again, I hadn't meant to torture him by trapping him in a lift almost exactly a week ago, either. I think Jasper brought out the worst in me.

"Is your brother home?" he replied, if you can call it a reply. It didn't remotely answer my question, anyway. "Or your mother?"

"Mum's in the middle of a long session in there." I pointed in the direction of the room I knew he'd correctly identify as the bathroom, seeing as his flat has the same layout as ours. "Beauty treatments," I added hurriedly, as Jasper was looking a bit horrified. "I have no idea about Jamie. As usual. Wait, how do you even know I have a brother? Or a mother, for that matter?" I remembered something about our last meeting. "And I hope you're not here to have another go at me about not really being Jewel's friend!"

"No, no. Jewel told me," he said, shifting nervously. "Listen, I just want to talk to you about something, and it's kind of... private, so I wondered..."

"Molly! Who's at the door?" Mum shouted from the bathroom.

"No one!" I yelled back, because it seemed like the right thing to yell, if Jasper was insisting on privacy.

Jasper gave me an odd look.

"I mean... no one SPECIAL!" I forced the volume down on my voice. "I mean..." I whispered.

Jasper seemed embarrassed. "This is really embarrassing," he said.

I am so astute.

"But I can explain, OK? Which might be even more embarrassing." He took a deep breath. "Can we go somewhere to talk, Molly? Would you mind?"

"What – now?"

His shoulders sagged. "Or later. Or never. I don't know. I..." He glanced back at the stairs. "Look, I'll go. This seemed like a good idea and I knew you were home this time last week so I thought you might be – and... Yeah." He turned away. "Never mind. Bye."

He took a few steps towards the stairwell.

"Wait!" I called. "Come back! We can talk right now, if you like." This whole conversation was off-the-scale weird, but I had to admit it was also intriguing. What could he possibly want to say to me?

He turned back, a tiny smile on his lips. "Yeah?"

I nodded. "Course. You can come in right now. Mum won't listen in. Much." Speaking of intriguing, I had a thought. "Or maybe she will... So we could go to yours instead!" I wasn't usually in the habit of inviting myself to strange boys' flats for secret chats, but... Well, it was Jewel's place too. And there were those interesting photos on the wall that I wanted to get another good look at. Plus it wasn't every day that strange boys proposed mysterious conversations at my front door in the first place. It was an opportunity. I'd been missing too many of those lately, what with lift jams and cheese splashes and everything.

"Oh. Er..." Jasper said, shifting awkwardly.

It was my turn to be embarrassed. "Or not," I added quickly.

The awkward pause that followed was interrupted by a familiar "ping!".

Jasper winced.

The lift doors opened and Jamie got out. "Hey, Measly," he said.

I rolled my eyes. So much for the new understanding my brother and I reached the other day.

Jamie seemed to register that Jasper was there. "Hello," he said, sounding a bit doubtful. His pause seemed to say: *"Who are you?"*

"I'm Jasper," said Jasper, who was obviously as astute as me. "I live upstairs. I was just leaving."

"Not yet, though," I jumped in. "We were... arranging something first."

Jamie straightened, narrowed his eyes and generally behaved like he wanted to drag me away and / or defend my honour from boys in scruffy t-shirts. Interesting. He's never been the type of boy who gets protective about his little sister. Then again, I've never been the type of little sister who needs protecting from boys. Mostly because I haven't had all that much to do with them, apart from lots of distant lusting that Jamie could (and should) never know about, especially since most of it was directed at his best friend Liam.

"Right," Jamie said frostily. Ooh-er. Did he disapprove of me seeing Jasper? Well! Even though I wasn't, it was none of his business.

That thought made me add boldly, "So, Jasper. Meet me at the coffee bar by the giant lily statue. It's always quiet there, even on a Saturday." I marvelled at my commanding voice. I almost sounded like one of those confident girls that hang around Jamie! "Tomorrow at one. OK?" I added, thinking it was a meeting time that would play into Jamie's suspicions. Almost like a lunch date, or something.

Sure enough, Jamie glared at me, and then at Jasper.

"Oh. OK, yeah," Jasper mumbled, retreating.

Jamie gave me another look and swept into the flat. I decided I'd have a go at him later about his attitude, or at least try to get him grounded by telling Mum that he hadn't been studying for his exams. It was probably true, after all. What exactly was his problem?

"It's a date!" I called loudly to Jasper, who was hurrying up the stairs. It seemed to make him move even faster. Inside, Jamie slammed his bedroom door. Ha, take that, suddenly overprotective brother!

It was only afterwards, as I stood in the hollow silence of the landing at The Lilies residential wing Level 5, that I thought about what I'd said and how I'd said it.

That's when I began to cringe.

Much later

All cringed out

I cringed and cringed for a very long time. My words echoed in my head. (*"It's a date!"* I mean, who says that? To a boy they barely know? Only a total mall girl, that's who! Wendy and Ameera are so right about me!)

After that, I wallowed about lost friendship, with a little light cringing on the side.

Then I got sick of myself and decided that a walk would do me good. I didn't even bother changing out of my school clothes. I grabbed my bag, called, "Bye, Mum, I'm going out!" and shut the door behind me before she could shout any questions at me.

I was slightly tempted to pop upstairs and see if Jewel was in, but I didn't really want to risk facing Jasper again. There would be plenty of time for that tomorrow, on our so-called (by me) "date". Cringe.

Instead, I took the lift down to the mall with the intention of wandering to the mini-market and buying some chocolate. It's on the other side of the complex and it's a route I often take in the evenings, so I knew the usual friendly security guards would be nodding at me and looking out for me on the way. They're practically family, that lot.

I didn't get very far. Right after I got out of the lift, I noticed a small group of strangely dressed people by Service Entrance D and there was something familiar about them. It was only then that I remembered: it was the night of Art Boy's second mural meeting, as seen on TV! Although there didn't seem to be any cameras around this week. But at least I hadn't missed it altogether this time!

I hurried over, hoping I could blend in with the arty crowd, despite the school uniform. Perhaps they'd think it was ironic, or something. I didn't see anyone I recognized, but I thought I could stand at the edges and try to work out what was going on.

A few people stared at me as I neared them. Then Art Boy himself looked up and gave me a huge smile that radiated pure

Art Boy hotness. He walked over as I reached the group.

"Molly!" he said. "You made it!"

"Art Boy!" I wanted to reply. "You've forgiven me for the cheese thing and for not turning up last week!"

I tried to think of an alternative and more intelligent response. Help – what if he was going to ask me questions about art, like he did the other night? I wasn't Google-ready this time! On the plus side, I wasn't wielding any dangerous canapés either.

"Yeah," I said, adding to my display of high IQ with, "I certainly did make it. And, in fact, here I am."

He nodded in agreement at my declaration of presence. "Well, great. It's a shame you and Jewel missed the first meeting, but really I'm happy for people to join in at any time." He made an open-palm gesture which may have been intended to display sincerity, or could equally have been a makeshift shield against possible cheese-attack. "Especially you two."

"Oh," I said. I might have swooned a bit then, if it wasn't for that little word he said after "you". The one that meant "Jewel". In fact, come to think of it, he was always mentioning Jewel to me. What was with that? And why had I only just noticed it?

Sure enough, he looked around. "Is Jewel on her way?" he asked.

"Oh. No. I only –"

"Oh no, of course not!" he said with a head-shake, looking at me like he'd remembered something I was supposed to know about. "Well, I hope they're OK. I'm sure everything will work out fine. And maybe next time she can come along? If she lets me know in advance that she's coming, that's even better. We meet weekly, and there will be extra sessions when all the exam fever dies down. It's a community-wide endeavour, and each group is assigned a section of the overall canvas..."

He went on for a while, telling me about the project in detail, and I was stunned to find that I understood nearly every word he said. It was like blinkers had been lifted. Er, from my ears. (Can you get ear-blinkers?) Now that I knew the truth, everything seemed much clearer. Art Boy was only interested in Jewel!

I thought back. Jewel certainly hadn't shown any signs of fancying him back. The opposite, maybe. I could possibly still be in with a chance with Art Boy. But did I want to be?

Sure, he was gorgeous. But he was also a bit... well...

"I see the canvas as an open space," he was saying. "A vast field, a green light, permission for ideas to take root, if you will, to germinate..."

A bit pretentious. That was it. I hadn't noticed back when I hadn't understood a word he'd said.

He was an artist though, so maybe it was the real thing and not actually any kind of pretence at all. If art students couldn't go on about "the symbolism of the seed of art in the wilderness of the mall's commerciality", then really, what kind of world would this be? A more understandable one, perhaps. But one with infinitely less... Art Boy in it.

Plus did I mention he was hot? He smiled at me again, as if to prove it. "So will you come again next week?" he asked as last week's gaggle of arty girls began to close in on us.

"Yeah, probably," I mumbled.

"Great! We might actually get started instead of just talking about it," he laughed.

I sort of doubted it.

"And bring Jewel!" he said before he shifted his sunshine smile away from me and onto the other girls.

"Yeah, we'll see about that," I mumbled to myself.

I hung around for a few more minutes trying not to ogle him too obviously before I sneaked away to buy that chocolate.

Saturday, 21st May
After a weird day out at the mall

Woke up to Mum's kitchen radio droning on about this thing called The Rapture. Apparently this meant that it was Judgement Day and the world was about to end. This was immediately followed by a report on the increasing price of oil, a bizarre piece about maintaining your shrubbery, and an interview with a spokeswoman for a middle-aged rock-star who was recovering from a car accident in LA, or something.

At that point, I tuned out the radio and my head filled instantly with thoughts of my "date" with Jasper today. After last night's Art Boy encounter, I'd managed to replace all the cringing with intrigue about the mysterious twins upstairs. What did Jasper want to talk to me about? Why hadn't Jewel been at school last week? And what was the deal with Art Boy – did he and Jewel have a past? I was dying to get some answers.

I got up and went to the kitchen, where Jamie was wolfing down his breakfast and apparently not caring that he was dripping chocolate milk on his work uniform.

"Good morning," he said politely, sounding nothing like

Jamie. Perhaps this was a sign of the end of days. "Measly," he added. So maybe not.

I frowned. "You said you'd stop calling me that!" I remembered to be in a mood with him about yesterday, too. "Oh yeah, and what was all that about with Jasper?"

"Sorry, I keep forgetting you have a real name." He grinned. "And who's Jasper?" His expression was all "it wasn't me, ref". Then a bit of guilt crept in. "Oh, you mean the music guy who was eyeing you up on our doormat?"

"He was not eyeing me up!" I pointed out indignantly. "He was talking to me."

Jamie coughed. "If you say so. But who is he? What exactly do you know about him, Molly?"

"Nothing much, apart from the fact that he lives upstairs, carries keyboards around and is scared of lifts. What's it to you, Jamie?"

"Nothing." Jamie shrugged. "Except that he was eyeing you up, I don't care what you say. And then you asked him out, didn't you?"

My cheeks went all hot. "Maybe. So what if I did?"

"So... So maybe there are other boys around, boys you know you can trust, and..." Jamie stirred his cereal. "Nothing. Forget I said anything."

"Oh no. Tell me what you're up to, Jamie Hart, or else I'll..." I tried to think of something. It was a lot harder to get at my brother now that he didn't care so much about his Lego constructions. "I'll tell Tasha something bad about you."

Jamie gave a hurt sigh. "I'm over Tasha," he said, looking

like he was anything but. "I told you, didn't I? I'm all work and study now. A whole new me."

"Ha! You were out yesterday!"

"In the afternoon, for about ten minutes! I went to buy gum. For concentration."

"And Wednesday night!"

"I was at Liam's! That's different. He got back early from that short break his family dragged him on. And we talked about work and study."

I roared with laughter. "OK, now I know you're full of –"

"And yeah, if you must know, he talked about you as well, Molly." Jamie shook his head in disbelief. "That's sort of why I felt strange about the music guy. I promised Liam..."

"What?"

Jamie sighed. "Liam likes you, Molly. He really likes you, though I have no idea why, personally, and the whole idea freaks me out bigtime. But he's a mate and I said a couple of weeks ago that I'd ask you along to one of our group nights out. I thought that way he'd see what a pain you truly are – no offence – and that would be that. Then you said you weren't going, and anyway he had that last-minute holiday." He shrugged. "He wanted me to try again but I told him he was on his own now. Then I saw you outside with that boy yesterday, and I thought about Tasha not liking me and... I don't know. It's weird."

"Weird," I echoed in shock. I vaguely considered swooning like a corseted lady from the Victorian costume dramas Nan likes to watch on TV, but I didn't want to miss whatever Jamie would say next.

"Listen, I promised Liam I wouldn't tell you. So I haven't. OK?"

I just stood there. My jaw might have unhinged itself a bit.

"But you did tell me about your friend Wendy, so I guess it's only fair," Jamie continued. "And I nearly blabbed to you about Liam more than once, anyway. The other day I pretended I was talking about Harry Bo. Good, aren't I?" He gave himself a smug smile. "So now you know. But you have to forget I said anything."

He stood up and left for work, leaving me standing in the kitchen until my phone startled me into action by warbling "Rolling in the Deep", in time with the swooping of my heart.

Wow.

I need a moment to collect my thoughts here.

Later
Weirdness continued

So anyway... it was Wendy on the phone. She said she really missed me and she was sorry she'd put all that pressure on me before with the Jamie stuff and the party stuff, and would I forgive her?

What a day. I smiled to myself. Then I realized what she hadn't said.

"What about Ameera?" I asked.

Wendy sighed and my heart sank.

"She's still... you know. Calling you a 'mall girl' and stuff."

"Wendy! You started that!"

"I know. I'm really sorry, I swear."

"I don't get why Ameera's being like this. It was your family's party I missed – and, er, sorry about that, by the way..."

"Oh, it's OK. I don't blame you for not going. My mum was unbearable and she would definitely have gone on at you about the evils of the mall. But I don't know, Ameera's taken it really badly. You know what she's like about loyalty."

I realized Wendy was right. Ameera doesn't often fall out with people, but when she does she really means it, unlike Wendy whose fiery temper fizzles quickly. If Ameera thought I'd let Wendy down, she wasn't going to forgive me just because Wendy said it was OK with her.

"Oh, this is pointless," I mumbled.

"Listen, I'm working on it, Molz, I promise." She sighed even more. "Take care, OK?" she said, and hung up.

And my rollercoaster day wasn't even over. I still had to meet Jasper. Though suddenly the whole "date" thing I was stressing about yesterday seemed really pathetic and I couldn't even bring myself to worry for a second. What was the point of Liam liking me, or of me accidentally asking out Jewel's twin brother – any of it – if I'd lost my best friends? That was what really mattered.

I moped all the way to the quietest coffee shop in The Lilies. I have no idea why no one ever goes there, but I guess most shoppers prefer the crowded places where they can feel like they're in the middle of the mall action. This coffee shop is poky with tiny windows and an opaque door, and inside it's like a little cave.

Jasper was sitting by the giant lily statue, shifting about

nervously in his black t-shirt and jeans. He saw me coming and jumped up as I reached him.

"Thanks for this, Molly," he said. His voice trembled. Oops, I must have really scared him yesterday. "I mean, it's great of you. But listen, I'm afraid I can't... I can't..."

Oh no, what next? Was he going to tell me he couldn't go out with me? That it wasn't me, it was him? My first accidental relationship, and we were already breaking up!

"It's OK," I said quickly. "You don't have to... Do anything... Or whatever." The cringing was most definitely back.

He smiled thinly. "Thanks, but I should at least try, shouldn't I? This is what I wanted to talk to you about. I hope you don't mind."

"Er... mind what?"

"Nothing." He nudged his head towards the coffee shop and took a deep breath. "So I guess I'll buy you a drink. After you."

I opened the door to the coffee shop and took a step inside. It was even darker and pokier than I remembered from the last time I'd been here. There was an old man reading a paper in the corner but no one else. It was the perfect place for a mysterious, quiet chat. Except...

Jasper wasn't following me. Instead, he was taking big gulps of air. Then he stepped forwards like it was a monumental effort. Just like the other day in the lift.

Oh!

I couldn't believe myself! Why hadn't I thought of this? I'd only chosen exactly the worst shop in the entire mall for someone who was scared of confined spaces!

I gave him a look that was pure apology.

He returned it with a look of solid determination. "No, I'm going in," he said, trembling.

"No, you're not," I replied. And then, because he wasn't moving, I grabbed his arm and nudged him over to the fountain next to the lily statue. A nice, wide open space, and rushing water to hide secret talking. Now this was perfect. I know my mall inside out.

I let go of Jasper's arm and sat with my back to the water. Jasper sat next to me with a long sigh. He shifted closer to me, maybe to make himself heard over the gushing sound.

"Guess it was too much, too soon," he said after a while. "You know, there are some malls I can't even go into."

"Seriously?" I said. He was the strangest "mall boy" ever. "And yet you live in one."

"This one's OK because it's all natural light and plenty of exits," Jasper said. "Besides, we haven't lived here long and I'm not sure whether we're staying. It's a temporary thing. My father only got us this place when Jewel came to live with us a few weeks ago, and Mum said... Oh, you don't want to hear about my crazy family."

"No, go on." I did, I did!

"Well, maybe I don't want to tell you." Jasper grinned. He looked down, hesitating. I noticed that his eyelashes were really long. "So should I say what I've been dying to talk to you about?"

"Yeah, course."

"It's just... the other day, in the lift – don't apologize!"

How did he know I was about to do that? Freaky.

"Anyway, this might sound weird to you," he continued, "but that was the mildest reaction I've ever had to being in a small space like that. Especially for that length of time."

"You are kidding," I blurted before I realized how rude it sounded.

He laughed. "Seriously. Sometimes I can't breathe at all. It's like my brain's screaming, you know?" His face fell. "Sometimes the screams actually come out, too."

"That sounds horrible."

"Yup." He sighed. "And really embarrassing. I hate people knowing about it."

"I won't tell anyone." Oops, had I already told Jamie?

"Thanks, Molly. The trouble is, it gets in the way of my life," Jasper continued as I swallowed my guilty feelings. "Like right now, for example, I should join Jewel... somewhere. Somewhere she is that I probably need to be, at least as soon as the exams are over, if there's no change." He sped up as if he wanted to skip over that part, which was wise of him because I nearly interrupted with a barrage of questions. "And Mum's offered to go with me, even though..." He skipped that bit, too. "But I can't face the plane journey. When I think about being shut in a tin with no way out..." He shuddered. "But see, here's the thing. The other day in the elevator with you... It wasn't like that. It's the best I've ever coped, even though we were there for ages. I know I must have looked like I was going to pieces, but I think you somehow really helped me."

"I helped you?"

"Yes. Seriously, Molly." He smiled. "I tried getting in the lift again by myself the next day but I couldn't do it. And I was reading this thing online about coping with my condition, and it said if you found anything that helped you should keep trying it, in stages, to see if you improve. Apparently some people totally cure themselves that way – and, believe me, I've tried everything. Mum even sent me to a really expensive hypnotist once, and it didn't work. But I thought, if you didn't mind...?" His brown eyes searched mine. "I mean, we could try a few small trips in the lift? Or in that coffee shop? Maybe a few minutes a day, if you had time? I could pay you in drinks or something? Though you might have to do the actual buying and bring the coffee out to me, at least at first."

"Oh." Well, this was weird. "Yeah, that sounds OK. You mean like an ongoing business arrangement?"

"No, I thought maybe more like a series of dates," he said, and his eyes sparkled to show he was joking. At least, I think he was. He was full of this cheeky kind of confidence when he wasn't scared. It was actually pretty attractive.

I shifted a tiny bit closer without even meaning to.

In the pause that followed, a thought about kissing him popped into my head. Which was crazy. I hadn't meant to ask him out, and he only wanted to see me for bizarre medical reasons. What was the matter with me?

"You want to try it now?" he said quietly, and for a second I thought he meant kissing and I went hot and cold all over.

Then he stood up and I realized that, of course, he meant the coffee shop therapy.

"OK," I said as a wave of relief swept over me. Or possibly a wave of disappointment. I wasn't quite sure which.

We made it to the doorway three times before he said that was enough for one day and anyway his mum was expecting him at home. Then we walked back together chatting about life and stuff. He relaxed more and more the further we got from the little coffee shop. He told me he was still officially at school in the town he moved from a few weeks ago, which was two bus rides away from Lilyford, but he was on study leave for GCSEs. His Mum had decided he shouldn't change schools in an exam year. It turns out Jasper's actually in the year above me, despite being Jewel's twin, because he was born on the last day of August and she was born on the first day of September. I know there's a whole lot of other weirdness going on in that family but that's as much as I managed to get out of him. Partly because I was enjoying telling him tiny details about my own life.

For the rest of Saturday, I almost forgot to obsess about Liam for the first time in absolutely ages. Almost, but not quite.

Sunday, 22nd May
Back from Dad's house
The most interesting thing that happened at Dad's today was when Nan looked up from her tea and said, "That Rapture thing didn't happen, then, eh? It's almost a bit of a disappointment after all that talk. Still, I suppose it's not the end of the world."

Jamie cracked up laughing and Dad explained carefully to Nan why what she'd said was funny. She listened with a patient expression on her face, though I suspected she knew exactly what she was saying all along.

I keep telling Nan she should be an actress. She always tells me she has her hands full being a "perpetual mother" and "grateful grandmother", not to mention tae kwon do champion. (I'm not joking. Nan's a black belt and she only took it up a few years ago.) Anyway, I'm glad she got me to start this diary. With all the writing I do here, I've managed to halve the amount of time I spend telling her stuff, which on Sunday meant about two hours instead of the usual four. Perhaps Nan needs a break.

Friday, 27th May, afternoon
After a fun-packed week (!) at West Lilyford Community College

Perhaps *I* need a break. This is a typical day at my school right now, whatever year you're in…

Teachers go on about exams and how important they are, complete with much studying of past papers and revision waffle.

At break time, people hang around in groups, with girls going on about how little they've studied and how they basically know nothing, and boys going on about how little they've studied and how they basically know everything.

Then it's back to lessons, where teachers go on about exams and how important they are, complete with much studying of past papers and revision waffle.

Repeat (Tuesday). Repeat (Wednesday). Repeat (Thursday). Repeat (Friday).

And that about sums up my week.

By the end of Monday, I'd drawn up a detailed revision

schedule using three different coloured biros. By Tuesday, I'd torn up the timetable and sat for hours staring at a pile of books instead, hoping to absorb their contents with the power of my gaze. On Wednesday and Thursday I got fed up with myself and actually revised, for hours, both in the library at break and later at home. In the space of one short week, I've become a total study-holic, living and breathing course guides and eating practice questions for breakfast. Next week is half-term, but the way things are going I bet I'll still be under the influence of the study rays.

They are wily, those teachers.

Wendy spent the week smiling at me occasionally but mostly hanging around with Ameera, who definitely wasn't talking to me. Jewel obviously wasn't back yet from the place Jasper mysteriously said she had to be, the one that was a plane journey away. I bet the teachers were managing to send her exam-importance beams anyway, all the way from Lilyford.

Jasper popped down to see me every day after school and he was managing entire seconds in a non-moving lift by Wednesday, and a takeaway coffee order with me holding the door open on Thursday. We got a few funny looks and a grumble from a lift-using shopper, but overall I recovered from the weirdness of being Jasper's sort-of therapist pretty quickly. I wonder what exam passes you need to be a proper one.

Meanwhile, Mum was off doing more beauty treatments and having a couple more mysterious nights out. I tried to ask Jamie what he thought of it all but he kept telling me he was too busy studying to talk. I pointed out that his computer screen was clearly displaying Facebook and he insisted it was part of his online study. Hmm. Despite what he says, I'm not sure my brother will ever change.

Liam was back, as I knew from Jamie. Like my brother (and Jasper), he was on study leave, but Year 12s have some optional revision sessions and I saw Liam around the school a couple of times. I had a lot more trouble than usual with my habit of sneaking sly glances at him in corridors. I found it hard to look at him after what Jamie said about him liking me. How weird. It should be a good thing, knowing this, but instead it has made me a thousand times more awkward around him.

I officially do not get life.

Later

Back home after my Jasper therapy session

Behold! Another illustration of me officially not getting life.

So I said goodbye to Jasper on the stairs and arranged to see him tomorrow, slightly distracted because my phone was warbling Adele at me. I was still shutting the door when I answered it and a voice went, "OMG, MOLLY!!!" in my ear.

It was Wendy. "Ow," I said. "What's up? Please tell me Ameera's over it and we can all go shopping tomorrow!"

"Ameera?" She sounded confused. "Oh. No. No! 'Fraid not. But you will never believe this. Your brother... your brother... on Facebook..." She couldn't seem to say any more, which was strange for her. She was good with words, which was why she'd done her GCSE English early.

"What's Jamie done now?" I asked suspiciously, mentally

preparing to have a major moan at him. But I could never have predicted what she said next.

"He friended me on Facebook last week, which was weird enough, but then he is your brother." Her laugh was a bit on the manic side. "But today, just now, we had a chat and... he asked me out! Jamie Hart asked me out, Molly! Isn't that fantastic? Aren't you happy for me?"

Well. Possibly for the first time in my life, I did not have the first clue what to say to her.

But I wasn't happy.

I made some excuse to hang up on Wendy and then I stressed about the whole situation for an age and a half. Should I say anything to Wendy? Or to Jamie? What would a good friend do? What would a good sister do? Was I either? Neither? Both? What was the question again?

OK, I knew I should probably tell Wendy everything Jamie had confessed to me about his unrequited love for Tasha.

Except that I was scared of hurting Wendy's feelings if I told her.

So I could keep quiet to Wendy, but have a quiet word with Jamie and demand to know exactly what he was up to.

But if I confronted Jamie, he might say, "You're right, Molly. It would be deeply wrong to go out with Wendy when I am in one-sided love with Tasha. Therefore and furthermore I shall hitherto break the date." (In this particular daydream, Jamie talked like one of Mum's legal documents from work.) Anyway, hencetoforth the end result would be the upset of my aforementioned friend Wendy.

In other words, either scenario would be bad.

So I didn't ring Wendy back.

When Jamie got home, I said, "Hey, I heard you asked Wendy out." And before he could answer I took the plunge and added, "So how about if I come along with..." It really did feel like diving into a swimming pool. One with a broken-down heating system and a STRICTLY NO DIVING sign. "With Liam. What do you think? You could ask him for me... or something."

Jamie looked horrified and a bit intrigued at the same time. "Are you telling me you want to go out with Liam? And you want me to ask him out for you?"

"I... well..." This seemed like something I should deny. "No, of course not. But I just thought that if you were seeing Wendy..." I had to pause then at the weirdness of it. "And things haven't been that good between me and my friends lately, I don't know if you noticed." Though I know he had, because he invited me into the sixth form room a couple of weeks back when I was lonely at school. "So I could come along, and..." The track I was heading down with these words didn't actually go anywhere, but Jamie didn't need to know that.

"OK, sure. Why not," he said in the silence I'd left. "I'll ask Liam. There's no way he'll say no. But Measly, I should warn you that he might not see something like this in the casual way that you do."

"Oh, don't worry," I'd replied then, after more secret gulping. *Casual?* I didn't think so! And – wait – shouldn't I say something similar to him about Wendy? "I'm sure it will all be fine."

And there it was. It was a selfless act, inviting myself and

Liam to Jamie's night out with my friend. This way, I could keep an eye on Wendy and step in somehow if things were going badly.

There was also the fact that I was going to go out with, oh, ONLY THE BOY I'VE HAD A SECRET CRUSH ON FOR YEARS!!!!

Result.

Saturday, 28th May

Verging on possible happiness at the Hart residence, 5th floor, The Lilies eco-mall, Lilyford

Woke up to Mum's radio droning the news, just like I did last Saturday. There was nothing about the end of the world or shrubbery this time, but they did mention the price of oil and also the same old rock star, who was apparently now "in a fair condition" and "progressing well" in a Los Angeles hospital after his car accident two weeks ago. The naff jingle at the end made it clear that Mum was listening to the local radio station. Well, that and the way the reporter tried desperately to connect the injured mega-star to the Lilyford area. (Apparently, despite residing in LA, he had "roots in East Lilyford", which probably meant some distant great-aunt of his once popped into the East Lilyford Services for a quick rest stop on the way to somewhere more interesting.)

Something about the whole radio thing niggled at me for a while, until I realized why it was weird. I knew Jamie would be getting ready for work, but he wouldn't have put the radio on – it's not a Jamie thing. He's more likely to stream tunes out of his smartphone. So Mum must have switched on Radio Lilyford, possibly before Jamie got up. So...

What had happened to Mum's lie-ins? Saturday mornings used to be sacred sleeping time for her! Jamie and I were trained from an early age to leave her well alone on a Saturday, seeing as she had to get up early to drive us to Dad's on a Sunday. (Dad used to offer to pick us up but she always refused, saying she'd "rather be in control, thank you very much".)

Mum was up to something, I was sure of it now! Mysterious nights out, extra beauty treatments, lack of Saturday lie-in... What did it add up to? Could it be... She couldn't have *met a new man*, could she?

Ugh!!!

But *who*? And *how*? She was almost always at work! And there was no way it could be any of her colleagues, the amount she moans about them, given half a chance. (Let's just say that when she accuses me of being a drama queen, I *could* tell her that I know where I get it from! Except that I'm not that keen on getting grounded.)

Anyway, it didn't completely make sense. Why would seeing someone new mean getting up earlier on a Saturday?

And wouldn't she have told me and Jamie about the revoltingly disgusting possibility that she had a boyfriend?

Hmm. Maybe not.

I sprang out of bed with the intention of capturing her for questioning, but I was distracted by my phone going off. The display flashed "Ameera".

Ameera! Now *there* was someone who always got up

freakishly early on weekends, mostly because she didn't want to waste valuable shopping time if she could help it. I almost missed her inviting herself over to mine first thing on a Saturday so that she could drag me around the mall. I'd started thinking it would never happen again.

I grabbed the phone before all my wistful pondering made me miss the call.

"Molly!" Ameera chirped, sounding so much like her old self that I wanted to hug the phone. "Listen, that was such a nice thing you did for Wendy."

"Uh..."

"And, you know what? I admit it. I was wrong about you. I'm sorry, Molly."

Yay! But also: oh no!

"What nice thing did I do?" I babbled, hoping I was misunderstanding.

I was not. "You know! Fixing her up with Jamie. She's over the moon about it!"

"Oh."

"And I just knew it had to have something to do with you. I know you're trying to make amends and I really respect that, you know? Oh, Molz, I've missed you!"

I really didn't want to tell her she was wrong, but I thought I should. The "make amends" got my back up a bit, but it was the "respect" that made me say it. "Uh, Ameera, I'm so glad you called, and I've really missed you too, but..." I took a deep breath. "But I need to tell you that Jamie asking Wendy out had nothing to do with me. I'm sorry." I bit my lip. "But it's true. In fact –"

"Aw, Molz!" Ameera laughed. "See, *this* is the Molly I know. Hello, BFF!"

"What? But I just told you I –"

"Yes, but I don't believe you. Come on, you said something to Jamie, didn't you? About Wendy, I mean? I bet you did!"

"Oh." I thought about it. "Yes, I suppose I *did* tell him that Wendy liked him, but..." But I didn't mean to blurt it out, and I was actually worried I was betraying Wendy's trust by saying it.

"See? I knew it. Molly, you rock!"

"Uh, Ameera, seriously, Jamie's decisions have nothing to do with me. Ever."

"There's always a first time." She giggled. "So – half term, baby! Are we going shopping or WHAT? Never mind studying for exams. We have to get Wendy sorted out! Just for herself, I mean – not for any *guy*. No offence to your brother. But just so that Wendy feels mega-confident by Friday. Life is all about inner confidence."

"Friday?"

"The big date, of course! Jamie and Wendy are going to Paolo's Pizza Place in The Lilies. Aw, I almost wish I could be a fly on the wall, be there for support, you know. Wendy is so nervous!"

"Uh... I might be going too, actually. I told Jamie I'd come and he could bring... Liam..."

Ameera squealed, though it was more of a scream, really. "You are awesome! You truly are! I can't believe I ever thought you weren't a real mate."

That made me feel terrible, and I almost told her about my

crush on Liam. But I've never told anyone, ever, and it seemed like a strange time to start. "Course I'm a real mate," I mumbled instead.

But Ameera wasn't really listening anyway. "So, I know it's not as exciting for you, but I'm taking this as a *double* project! I am going to get Wendy *and* you so ready! Yay for a whole week off school for preparations! We are going to have an *ace* week, the three of us!" She started reeling off a list of places in the mall we could go to for new styles and even some beauty treatments she had vouchers for, thanks to her mum and older sisters who had "frequent user" points. Being a fashion expert runs in Ameera's family, and even her nine-year-old brother is mega-stylish.

She made arrangements to meet me later for "planning", seeing as Wendy couldn't get out of family stuff on a Saturday and would probably need to tell a few white lies about "studying with her friends" in order to come out with us later in the week, too. Ameera pointed out that this would be pretty close to the truth because Wendy *would* be studying with us – only she'd be studying STYLE! Then she laughed a lot.

I had to admit that it all sounded brilliant. Me and my two BFFs, hanging around in the mall and back together at last.

Later

The Ameera part of my day

Had an awesome time with Ameera, flitting in and out of her favourite boutiques and making appointments for various treatments next week, including one at this weird place called Perfect Feet where you get special fish to nibble at your toes to make them smooth. As we left that place, I asked Ameera why it would matter whether our feet were rough when they were going to be firmly packed into shoes anyway, and she repeated this whole thing about it being all about how we feel about *ourselves*, and inner confidence was what mattered.

"Wendy thinks she's not good enough to go out with Jamie Hart. She thinks he belongs with one of those glamorous girls, like that Tasha who used to work at the kiosk."

I swallowed hard and focused on the rail of clothes that Ameera had stopped at. "Doesn't Tasha work there anymore?"

Ameera shrugged. "Haven't seen her there for a while. Anyway, I want Wendy to realize she's every bit as good as Tasha. It's all about confidence," she repeated, triumphantly picking out a bright red shirt and pointing out how great it would look with Wendy's dark glossy hair.

"I'm sure you're right. About everything," I mumbled, hoping that Tasha had emigrated or something, and Jamie would instantly forget she'd ever existed.

We looped around the mall several more times, and then Ameera dragged me down the lane near Service Entrance D, where she said she'd located a tiny new boutique.

"You have to see this place!" she said. "I only discovered it because Mum saw it on TV the other week. Apparently it was in the background in this local news thing about a loony art project, or something. Some mural based on collecting rubbish from the mall."

Art Boy's project! I'd completely forgotten to go along to the meeting on Friday because of the Wendy/Jamie news! And I couldn't go next week either, if Friday was the night of the big date. Poor Art Boy. If I wasn't splashing cheese all over him or failing to bring Jewel along despite his pleas, I was ignoring his meetings completely (or watching them from a glass lift).

"I know about that," I told Ameera. "It's run by the boy whose private view I went to that day..." I trailed off. What was I doing, reminding her of the day she fell out with me?

"Oh, you know that art guy?" she asked, barely looking up at me as she held a patterned dress against her. "He looked pretty hot on TV."

"He's pretty hot in real life too," I said.

She gave me a long, knowing look. "OMG, Molly, why didn't you *say* he was the reason you were missing Wendy's party? I still would have been miffed but at least I wouldn't have thought you preferred that Julie mouse to your real mates!" She laughed and cast her eyes towards the changing rooms. "Come on, I want to try this on. Even though I can't afford it. Ssh."

The little cubicles and the mention of Jewel/Julie reminded me that I was supposed to be meeting Jasper. We had one of our regular appointments by the giant lily statue at two o'clock. I couldn't believe I'd almost forgotten him in all the excitement of having mates again.

I glanced around but couldn't see any clocks so I got my phone out of my bag.

Ameera gave me a curious look. We've always been in the habit of sharing texts with each other, and as they're usually from our mums keeping tabs on us, we often read them out in silly voices while rolling our eyes.

"I'm just checking the time," I explained. It was five past two and we were at the wrong end of the mall. Argh!

"Got somewhere to be?" Ameera teased in a mock teacher-voice, though I did detect a slight edge of something less jokey.

What should I say? After what she'd said about Jewel, what would she think of me meeting Jewel's twin brother? Especially when I couldn't tell her the real reason, as he'd sworn me to secrecy.

I took a deep breath. "Um, yeah, actually. Sorry, Ameera. I've got to run. But I'll see you on Monday for more shopping, OK?"

"OK," she said, eyeing me suspiciously. And then she added, "It's not that boy, is it? Art guy?"

"Oh. No. A different boy," I blurted. "But it's not like that!" I added hurriedly. "I see him every day for..." I remembered not to go into details. "...study," I finished unconvincingly.

"And then you're seeing – sorry, *studying* – Liam on Friday?" Ameera shook her head and I held my breath a bit. Would she storm off again, calling me "boy crazy" as well as "mall girl" this time? Instead, she smirked. "OMG, Molly. I don't think you *need* your confidence boosted. But you'll help me with mission "makeover Wendy" next week anyway, won't you?"

"Course I will," I told her, before I said goodbye and chased across the mall to meet Jasper.

Later still...

The Jasper part of my day

Jasper was in a weird mood.

I said sorry about five times for being late and he told me

as many times that it was fine, no problem and he was glad I'd made it anyway, better late than never, etc. But he didn't smile once, any of the times he said it. I ended up beaming like a beacon at him, attempting to smile enough for both of us.

All the way through this exchange, he aimed repeated gentle kicks at the wall by the fountain, though he looked like he wanted to boot it – or something else – much harder.

"Are you OK?" I asked when I decided I'd apologized enough.

He stopped kicking the wall and looked at me, his eyes deep and troubled. "Yeah. Maybe. Or not." He sighed. "Listen, Molly, about our meetings. I've had some good news. It means Jewel's coming home and I won't have to take that plane after all..." He hesitated like he was waiting for me to fill in the blanks.

"Oh. So you won't be needing my pretend-therapy anymore?" I supplied, wondering why disappointment was flooding through me. "OK! That's cool! Glad you've had good news!" My voice sounded over-bright. What was all that about? Though also, why was Jasper acting like his news was anything but "good"?

He didn't take his eyes off me, but he did finally smile a bit. "It's not that I don't need our meetings. I still want to get better, and you're definitely helping." He sighed. "I guess it might be kind of hard to explain it to Jewel, though..."

I felt an irrational urge to say something like, "Who cares what Jewel thinks! Besides, she's your sister. Why would it be difficult to tell her you're getting some kind of amateur therapy from a neighbour?" But it's not like I tell my brother everything about my life. Or, in fact, very much at all. Also, it didn't take a genius to work out that Jasper and Jewel's relationship – and everything about their family – wasn't exactly ordinary anyway.

"I only wanted you to know that... it's less urgent now," Jasper said. "So we could cut back on the meetings if you like."

"Oh. Yeah. Yeah, sure! Whatever!" The over-brightness was still there. I fixed my eyes on the water in the fountain. *"But why would I like that?"* I thought.

I glanced over at him. He was kicking at the wall again. "Look, sorry, Molly. I'm not completely with it today. Even though the news I heard was good, it's kind of... thrown me. It's hard to explain. Maybe we can meet later in the week instead? After Jewel's got back and got over the jet lag, maybe, so that things are back to normal..." He paused and smiled. "Or as normal as my family ever gets, anyway."

I was so right about the weirdness of their family. And what was all this about jet lag – how far away *was* Jewel? I decided to ask him, but Jasper spoke again just as I opened my mouth.

"We could do something on Friday?" he suggested. "If you're free? I should be around late afternoon, and evening too."

"Friday?" Ameera would not be happy about that. She had plans for me and Wendy that took us right up to the hour of the big date. I wouldn't be surprised if she ended up spending the evening outside Paolo's Pizza Place peering through its open-fronted entrance and admiring her handiwork.

I suddenly wondered about telling Jasper the reason I couldn't see him – after all, he was a friend, wasn't he? Maybe I should say, *"No, I can't make it on Friday as I'm preparing for a date with the love of my life!"* But that would be more than I'd even told my best friends... and anyway, there was something about the way he was looking at me. It was a look I'd caught from him before sometimes during our therapy meetings and it was intense and, well, kind of made my stomach flip every time I thought about it. Like right now. Except that it never lasted long and I wasn't sure whether it was all in my imagination.

He looked away, making me think I'd imagined it again.

"I'm not sure about Friday," I mumbled.

"OK," he said, his voice sounding kind of weird and flat. "I guess I'll be seeing you around, anyway, with Jewel back in town. Bye, Molly." And he turned and walked off, disappearing almost instantly into the Saturday shopper throng.

"See you around," I told the fountain. The flowing water was unresponsive but way less confusing.

Friday 3rd June, morning

Makeover musings at the Hart residence, 5th floor, The Lilies eco-mall, Lilyford

Ameera was not kidding about her plans for me and Wendy. Though Wendy got out of half of it by saying she couldn't escape her parents and the study timetable her mum had stuck to the fridge. I'm sure it was at least partly an excuse, because I could tell that Ameera had spooked her with a detailed description of the "crystal dermabrasion" she'd booked for us on Monday afternoon.

So I ended up undergoing the majority of the makeover for both of us. (I did study a bit in the evenings, though. I couldn't get over the exam fear that the teachers had so expertly instilled in me, despite it being half term and my friends being back in my life.)

By the middle of the week I'd had three facials, a manicure, a spray tan and weird multi-coloured extensions weaved into my hair. My new look was reminiscent of early Cheryl Cole, but crossed with a drunken sheep on a bad hair day.

The Perfect Feet treatment yesterday afternoon was particularly weird, and not just because of the tickling sensation of fish nibbling on my toes in a freaky tank. Also because while I was in the waiting room I saw a familiar woman walk in and hover by the price-list poster. It took me a few seconds to register that she was my mother.

"Mum!" I called out. "Shouldn't you be at work?" Mum's work is really high-powered and she's always complaining that she barely gets a minute to grab a sandwich at lunchtime, let alone go to any of the shops. But it was way too late for lunch anyway, and too early for hometime. (Or whatever the end of the day is called at work.)

She looked startled but she recovered quickly. "Molly!" she said. "Shouldn't you be revising for your exams?"

"Uh... yeah, but Ameera had a voucher for this treatment and..."

This was kind of a sneaky trick because Mum has seen (and heard) me mope around about how my life is over without my best friends, so I knew she'd be a bit more forgiving than usual, in her delight at my BFF reunion.

Sure enough, she waved at Ameera and said, "Oh, hello.

Nice to see you again. You must come round some time."

"I've been round every single day this week," Ameera said brightly, and I nudged her. There was no need to push it.

"Oh, good. Don't forget to study for your exams, girls," said Mum vaguely. "See you later, Molly."

And she left without making an appointment or having a treatment or anything. What was she doing there during working hours in the first place?

Then Ameera and I were called to the fish tanks and I was soon distracted from my family mystery by the freaky foot-smoothing process.

And now it's finally Friday, and tonight... is IT. The big date.

Argh, what am I doing?!

Friday, 3rd June, late

What WAS I doing?!

"Ready?" Jamie asked me as he stood by the front door, looking like he'd made a surprising amount of effort with his clothing and hygiene.

What a great question. All the way down to our meeting point at Paolo's Pizza Place on Level 1, I kept imagining the evening playing out like one of those disrupted wedding scenes from a film, when the vicar asks whether anyone knows any good reason that the couple should not be wed and someone bursts into the church at the last second, bleating, "Stop the proceedings! This isn't right!"

I mean, obviously the fact that Jamie was on a first date with Wendy wasn't quite as serious as that, but I was still waiting for someone to pop out and shout, "Molly Hart! WHAT DO YOU THINK YOU'RE DOING?! You can't let Jamie go ahead with this! You know full well he's (inexplicably) in (one-sided) love with Tasha. Why are you letting him go out with Wendy! She's your friend! She has a massive crush on him! She's only just started talking to you again! Shouldn't you warn her about your brother and the way he's been moping over another girl?"

Apparently not. Because here we were, on our way to a double date.

My stomach fizzed with excitement and nerves, and possibly also the after-effects of the "beauty from the inside" wheatgrass drinks Ameera had bought me earlier.

There was no sign of Liam, but Wendy was waiting for us outside the restaurant. Or at least an ultra-glossy, super-groomed version of Wendy was there, anyway. The small amount of Ameera-led treatments she'd received had obviously had an effect on her after all, or maybe it was all natural radiance due to her happiness at seeing my brother.

Oh, I hoped not.

I hoped not even more when a waitress sauntered over to greet us and I recognized who it was.

"Hi, I'm Tasha and I'd like to welcome you to Paolo's Pizza Place!" Tasha trotted out, clearly concentrating hard on a speech she must have learnt recently. She swung her blonde ponytail about as she spoke, and Jamie stared at it, hypnotized. "Table for three?"

I wanted to hit my brother. Had he *known* she worked here? Coming here was *his* idea! This was the stuff of nightmares!

"Jamie," I whispered furiously at him.

He didn't react. His eyes were fixed on Tasha and his cheeks were bright red.

"What's wrong, Molly?" Wendy asked brightly. She was staring at Jamie and beaming, apparently not noticing the way Jamie was mesmerized by Tasha's perfect hair. I wanted to grab Wendy, drag her away and apologize for at least a year about having been born into the Hart family.

"Table for three?" Tasha asked again slowly and deliberately, oblivious to any tension.

"Four," said a voice behind me.

Liam! I turned around and temporarily forgot all my worries about Jamie and Wendy. Liam was here! And he liked me, and he was here *with me*! This was the stuff of dreams!

"Hi, Molly," he said with a shy smile. He smelled of manly body spray and he looked awkward and nervous in extra-clean and slightly-too-smart clothes, like he'd made a big effort for tonight, so it had to be a dream.

I tried to say hi back but my lips couldn't stop smiling for long enough.

Meanwhile, our waitress was glaring at me. The look on her face said: *"You've got to be kidding me!"*

Oh, no, of course! Jamie had told me Tasha had a thing for Liam. I changed my mind again. This was a nightmare.

"Uh, can we go somewhere else?" I asked, but my voice came out small and squeaky and Jamie didn't even seem to hear me. Probably because he was in a Tasha-induced trance.

"Why?" Wendy asked, at the same time as Liam said, "Sure,"

and Tasha said, "Come with me!"

Tasha's voice was the loudest and most commanding. Before I could object, Jamie was following her like a zombie and Wendy was shrugging and going into the restaurant after them.

"Are you OK?" Liam asked me with another of those hot, shy smiles and I squeaked, "Yes!"

Then Tasha called out, "Liam, over here!" and I swear she did this little wiggle thing with her annoyingly perfect curvy hips to summon him.

Liam and I (*Liam and I!*) trooped over to Tasha. She'd seated us right at the back by the swing-doors to the kitchen and I couldn't help wondering if she was up to something. Especially when she pulled out a chair for Liam, giggling as she did so.

We sat down and picked up our menus. Tasha stood over us – or rather, over Liam – fiddling with her hair and adjusting her uniform. Jamie's eyes slid away from his menu and back to Tasha.

Liam smiled at me. Tasha glared at me. Jamie smiled at Tasha. Wendy looked confused. I wished I could rescue her. Wasn't that the point of me coming tonight? I had to *do* something. Liam smiled at me again. I forgot about Wendy.

"Are you ready to order?" Tasha chirped at Liam.

"Could you go away a minute?" I said bluntly. Everyone stared at me. "I mean, could you *give us* a minute. You must have other customers," I mumbled. I didn't want Liam to think I was rude. On the other hand, I really didn't want Tasha to hang around any longer if at all possible.

"I'm ready!" Wendy declared.

Nooooo!

Tasha gave me a smug smile as she took Wendy's order. Jamie stared at Tasha the whole time, before he randomly named a pizza. Then Tasha beamed at Liam and simpered over his menu, recommending specials. Oh, this was horrible!

And so it went on for the whole, impossibly long, meal. I soon understood that the reason Tasha had put us near the kitchen was so that she could sashay in and out a lot, pausing to pose prettily exactly by where she'd seated Liam. Jamie had his back to most of this but it didn't stop him swivelling around every two minutes. Any conversation the four of us managed was stilted and interrupted by the swinging kitchen doors and the appearance of my brother's crush, who had a crush on my date.

Finally, *finally*, the ordeal was over, and I wished I was already at home. Or stepping in and out of lifts with Jasper. Anything had to be better than standing about awkwardly outside Paolo's Pizza Place while Tasha shifted her waitressing duties to the front of the restaurant.

"So... what should we do now?" Liam asked. I suddenly felt really annoyed with him. Hadn't he even *noticed* what had been going on? How dim *was* he?

"I... can I just talk to Wendy a minute?" I blurted. I'd been dying to speak to her alone all night but she hadn't been getting any of my not-that-subtle signals and even when I dropped a big hint about her following me to the toilets, she'd stayed in her seat and was still sitting there fiddling with her phone when I gave up and came back.

Now she looked a bit surprised as I marched her towards Service Entrance B and out of earshot of the boys.

She spoke first. "What's up, Molz?"

I didn't know where to begin. "Wendy, I am so so so so so sorry about my brother..."

And then, to my complete surprise, she roared with laughter. "Molly, I am so so so so so sorry, but that was the most boring hour-and-a-half of my *life*! Double *maths* is better than that!"

I looked at her. "Are you kidding? You're not... like, heartbroken or anything? I don't have to kill Jamie for you? Because I've been thinking about it, you know."

She shrugged. "OK, he's gorgeous –"

I made a face.

"He *is*, Molz, there's nothing you can do about it. I still find him attractive. Who wouldn't? Except you. But I have nothing to say to him. I swear, I could not think of a *single* thing. And he didn't seem remotely interested in me, either. Which is a bit off-putting." She nudged me. "So I'm sorry, and I was flattered and really happy when he asked me out... but I've gone right off him. You don't mind, do you?"

"Me? Mind?"

"You don't think he'll be upset, do you?"

"I... don't know." I doubted it, but I understood my brother even less than usual that night. Why had he asked Wendy out in the first place, especially if he was going to stare at Tasha all night?

Wendy laughed. "Guess me and Jamie are never going to be star-crossed lovers after all, and you and I are never going to be double sisters-in-law, Molz." She glanced at her phone. "Oh hey, Harry's waiting for me outside right now. I sent him a text when you went to the loo earlier."

"Oh. Right."

She looked at the exit. "Do you think you could tell Jamie something came up and my brother's taking me home? And tomorrow I'll have to break it to Ameera that my crush is over and she put all that work in on us for nothing."

"She did it for our inner confidence, not for any boys," I pointed out, quoting Ameera's words.

"Well, then it worked, because I definitely have the *confidence* to get out of here right this second without a backward glance." She laughed again. "Though maybe I'd have had that anyway. I don't mind admitting I was wrong about Jamie. I'm starting to realize that crushes are weird things."

I glanced back at the boys. Liam was looking absolutely hot. This was how I was used to admiring him – from across corridors as he stood chatting to my brother and looking relaxed. Not sitting nervously pretending to be a grown-up in a mall restaurant with a waitress simpering over him. Which wasn't *his* fault, after all.

Wendy seemed to have recovered from her crush – her *friendship-damaging* crush, a grumpy part of me couldn't help noting – almost as suddenly as she'd developed it in the first place, just a few short and eventful weeks ago. But I've liked Liam for so long that my feelings couldn't possibly disappear that quickly. OK, hanging around with him up close – and knowing that *he liked me back* – did seem to have changed things.

He wasn't the perfect boyfriend from my imagination, maybe, and we were extremely nervous around each other. But that was a good sign. Wasn't it?

A little thought about Jasper popped into my head then, weirdly enough. I thought about how comfortably we'd chatted, and the times I'd caught him looking at me during our therapy sessions and how it made my stomach flip. Except that I might have been imagining it. Also, the way our conversation ended earlier in the week, we sure didn't sound like two people who had any kind of future connection. If anything, it had played out more like an awkward break up.

And Liam was waiting for me, looking gorgeous, and quite probably wanting to continue our night out – hopefully without Jamie, now that Wendy had gone.

Though I bet he and Jamie would want to go and do something laddish like they normally did on a Friday night. They'd probably meet up with the rest of the guys in their group, who were bound to be somewhere in the mall right now, and they'd go and laugh loudly about nothing-at-all outside some burger place.

In which case, I could easily say goodbye to the Liam portion of my evening and... well... I could maybe see what Jasper was up to? Just in a friendly way. After all, he'd said he was free tonight and it was strange to think he was only a few floors up from me right now, being intriguing.

Maybe Ameera's confidence thing was totally working for me, too.

Friday, 3rd June, continued

Letter from Past Molly, the Hart residence, 5th floor, The Lilies eco-mall, Lilyford

Dear Future Molly,

I'm interrupting this account of the night I finally went out with the biggest crush of my life, aka my big brother's (now possibly former) best friend Liam, to ask you something.

I wish you could tell me the answer, from your position of future wisdom and sorted-ness. Or just because you're older, and a survivor of teenhood. (This strikes me as a superpower in itself – one that's at least equal to mega-strength, shape-shifting, or the ability to sit through Monday morning at school without yawning.) Anyway, here is the question:

Was it right to dump Liam and go to find Jasper instead?

Did I do the right thing? I wish I knew. Because I sure feel out of my depth right now. In fact, I've jumped into a whole different pool from the one I started out in tonight.

OK, my night out had some amazing moments. But it also contained many less awesome parts and one *way* less awesome person, mentioning no names. (Tasha.)

Future Molly, do you even remember anything about this night from your past? Wow, on one hand that's a frightening thought, and on the other, woo hoo – I've forgotten Tasha!

Anyway, read on, because I'm about to remind you about everything in some detail

In the meantime... Help!!!

Yours,

Past Molly

Friday, 3rd June
End of interruption

So there I was, in the ultra-bright lighting of Service Entrance B, thinking about the confidence Ameera had magically instilled in Wendy with her week-long makeover mission. Or possibly the confidence that Wendy already had by the bucketload anyway, considering she escaped the majority of the beauty treatments and style advice sessions last week, leaving Ameera to fuss over me instead.

Either way, this confidence had led Wendy to dump my brother after what was admittedly a pretty disastrous date (seeing as he'd spent half the meal drooling over another girl – i.e. Tasha!). But Wendy was supposed to have had a massive crush on Jamie, the kind that meant ignoring his flaws. The same way I was supposed to have a massive crush on Liam, the kind that meant overlooking the way he didn't seem to mind that Tasha was totally flirting with him right in front of me.

I was also quite probably not supposed to be thinking about Jasper.

Liam smiled shyly over at me from outside Paolo's Pizza Place, shrugging a bit as if to ask me what was going on. I did fancy him, I *did*. But what was going on, apart from the Tasha issue, was this:

Now that I'd started thinking about Jasper, I couldn't seem to stop.

What was I going to do about *that*? If I went somewhere else with Liam but daydreamed about Jasper the whole time, wouldn't it be exactly like what I'd been fuming at Jamie about all evening?

I took several deep breaths and focused on Ameera's idea of inner confidence as I walked back to the boys. I was going to sort this out somehow, however hard it seemed.

Jamie spoke first. "Where's Wendy gone?" he asked. Like he cared. (Or did he? I really did not understand my brother, or why he asked Wendy out when he was clearly obsessed with Tasha.)

"She had to... go. Her brother was waiting for her."

"She left, just like that?" Jamie narrowed his eyes at me. "OK, what did you say to her, Measly?"

This was probably not something to discuss in front of Liam, but I couldn't help it. "*Me?* Have you thought that it might have something to do with the way *you* were behaving?"

"What do you mean? You're the one who's been in a mood all night! I saw the way you were looking at Tasha!"

"OMG, Jamie!" I wanted to hit him. Instead, I found myself stamping my foot and probably looking about five years old. I hate the way my brother does that to me! "You are a complete –"

"See? Strop, strop, strop. Honestly, I can't believe I agreed to spend Friday night with my whiny little sister!"

"Hey..." Liam said quietly.

"Hey!" a voice called loudly behind us.

We all turned.

It was Tasha. She was shaking her hair so that it fell prettily over the shoulders of her super-stylish designer jacket. She'd undone her ponytail and changed out of the black and white uniform. She stood with one hip jutting out in an effortlessly stunning way. I would definitely fall over if I tried to pose like that.

"My shift's over – at last!" She giggled, looking right at Liam. "I'm meeting Hannah, Livvy and some of the others at the fountain. We'll probably hit one of those late-night cafés by the food court. Want to come?"

Jamie said, "Sure."

I rolled my eyes. Liam looked even more uncomfortable than before. "Molly?" he mumbled.

Before I could reply, Tasha strutted over to him and looped her arm through his. "Course you're coming!" And then she whispered something in his ear.

He went bright red and his eyes clouded with a cornered expression. But he didn't pull away.

Oh, *honestly*! I'd been fully intending to think of an excuse to leave anyway, but I hadn't expected it to feel so *easy*.

"Sorry, I'm leaving," I announced. I felt a bit guilty about my stroppy tone, so I added, "Night, Liam."

"Molly..." Liam said, but Tasha started whispering again and I couldn't be bothered to hang about and wait for her to finish flirting with the boy I was supposedly out with.

As I walked off, I heard Liam say, "Shouldn't one of us walk her home?"

This was followed by a dismissive, "She can take care of herself," from Jamie, although he did add, "We practically grew up in the mall, remember."

"So, in a way, Molly's home already?" Liam said.

Tasha's laughter grated on me, even from a distance.

I took huge strides until I reached Service Entrance D and the lift to the residential block. My ears were ringing with the voice of the boy I'd dreamed about for years. *"Shouldn't one of us walk her home?"* Not Liam himself, but *"one of us"*. So this would include my annoying brother, and the even *more* annoying Tasha. Thanks a *lot*, crush of my life!

The sensible thing then would have been to go home. Boys – who needed them?

However, at that exact moment, and with Liam's words in my ears, there was no doubt in my mind about where I was going and who I wanted to see. Even if I'd been totally imagining the way he'd looked at me and he only ever thought of me as a friend, right then I didn't care. Jasper always had time for me. Jasper never made me feel like he'd rather be with someone else.

Plus I couldn't get him out of my head. I had to talk to him.

I pressed the button for Level 6 – Jasper and Jewel's floor.

It was only when the lift shunted past my floor that I started to reconsider. It was late. Not late enough for anyone of our age to be asleep yet, but late enough for it to be seriously weird to turn up at someone's front door. I had no idea what Jasper and Jewel's parents were like, except that they liked to line their walls with pictures of rock stars. But I'd imagine nine out of ten parents would frown at the doorbell ringing after a certain time, even on a Friday night.

Unless...

The lift doors opened and a strong beat filled the air. The track that was playing sounded like an acoustic version of a song I didn't recognize. But it was brilliant and it was definitely coming from Jasper's flat.

...unless you thought someone was *having a party* or something. Then, surely, showing up late would be fine.

Maybe if Jasper's mum answered the door and looked annoyed, I could pretend I was on my way to some party and had the wrong house. I could blame it on the great music.

Before I had time to think it through, the track came to an end ,so I took a deep breath and rang the bell.

I waited as a new track started, and then quickly ground to a halt. It didn't sound abrupt, though, like someone switching off a stereo. It was more like the gradual way musicians finish a concert. I half-expected to hear a voice say, "Thank you, Lilyford, and good night!"

I heard footsteps on the tiled corridor that I knew matched ours. They got closer.

The door opened a tiny bit.

Jasper peered at me through the gap he'd allowed himself. "Molly? What are you doing here?"

He was wearing another of his faded band t-shirts and his usual black jeans, but there was something about him that looked different. He seemed dazed and extra-rumpled, like I'd just woken him up. It was super-cute. But surely he couldn't have been sleeping through that loud, wonderful music?

"I, er..." I realized I had my "party" excuse ready for his parents, but nothing for him.

He filled in my silence with the perfect get-out. "Jewel's not in, I'm afraid. She said she wanted to go shopping, believe it or not. She's still on California time. I think she's at the 24-hour mini-market if you want to look for her."

It would have been so easy to leave at that point. Finding Jewel might be fun – plus she'd been in California! Now that was interesting! I wondered if she would tell me all about it, or whether she'd be as secretive as her brother.

But instead... I decided to tell the truth. "No, I... I'm here to see you. You said you'd be around tonight?"

He gave a confused smile. "Oh. Yeah. But you said you weren't sure about it? And, er, you didn't show up. So I was just practising." He rubbed his eyes. "Sorry, I lose track of... well, *everything*, when I'm on my keyboard. What time is it, anyway?"

I decided that telling him would only highlight the weirdness of me turning up like this. "That music was you? It was seriously fantastic," I blurted instead. Well, it *was*.

Jasper's smile broadened. "Thanks."

"I wish I could play like that. Or do anything that well."

"Oh, I bet you could."

"I bet I couldn't. I struggled with recorder at primary school."

"It's all about practice," he said. "I've been playing since before I could walk. Mum's a music teacher. Hey, she could give you lessons! Or... or I could?"

"Wow, I'd love that!"

He smiled even more. "Great."

The silence that followed should have been awkward, but somehow it wasn't. We just stood there looking at each other and smiling. It was weird. In a good way.

Eventually, Jasper said, "Listen, Molly, I'd invite you in but... I sort of promised Jewel..." He seemed to backtrack. "I mean, really it was because I told her..." He shook his head. "Never mind any of that," he said. He grabbed something from a table by the door – a phone or a wallet, it looked like, or possibly both – and shoved it into his pocket before he jumped out, shutting the door firmly behind him. "You want to go out? With me, I mean? I mean, do you want to go out with me?"

I smiled at the odd way he was speaking, obviously because he was still dazed from the musical interruption. The thought of heading back into the mall and possibly bumping into Jamie and Liam with those girls wasn't very appealing. The thought of going somewhere, anywhere, with Jasper, on the other hand...

"OK," I said.

Jasper grinned. "Really? You do?"

"Sure," I said. I turned and headed for the stairs.

"No, this way," Jasper said quietly, pressing the button for the lift.

Oh! Did he think I'd come round for another of our therapy sessions?

Well, of course he did – that's what we'd been doing together daily, up until the day things went a bit weird. There was nothing else going on between us. It was all a business arrangement, like I'd originally said.

The lift arrived with a ping! sound.

I stood near the doors with Jasper. "Right, what are we going for this time?" I asked him. "Three seconds in the lift? Or five?" I remembered his increasing bravery before we'd stopped meeting. "Or do you want to try a whole floor?"

Jasper gave me a determined nod. "Yeah. Let's go for it," he said. "I think I'm ready." He took a deep breath and stepped into the lift. I followed him. He backed into the glass wall as the doors closed, but his breathing seemed steady.

"You're doing really well," I told him as I reached to select Level 5 from the panel.

But before I could press the button, Jasper grabbed my hand and held it. "I know," he said. He reached over with his other hand and pressed the button numbered 1. The food court, five whole floors down. "Let's go for a drink."

"Jasper!" I widened my eyes at him as the lift started moving. "Seriously?"

"Seriously," he replied. "I've figured out why this is working." He glanced at our joined hands and then back at me.

That's when I knew for sure that I hadn't been imagining the intense looks before. This most recent one could be filed under "positively smouldering" in a database of hot looks (which hopefully exists somewhere).

"I read about it," he said in a low voice. "It's to do with distraction. It's harder for the panic to take hold if I'm thinking about something fantastic. Or..." He tightened his grip on my hand. "You know. *Someone...*"

I was so shocked that I barely registered how wonderful it felt to hold his hand. Though my version of "barely registered" included my head screaming: *Jasper is holding my hand!!! Jasper is saying amazing things!!!*

"What do you mean?" I asked him as casually as I could manage through the inner screams. I'd done plenty of embarrassing things in life, but misunderstanding something like this would surely win some kind of prize. Maybe I'd make the front cover of one of those magazines Ameera always reads in beauty clinic waiting rooms: "SO EMBARRASSED, I ACTUALLY DROPPED DEAD! Read my full story inside!"

"I mean..." His lashes seemed extra-long as his eyes settled on my mouth. He shifted closer and murmured, "Molly..."

OK, no *way* was I imagining this! Any worries about embarrassment flew out of my head as I moved towards him. Our lips met.

And... yeah. Wow. I was in serious danger of dropping dead from *that*, instead.

We kissed for a few awesome seconds, until the lift doors pinged open. The first thing I saw after I blinked a few times was Tasha, sitting on a bright green plastic table in the mostly deserted food court, surrounded by her friends. She was dangling her legs over the good-looking guy sitting in the attached seat. The good-looking guy was Liam.

Also, Jamie was thundering towards the lift, looking a lot like he did when he was ten and Mum accidentally hoovered up a crucial piece of his Lego Rebel Trooper Battle Pack. I'd actually given him half of my favourite ice cream that day, I'd felt so bad for him.

Jasper looked even more dazed (and, yes, even more super-cute) than before as Jamie approached. "Isn't that your brother?" he asked me. "He looks upset. Should I go so you can talk to –"

"Oh. The music guy," Jamie said, stopping in front of us.

The lift doors started to close and Jasper moved away from me to tap a button and keep them open. His other hand didn't let go of mine, though.

Meanwhile, Liam seemed to have finally detached himself from Tasha's clutches and was bounding after Jamie. "Jamie, mate!" he was calling. "Are you OK?"

Jamie pretended he couldn't hear him. In fact, he totally stared at the ceiling and acted like Liam didn't exist. I didn't realize boys did that kind of thing to their friends. When I've moaned to Nan in the past about Wendy and Ameera blanking me, she always tells me it's the female equivalent of a big punch-up and she sometimes wishes girls would find a quicker way to settle their differences. Even though I was still furious with Jamie, I was kind of relieved to see that he fought like Nan's idea of a girl.

Liam got closer. "Don't go!" he said. "Look, is this about Molly? I swear I don't understand what happened on our date tonight. Next time we're out together – soon, I hope – I'll ask her..." He noticed me. "Oh! Molly. Hi." His eyes moved down to my hand in Jasper's.

I sort of gasped a bit before I detached myself from Jasper.

Jasper stared at Liam, and then at me. "Is this... your *boyfriend*?" he asked, stepping out of the lift. The dazed expression had gone and now he just looked... crushed.

"No, we... went out tonight..."

"Oh," Liam said at the same time. "Jamie didn't tell me you were seeing anyone... else."

Jamie made a little "huh" sound.

"I'm wasn't," I said.

Jasper turned away from me.

My heart sank. "I mean, I'm not."

Liam stared at the ground.

How had I got myself into this mess, and so quickly too? I truly did deserve some kind of world record for the speed at which I was able to wreck everything.

Jamie marched into the lift and pressed the button marked "5". "Measly, you coming?"

"You know, I'm kind of tired. I think I'll take the stairs back," Jasper said quietly, still not looking at me, or at anyone else.

Maybe I shouldn't have got in the lift. I should have followed Jasper or stayed and sorted things out with Liam, but suddenly I couldn't bear the way the boys – the guy I've had a crush on forever and the guy I'd just had the most amazing kiss with – wouldn't look me in the eye. I jumped in next to Jamie.

"I don't get it," Liam said, mostly to himself, as the doors began to close. "Any of it."

"Tasha likes you and Jamie likes Tasha!" I shouted just before the doors closed and he disappeared from view. Well, someone had to give him a clue.

"I can't believe you just said that," Jamie growled as we started to ascend, leaving the mess of my love-life on Level 1. "I am never talking to you again."

"Good," I fumed. "Because I don't want to talk to you either. This is all your fault! Why did you ask Wendy out in the first place, when you're so crazy about Tasha?"

He shrugged and completely forgot he wasn't talking to me, probably because of the mention of the great goddess Tasha. "I wanted to be a whole new person, remember? All about the work and study, that's what I said. But you told me about Wendy and, you know, she's not bad-looking."

"Jamie!"

"What? She's pretty. And clever. I thought if we got together it would help with my new, serious image."

I shook my head. "Jamie, you do realize how crazy that sounds? And how deeply wrong it is to play with people's feelings like that? Anyway, what were you even thinking, taking her to the place Tasha worked?"

"I didn't know Tasha would be there! I swear! She didn't tell me she'd changed jobs. She's never even replied to a single one of my texts."

He looked so miserable that I believed him. "Even so. Wendy *really* liked you!" I nudged him. "Before she saw what you were *really* like."

Jamie raised his eyebrows and gave me a long look. "Oh, and this from the girl who strings my Molly-obsessed ex-best mate along and then goes off with another random guy as soon as his back's turned?" He nudged me back. "The very same *night*? Isn't that the kind of thing you used to moan at me about?"

I resented that! I was *nothing* like my brother. Though maybe it was because I'd never been an admirer-magnet like him. (Harry Bo doesn't count.) The minute two boys I liked actually seemed to like me back, everything went horribly wrong.

"It wasn't like that," I told him. "Besides, I was sick of Liam not telling Tasha where to go."

Jamie sighed. "Yeah, me too."

"Oh? I thought you were too busy drooling over her to notice."

Jamie gave me a soft shove as the lift doors opened at Level 5. "Measly, please remind me never, *ever* to talk to you." He smiled a tiny bit, though, as he let us into the flat.

There was no sign of Mum – again – but I decided to worry about that another time. Jamie went to his room and I went to mine, where I've sat writing this and wondering at what point in the future I'm going to stop messing everything up. And how a night can be so fantastic and so totally rubbish at the same time.

And how I could start an evening all ecstatic about seeing Liam and end it with pining over Jasper.

Saturday 4th June

Moping at the Hart residence, 5th floor, The Lilies eco-mall, Lilyford

The only noteworthy thing that happened today was that Radio Lilyford woke me up this morning. Again. I thought about leaping into the kitchen and questioning Mum about her new habits, but I was a bit too busy wallowing in misery. Some other time, perhaps.

I went round the mall with Ameera for a bit and she chattered endlessly about how relieved she was that Wendy had dumped Jamie because he wasn't good enough for her, no offence, and did I think I had a future with Liam? I told her I had no idea.

We had lunch in the food court, where Jamie was making a great show of ignoring Liam. The stalls they work in are next to each other and normally they chat and joke and throw burger buns (Liam) and baguettes (Jamie) at each other when their bosses aren't looking. But today there was a clear and frosty divide between the baguette stall and the burger stand. At least, a one-way one. I kept noticing Liam trying to make eye contact with Jamie, which only seemed to make Jamie concentrate harder on slicing tomatoes. Then I had to stop looking because Liam caught my eye and quickly looked away.

Ameera noticed. "He likes you," she observed. "I reckon he's going to ask you out again."

"I really don't think so," I said, though I didn't tell her why. I hadn't mentioned the Jasper part of last night, and I knew she assumed I'd gone home when Wendy did. I'm not sure exactly why I didn't tell her – it just seemed easier that way.

As we left the food court, I caught Liam staring at me and I thought Ameera might be right. I just wasn't sure how I felt about it.

Sunday, 5th June
After a day with Dad and Nan

Had a chat with Nan about what happened on Friday. Told her everything except the fact that I've mega-fancied Liam for ages. And the way I can't stop thinking about Jasper and wishing I could see him again, but I'm afraid of what he thinks of me. And the part about kissing Jasper in the lift and how I keep torturing myself with memories of how delicious it was. And how I think Liam might try to ask me out again and I don't know what I'd say. And how maybe I should just walk off into the sunset – or the bright mall lights – with some other guy, like possibly Art Boy. Except that he seems to have a thing for Jewel and he might not like me anyway. I'm getting a bit big-headed, now that two gorgeous boys have shown an interest in me, at least temporarily. I should probably give up *all* boys, forever, the way that Jamie has actually given up girls (at least for one night – he definitely stayed in last night). Except that I don't want to. I want Jasper. And here I go again...

I didn't tell her any of that, so basically I told her nothing at all. I did mention that Jamie had actually gone out with my friend Wendy, though, and what a disaster it had turned out to be.

She said, "Your brother will change when he grows up a bit, Molly. You'll see. I think his heart's in the right place but he's not going to commit himself to one girl right now, is he?"

So then I felt bad about that too. I'd given Nan a false impression of New Jamie, who was so utterly committed to one girl that he was acting like his best friend had ceased to exist, just because this girl liked the wrong guy.

I said, "Jamie's not that bad, Nan."

She called me a "good girl" and then instantly apologized for treating me like I was still about eight years old. I sort of liked it, though. I wished I *was* little again. Life was easier back then, even though I did fall out with Wendy and Ameera about as often as I do now, if not more. Wendy still swears I ruined her skipping rope when I used the end to nudge Ameera's lunchbox out of the puddle it had fallen into.

Jamie and I revised for exams all evening. I know he was properly studying for a change because his computer wasn't even on when I brought him a drink. He was sitting on his bed staring at a pile of open books. His face displayed a miserable expression that obviously matched mine, because when he brought me a drink later to pay me back, he said, "Chin up, Measly," and ruffled my hair. It could have been sweet if it hadn't been so annoying.

Monday 6th June
Typing at the resource centre during "study time" between exams, West Lilyford Community College

Back to school with a bang! Exams started today. Urgh.

I bumped into Jewel in the lift this morning and we walked all the way to West Lilyford together. I wondered why that had never happened before and she told me that her mum usually drove her to school so they left a bit later, but her mum wasn't very well right now.

I asked how her holiday went. She mumbled something about how it wasn't a holiday.

"Oh, sorry," I said, remembering Jasper's mysterious conversation about needing to fly somewhere, and then things suddenly being better. "I hope everything's OK. I heard you were in California."

She did a double-take. "Who told you that?"

I suddenly worried. "Er... Jasper," I admitted.

She shook her head. "He's incredible. The way he goes on at me not to say anything and then..." She gave me a suspicious look. "What did you do to him, anyway?"

I jumped on and off the pavement a couple of times to control my nerves. "What do you mean?"

She touched my arm, probably to stop me hopping about. "You know what I mean, Molly," she declared. "OK, my brother and I didn't exactly grow up together, plus I know he has natural emo tendencies, but I can still tell when there's something wrong with him. He's been moping around so much these last couple of days that he hasn't even played his keyboard. It was the quietest weekend I've had since I moved in with him and Mum!"

"Oh," I said, wishing I could change the subject. I hopped about even more to disguise the way my heartbeat had gone crazy. "Hey, did you get a chance to study for the –"

"I saw you, you know."

"What?" I narrowly avoided jumping into a lamppost.

"I saw you on Friday night. I was on my way back from the mini-market and I took a small detour to see how that mural project was going..."

"Art Boy – er, the organizer – really wants you to get involved in that," I babbled.

She ignored me. "So I was in the lane by Service Entrance D and I was glancing up at all these funny angles, squinting at where the mural's supposed to go, and I saw you in the elevator with Jasper. And it looked like you were... I don't know. *Close*."

I gulped. I also inwardly swooned a bit, remembering.

"Did you hook up with Jasper, Molly?" Jewel asked. "And then ditch him?"

She was so direct! Luckily, we'd reached the school gates. "What's your first exam?" I asked, taking my timetable out of my bag.

She gave me an odd look but she found her timetable and

held it out next to mine. I studied it for a couple of seconds, collapsing into a bit of a daydream when I saw her full name at the top. It said "Julie Stone" and I wondered whether the last name was as fake as the first name. If it wasn't, then maybe Jasper was called "Jasper Stone" and... I don't know. Just maybe that was his name. I allowed myself an extra inward swoon.

While I was doing all this, Jewel worked out our first exams were at opposite ends of the school, and we both had to leave right now if we wanted to get there in time.

"See you at lunchtime!" Jewel called, rushing off.

I extracted myself from my daydream and plodded over to the hall, where Ameera and Wendy were waiting for me. As soon as I saw them, I added a new worry to my long list. Now that I was back with my BFFs, and Jewel was here too, who was I going to hang around with at lunchtime? How was I going to avoid upsetting anyone?

Life is so hard.

Thursday, 9th June
After another exam-filled day at West Lilyford Community College

Exams. Exams. Studying. Exams. More studying. More exams. Zzzzz.

At least the exam-time fever has worked in my favour. My fears about mixing my new friendship with Jewel with my long-standing BFF-trio have been unfounded, at least for this week. Our normal school routine has been totally disrupted by extra-long papers and odd lunch-breaks. Plus the social order of our year-group is all over the place. It's like this programme I saw on TV once about how strangers on a train suddenly start talking to each other if there's a crash or something. Disaster mentality unites people. Everyone talks to everyone at exam time.

So this week Jewel hung around with me, Ameera, Wendy and quite a few other random Year 10s we don't normally speak to. It was actually quite nice.

Friday, 10th June
After-school mall madness

It was quite nice until late this afternoon, anyway. Then I wondered whether my friends – well, one of them in particular – had gone a bit loopy. It happens sometimes, at exam time. But if anyone was going to cave under pressure, I would have expected it from Wendy, not my "yeah, whatever" mate Ameera.

Ameera came home with me and Jewel because she was meeting her mum and sisters for some new skincare treatment they'd booked. She chatted about it all the way back and Jewel listened politely. We'd all survived a full week of exams and we were happy. I was almost thinking that this friendship thing wasn't going to be a problem after all.

We were just going into the mall, getting ready to go our separate ways, when Ameera's phone blared a bit of Rihanna at us.

She plucked it out of her bag and went, "Oh, 'scuse me!" to us, and then "Yes?" into the phone. "Yeah. Yeah. OK. Yes, right now! No! Whaaaaat?" Big pause. "Yeah, I suppose." Bigger pause. "OK, I'll try!" Then she pressed a button and turned back to us, looking a bit shocked, but smiling.

"Are you OK?" I asked.

"No. Yes!" Ameera giggled. "Sorry." She kind of shook herself. "That was just my big sister. Mum found out she was getting out of work late, so they changed the appointment." She glanced at her phone. "It's in about half an hour. So... can I go round to your place and wait there?"

This was already strange. Ameera would always rather crawl round the mall than sit in my poky bedroom.

But then I noticed she wasn't looking at me. She'd directed that question at Jewel.

"Oh!" Jewel seemed to realize at the same time as I did. "It's, er, not a good time. My mum's not very well. Sorry. She, er, hasn't been well for a couple of weeks now."

Ameera's face fell. "Aw!" she said, glancing around. We passed a flower stand shaped like a wheelbarrow and parked in front of a large hardware chain store.

"You can come to mine," I pointed out.

"Hmm," said Ameera. "How about if we buy Julie's mum some flowers, though? Cheer her up a bit?"

I narrowed my eyes at Ameera.

"That's a cool thought," Jewel said. I suppose she didn't know what was and wasn't strange behaviour from my BFF. "She might like that, actually. It's worth a try."

Ameera and Jewel wandered over to the wheelbarrow and spent a while choosing. I stared at them the whole time, wondering what was really going on.

"Come on, then!" Ameera waved a multicoloured bunch of

flowers at me. "We're taking these to Julie's mum."

"Oh..." said Jewel. "Actually, I'd better go by myself. It's just that..."

"It's OK, said Ameera. "We'll wait outside yours and then we can all go to Molly's together. Right, Molz?"

"I suppose," I mumbled. This was definitely weird. Plus going round to Jewel's house meant the possibility of seeing Jasper. I wasn't sure how I felt about that, and especially not with Jewel and Ameera in tow.

We got out of the lift on Level 6. I was scared that Jasper would appear at the door, but he didn't. And then I was disappointed. In fact, I was starting to feel a bit annoyed with him. It was like the other side of the coin to the guilt I'd been feeling all week. I hadn't done anything *that* bad, after all. I bet *he* wasn't perfect either!

While I fumed irrationally along those lines, Jewel said, "Back in a minute, then," and disappeared into her flat with the flowers, leaving the front door ajar but definitely more closed than open.

"Ameera, what's this about?" I asked her quietly as Jewel's footsteps died down.

Ameera lowered her voice, too. "Something my sister said about Boring Julie. I thought I'd take a quick look at the inside of her flat." She sidled closer to the door.

"What are you doing?" I whispered. "You can't just go in there uninvited! It's wrong. Besides, what if Jewel...ie sees you?"

"Why would she mind me taking a quick look around?" Ameera said. "I'm not going to go rifling in drawers or anything,

Molly! Relax."

"But what are you even looking for?"

"I don't know," she said. "I'll know when I see it."

I remembered my curiosity about the photos on the walls. We could probably glance at those pretty quickly, and Ameera might even recognize some of the artists in them. She was miles better at that kind of thing than I was. If a band hasn't brought out a download chart-topper in the past few years, I'm unlikely to have heard of them, but Ameera is properly into music and likes all sorts of older stuff.

"What did your sister say, anyway, to make you channel your inner spy-girl?"

"I'll tell you later. Come on, we haven't got much time. And if Julie sees us, we'll just say..." She pushed the door to Jewel's flat wide open. "...the door blew open and..." She knocked a letter that had been propped on a tall table by the door. It fell onto the tiled flooring. "...this letter flew across the room, so we thought we'd pick it up for them. Are you coming?"

I peered inside. There was no sign of anyone around, and presumably Jewel had had time to put the flowers in water, or whatever, and take them to her mother. If Jewel's mum's room was the same as my mum's, then I knew it was the furthest from the entrance. But even if it wasn't, all the bedrooms were down the corridor from us anyway.

"There are no breezes on the inside of the mall," I grumbled as I followed Ameera. Well, *someone* had to keep an eye on her.

Besides, "curious" did not cover the way I was feeling…

Argh, Mum's calling. She seems to be making a rare

appearance in her own family's life and is offering me something she's calling "dinner".

Back after I've wolfed down today's gloop.

Friday, 10th June, continued

After polishing off suprisingly non-gloopy dinner

So there we were. Entirely uninvited.

"Ameera Hassan," I hissed at my trouble-making, snooping friend, "I can't believe you've got me doing this! I am *so* blaming you if we get busted!"

As I said this, I was craning my neck all over the place, trying to get a good look around Jewel's flat. Which, of course, was also Jasper's flat. This thought made me go part-melty and part-indignant inside. My feelings about Jasper were totally mixed. The first time we met, he'd jumped to all sorts of rude conclusions about me, but once that was cleared up he'd been super-friendly, if mega-mysterious.

And then there was that kiss in the lift last Friday. Sigh. Until we bumped into Liam and it all went horribly wrong.

It seemed to make sense at the time – I suppose snogging someone straight after a date with someone else is generally a bit frowned on. But a week had passed, and I was starting to think that Jasper was actually being rude. I mean, why hadn't he come round to see me, to give me a chance to explain? (I'm not sure what exactly I could say by way of explanation, but that wasn't the point.)

What kind of boy *was* Jasper, anyway?

I have to admit, I was hoping for some clues, hidden

somewhere within this funkily bohemian, colourful flat. Or hopefully not quite so hidden. Ameera might have promised she wasn't going to go through any drawers or anything, but now that I'd taken that first big step and actually followed her inside, it did seem a shame not to conduct a more in-depth investigation. I stared in the direction of the room I suspected was Jasper's, judging by the fact that I'd heard the door slam there on the first night I met him. Was he in? He was always so secretive. What would he think if I appeared at his door? Would he be horrified that I was in his flat at all?

While I was thinking about Jasper, Ameera was gazing at all the rock star pictures on the walls, her mouth hanging open. (I'd like to say "unattractively", but really Ameera could never be unattractive, even when she was doing an impression of a shell-shocked goldfish.)

"OMG," she whispered.

"What?" I said, shaking myself out of my "Jasper's room" daydream. And then, when she didn't reply, "WHAT?!"

"Ssh," said Ameera. "Rukshana is right! OMG. OMG!"

I mentally scrolled through the names of Ameera's big sisters. "Was it Rukshana who called you earlier?"

"Yes. OMG," said Ameera. She was in some kind of weird trance. Then she practically jumped up and down on the spot. "Look! Look! Boring Julie! OMG!!!"

"Ssh," I said back to Ameera. Then I looked. And there she was. My new friend Jewel, posing with her arms flung around the neck of the rock star I'd vaguely recognized last time I briefly visited this flat. She was pouting jokily at the camera and looking a couple of years... well, sort of younger, but also sort of older, too. No, no, she was definitely younger, despite the tons of make-up and skimpy clothes she was wearing. She looked like a rock star herself. A very young teenaged one. She looked totally glam and confident.

"So?" I asked Ameera. "Looks like she went to some gig a couple of years ago and got her picture taken with someone in the band. So what?" The closest any of us had ever got to a mega-star in Lilyford was when a children's TV presenter opened a new chain store a few years ago, but Jewel was probably from some proper city, the kind that famous bands actually went to.

Ameera added some pointing to her staring. "Does that look like it was taken at a gig?"

I squinted closer, trying not to think about the fact that we could get caught by Jewel – or Jasper, or their parents – at any second. We really should be getting out of here instead of scrutinizing the Stone family's gig snap collection.

Then I saw what Ameera meant. The background was all wrong. There was wooden flooring and a wide staircase. It reminded me of one of those huge open-plan apartments I'd seen in American sitcoms. I could also make out a large black leather sofa and a television set in one corner. In front of the sofa was a glass coffee table which held a tall silver mug and a pack of breakfast cereal, the kind that Jamie ate. I remembered Jewel telling me she liked it, too. There was also a bowl by the cereal, and a spoon in the bowl. As if Jewel had just been having breakfast, for example, and someone had taken her picture before school. *Rock* school, judging by her clothes and make-up.

"Do you think she was staying in a rock star's house?"

Ameera pointed a bit more. "I think it's *her* house. Julie's. Look!" She outlined a series of small photos on the walls within the bigger picture. They were professional-looking shots of a little ringlet-haired girl gazing at something in wonder, and they looked extremely familiar. One was poster-sized and you could just about make out that the girl in them really did resemble a much, much younger Jewel.

"This is it," my friend half-whispered, her face clouded with awe. "It's the kind of thing Rukshana was hoping I'd find."

"What?" Ameera and her sister had talked about this? "You mean you planned this... this *snooping*? How could you?" I fumed, though the fire of my fury was being squirted at by the waters of intrigue. I was pretty sure I knew what Ameera was thinking she'd discovered, and it did sort of fit with some of the things Jewel had said to me in the past. Especially when we'd made up ridiculous stories about shoppers in the mall, and Jewel had come out with wild things that belonged... well, in another world. A world of glamour and movies. Stuff she seemed to know a lot about.

"My sister told me she'd heard rumours that the daughter of a famous singer had moved to Lilyford," Ameera said softly.

My anger fizzled out. I also gave up the pretence that I didn't believe a word of it and/or was completely unimpressed. "No way," I breathed.

"Seriously. One of her mates from the office has got involved in that mural project that was on TV. You know, the one with that super-hottie art guy?"

I nodded. I certainly did know.

"Well, apparently he was bragging to Rukshana's friend, all this ridiculous stuff that she didn't believe at all. But Rukshana – she's proper bright, you know, she wants to be a lawyer when she saves enough for college – well, she remembered something I'd said about Boring Julie appearing out of nowhere and taking my best mate away from me, to some art thing." Ameera looked a bit embarrassed, but she went on. "So, well, that art guy said he could get special publicity for the project through his famous connections."

I remembered the way he was always asking me to bring Jewel. "Famous connections?"

"Yeah. He said he knew that a certain newsworthy girl had recently moved to Lilyford. The daughter of a member of The Red Sardonyx." Ameera nodded at the rock star pictures that we were still rooted in front of. (And probably shouldn't have been.)

"The who?"

"They *wish*!" Ameera laughed. "The Who were one of their biggest influences! Ha, get *me*, knowing that!" She gave a self-congratulatory smile before she went on. "The Red Sardonyx were never as big in Europe as they were in the States, but that doesn't change the fact that they were mega-stars. Still are, really – they re-form for charity gigs sometimes. The guy in the photos is Zircon, the lead singer. Remember him?"

I felt my usual ignorance in the face of Ameera's superior musical knowledge. "It sounds familiar," I bluffed. Though now that she mentioned it, I was sure I'd heard that name somewhere recently.

"I read that his real name is Alan Stone! Alan's a bit different from *Zircon*!" She sniggered. "Rock stars! They're such –" She stopped herself. "He's her dad. Her *dad*! OMG."

"We don't know that for a fact!"

"Molly, come on. Rukshana was doubtful too, but her lawyer skills sensed something and she asked me to see what I could find out. And look at that picture!" She nodded at it. "Nope, it's true. Boring Julie's dad is in The Red Sardonyx. And mine works for the council." She looked like her world was in the process of being rocked.

I heard a door open in the distance.

"Ameera, we really should get out of here," I said. Another clicking sound – maybe the same door closing again. I jumped and pulled her arm. "Now."

She let me drag her towards the front door. We were back outside with the door mostly shut when I remembered the letter that Ameera had pushed to the floor, supposedly as our (highly dubious) excuse for being in Jewel's flat. If Jewel saw it, would she suspect we'd been snooping?

Should I put the letter back? I thought I heard footsteps. My heart started pounding.

Meanwhile Ameera was still talking, in a total daze. "OMG. But Zircon was in that horrible car crash in Los Angeles a couple of weeks ago! You must have heard about it?"

I forgot about the letter when I realized what Ameera was saying. "Oh... yeah. Of course." The crash that I'd heard about on Radio Lilyford! That had to be where Jewel had gone – to be with her father. And where Jasper had been planning to fly to, as well. Poor them. No wonder Jasper had been behaving a bit weirdly.

"They said Zircon was much better now, though. They really went on about it on the local news, because they said he has some distant family in Lilyford, or something..." Ameera gasped. "They can't mean Julie, though, can they? A daughter isn't "distant". Besides, it would have been *everywhere*! There would be paparazzi hanging around school and stuff. Wouldn't there?"

"Maybe the family have been keeping it really secret. But Art Boy is leaking information. Maybe he's breaking a super-injunction, or something!" I'd heard about that sort of thing on television.

"But no one believes him!" Ameera laughed. "Rukshana told me her friend thought he was a pretentious wannabe."

I felt a bit sorry for Art Boy then, but my mind was on other things. It was still reeling with the thought that Jewel and Jasper had a famous singer for a dad, for a start, but it was also registering that Ameera might know more about the whole family. She was forever reading gossip magazines and telling me and Wendy things we didn't particularly want to know, all about the family tragedies of film stars, where they'd been on holiday and what shade of lipstick they liked best.

On the other hand, she didn't seem to know that Jewel's name wasn't Julie, and she hadn't shown any signs of knowing that Jewel had a twin brother. (Why wasn't Jasper in any of the photos anyway?)

I would have to ask Ameera exactly what she did know. Some other time. There were definite footsteps now, getting louder. It was too late to pick up the letter.

Jewel appeared at the door, smiling and not seeming to notice the guilt on Ameera's face, an expression that probably matched mine.

"Hi, guys," Jewel said, holding the door a tiny bit open. "Sorry that took a long time. Mum wanted a bit of a chat. Which is brilliant. Seriously. She hasn't wanted to talk since... ages."

I wondered about Jewel's mum. Where did she fit into what Ameera and I had just found out? I remembered Jasper saying that his mum had offered to get on the plane with him, but it had sounded like something he didn't think was such a good idea. Maybe their parents weren't together anymore, like mine. But that didn't explain the photos all over the walls. I really couldn't imagine Mum plastering Dad's picture all over her living space. Not unless she made it into a dart board, or something.

"She loved the flowers," Jewel continued. "Great idea, Ameera. Thanks."

"Uh... Y-y-yeah," Ameera stammered, looking everywhere but at Jewel.

"So, do we still have time to go to Molly's?" Jewel asked brightly.

"Uh... no, sorry. I think I have to... see my sister now," Ameera said, fiddling with her bracelet-style gold watch. "It's got late and... I have to tell her something."

Jewel seemed distracted, glancing back into her flat through the nearly-closed front door. "Oh, OK. Hold on, I've just seen some mail on the floor over there. Weird. I must have knocked it. I'd better put it back or... Just a second!"

"Don't!" I mouthed when Jewel turned her back to us and disappeared into the flat. I continued in a tiny whisper, "Please, Ameera, don't say anything to anyone. Not yet, at least. What if we're wrong, or if there's a proper reason that it's a secret?"

Ameera's eyes widened with the mystery of it all, just as Jewel appeared again. This time, Jewel shut the door firmly behind her.

Ameera said, "Sorry, I meant that I *don't* have to tell my sister anything. Yet. But I do have to see her." Then she giggled. "Can we get together another time? Please?" she added eagerly. It was the friendliest I'd ever seen Ameera be to Jewel. I narrowed my eyes at her.

"Oh, OK," said Jewel.

"Great! Fantastic!" Ameera beamed at her. "I can't wait!"

Jewel didn't seem to notice that she was behaving weirdly. "We still going to yours, Molly? Or do you want to do something else?"

"I... don't mind," I mumbled. "Yeah. Either." I was having a hard time acting normal, too. Not just because of what we'd found out but also because of the guilt of snooping in Jewel's flat.

At least we'd got away with it, and thanks to Ameera I'd finally satisfied my curiosity about the pictures on Jewel and Jasper's walls. And I knew the likely reason that they'd never invited me in.

Wow.

Saturday, 11th June
Weirdness is normal at the Hart residence, 5th floor, The Lilies eco-mall, Lilyford

A weird day. Except that "weird" is starting to seem normal nowadays. In which case, a *normal* day would be *weird* for me right now, and a *weird* day would be *normal*. Or something.

In any case, today was weird whichever way you look at it.

First there was Radio Lilyford blaring again in the morning, reminding me that I still hadn't confronted Mum about her unusual new habits. But I was pretty sure Mum's explanation would be run-of-the-mill compared to what Ameera and I had discovered about Jewel yesterday. The whole world seemed kind of flat and boring compared to that.

I knew Ameera felt the same because she called me even earlier than usual, full of plans for crawling around the mall. So far so every-single-Saturday. Except that she wanted me to invite "Julie".

Huh. I know I joined in with the snooping and everything, but it was still seriously annoying that Ameera had planned it all without even telling me. In fact, it was only a rapidly approaching wave of guilt that prevented me from having a total go at her. Instead, I told Ameera I didn't have "Julie's" number, which was true, so then Ameera begged me to go round and speak to her. I said I'd see what I could do. To be honest, I was starting to think I preferred it when Ameera was mega-annoyed with me for skipping Wendy's party to go out with Jewel.

I wandered into the kitchen, where I was obviously too late to catch Mum, but just in time to see Jamie scoop in his last spoonful of cereal and say, with his mouth still disgustingly half-full, "By the way, Molly. You and your mates are invited to an end-of-exams house party with most of my year on Friday night."

I waited for him to finish eating properly before I pointed out, "But haven't some Year 12s still got exams after Friday? It's us lot that will have finished." Also, we had work experience coming up the week after next, whereas Year 12s still had study leave – i.e. nothing to do. It was so unfair. Still, a party was a party, even if there wasn't much reason to celebrate.

Jamie shrugged. "Yeah, well, that's probably the idea. This party seems to be kind of targeted at you."

He gave me a "got to run" look, ruffled my hair and headed for the door.

"Where's the party, anyway?" I called as he left the room.

He popped his head back round the door. "Liam's," he said. "His parents have gone to Spain without him this time."

"But I thought you two weren't friends anymore!"

He gave me a funny look. "What made you think *that*? We don't all live your dramatic life, Measly! I don't even care what my friends get up to." He shrugged and contradicted himself immediately. "Liam got this ace new game, so he invited me over last night, and when we were playing he mentioned that he wasn't into Tasha. So we're cool. Course, it was never a problem anyway!"

I rolled my eyes as Jamie left. He slammed the front door a bit harder than usual. Yeah, *right*, Jamie. Never a problem.

I got ready and wandered up to Jewel's flat, taking the

stairs. It wasn't because I was hoping to run into Jasper but just because... Oh, OK, I was hoping to run into Jasper. I didn't know what I'd say to him if I did, but I knew I wanted to. Maybe it wasn't the *day* that was weird, after all. Maybe it was *me*.

I didn't bump into Jasper but Jewel answered the door, and she happily agreed to go mall-crawling.

There followed a day of Ameera's over-bright, chirpy conversations with Jewel as we flitted in and out of shops. I knew my BFF was struggling with the enormity of finding out that Jewel was related to a rock star, but she was doing a truly terrible job of hiding it. Not for the first time, I found myself feeling grateful that Jewel didn't know what Ameera was usually like.

We went for lattes and I invited them both to Liam's party, partly to shut Ameera up.

Ameera said, "I'll go if Julie goes!" and Jewel said, "I'd love to, and can I bring Jasper? He'll have finished his GCSEs and he seriously needs cheering up." She swilled her drink in its mug and didn't meet my eyes.

I wondered about the wisdom of taking Jasper to Liam's party after what had happened on that fateful Friday after the amazing kiss in the lift, but I was quickly distracted by Ameera's next line of attack.

"Is Jasper your boyfriend?" she asked Jewel cheerfully.

Jewel stopped examining her latte and gave me a strange look. "No, he's my brother. Hasn't Molly ever mentioned him?"

Ameera tinkled a laugh. "Molly never tells me anything!"

The way Jewel was looking at me turned to friendly approval, as if she was thanking me for keeping her life secret. A wave of guilt washed over me. It was combined with the realization that Ameera definitely didn't know much about this rock star's family despite all the glossy magazines she read.

Meanwhile, Ameera had latched dangerously onto the "brother" thing. "So your brother's older than you?" she started, innocently enough.

"We're twins," Jewel said.

"Oh, wow! Is he doing GCSEs early, then? When's your birthday, because I'm a couple of months older than Molly and –"

"Ameera!" I said, at the same time as Jewel started to explain about their birthdays putting them in different school years.

"What?" she said, still with that innocent look. "I'm just trying to work out whether I'm too old for him. You don't mind if I'm interested in your brother, do you, Julie?"

Jewel looked a bit shocked, like no one had ever asked her anything like that before in her life. I suppose my friend Ameera is pretty unique. She's also usually very picky about boys, fancying only the hottest of film stars and no real-life schoolkids. Me and Wendy tease her about it and call her "Ameera Lautner".

"Ah... I guess not," Jewel said, "But you haven't even met Jasper. Have you? He's very..."

I couldn't say a single one of the words that popped into my head to complete Jewel's sentence. (And some of them were *way* slushy. Oops.)

Meanwhile my BFF continued her bizarre bid for the boy I had wonderful mixed feelings about.

"I don't care what he's like!" Ameera chirped, and I realized this was it. She didn't! She was just thinking of what it would be like to go out with a rock star's son! I felt guilty again, as well as annoyed with Ameera. What a mess. We should *so* not have snooped in Jewel's flat.

Ameera added, "I know he must be great if he's related to you!"

It didn't even make any sense – Ameera didn't really know Jewel either – but Jewel gave a confused smile.

I could have killed Ameera, but after another wave of guilt, I tried to hide my murderous thoughts from Jewel.

The rest of the day passed in a similar way. Weird, and more than a bit terrible.

Sunday, 12th June
After a day at Dad's

Gave my dad extra hugs today because I was grateful that he hadn't just been in a scary car accident in California, unlike certain dads of other Mall Girls. He ruffled my hair in the annoying way his son has obviously learnt off him, and uttered one of his random Dad phrases. This time it was: "A bird in the hand is worth two in the bush!"

"What?" I asked.

He said, "You've got bird's nest hair, Molly! Ha ha ha, just teasing my little girl!" Ruffle-ruffle-ruffle.

I wonder if rock stars with sci-fi names ("Zircon", I mean, not "Alan Stone") ever speak to their daughters like that. Or deliberately ruin their hair.

Friday 17th June
After school

School was weird all week, in exactly the same way that the mall was weird on Saturday. That is to say, Ameera *made* it weird with her attentiveness to Jewel's every move.

We had exams every day. I never thought I'd say this but I was almost glad about that. It meant there was much less time for Ameera's over-bright chatting at Jewel. It also meant that Wendy was too study-stressed to notice our BFF's odd behaviour and question us about it.

Jewel's mum was obviously still not much better despite the flowers, because Jewel walked in with me every day. I thought about asking her some personal questions so that I could work out exactly why she wanted to keep the identity of her dad secret, the way I'd suggested to Ameera. I'd been stalling Ameera all week, saying I'd try to find out soon. I could never think of the right words, though, and I was scared of upsetting Jewel – or worse, of having her suspect that I'd been snooping in her flat. I couldn't bear to think of how betrayed she'd probably feel about that.

Meanwhile, Jewel seemed way less worried about what she said to me. On Thursday, she asked me another pretty direct question about Jasper. She started with, "So is Ameera really interested in my brother?"

"Uh-huh," I said. She'd mentioned him several times a day, much to my annoyance, though she'd still never met him.

"How do you feel about that, Molly? I mean, you and Jasper *did* get together, didn't you? I know what I saw. I'm no expert on this high school dating stuff, but isn't it a problem if your friend goes after a guy you hooked up with?"

Sometimes she talked like she'd just landed from Mars. "Why aren't you an expert on high school dating?" I asked her, secretly congratulating myself for deflecting the question in such a natural way. Plus now was her chance to reply something like, *"Because I'm the daughter of a rock star and I'm more likely to date an A-list Hollywood actor than a boy with a Saturday job at The Lilies food court."* Then I could stop pretending I didn't know, and Ameera could relax and start acting normal again. (I hoped.) And maybe we could just *ask* Jewel why it was a secret, and Ameera would stop wanting to tell people. (I double-hoped.)

"Oh, I've... ah... been to a lot of different schools," Jewel mumbled. "I travelled a lot and... Hey, did you study for today's tests?"

After that, we mostly talked about exams instead. It turns out I'm not the only one who uses them to avoid awkward conversations.

Friday 17th June
After Liam's party

Oh. No.

Aaaaaaaaaarrgh!!!

Nightmare, nightmare night!!!

Here are a couple of highlights of Liam's party. (Or should I say "lowlights"?!)

I went to the party with Jamie because Ameera and Wendy live near Liam and were going together. Well, actually because

I didn't fancy meeting them at Ameera's first. I knew she was in "makeover mode" and I quite liked the idea of going out dressed as myself for a change. Jewel had said she needed to wait for Jasper to finish an evening music lesson and she'd join us there later. I got the impression that Jasper was teaching the lesson, not being the student, and it made me think wistfully that he'd offered to teach me, too, but that was probably never going to happen now. Then I got annoyed with him again for overreacting about Liam.

After that, I remembered to worry about Jasper going to Liam's party and both of the boys I liked being in the same room for the first time since the night I went out with Liam and kissed Jasper. But Jamie appeared at my door to say he was leaving so I pushed that thought out of my mind.

Jamie and I were almost the first people there, which is possibly a bit uncool but then Liam was Jamie's best friend (again) after all.

I left them in the kitchen talking about blowing up starships or football or whatever, and I wandered off to find somewhere to leave my jacket, though this was actually an excuse to nose around a bit. I'd been to Liam's with Jamie before, but not for a while, and not since I'd found out he liked me back. (If he still did. I wasn't sure about that. He'd been friendly to me so far this evening, but not overly so.)

Liam's house was extremely normal, especially in contrast to Jasper's place. The walls certainly weren't plastered with any kind of shrine to old rock bands. The nearest Liam's super-normal parents got to the decor of Jewel's flat was an old school photo, perched on top of the television. It was from last year and featured Liam and his little brother, who's now in Year 8. I'd almost forgotten how cute Liam looked in his school uniform. I was wandering off into a daydream, remembering all the extra opportunities I'd had last year to gaze at Liam across crowded corridors, before Sixth Form meant he was separated off into a different part of the school. Those were the days.

My daydream was interrupted by a familiar grating voice. It was Tasha, talking loudly to her mates on the garden side of the open patio doors. I couldn't believe she'd been invited, though I knew her friend Livvy was in some of Liam's classes at school and might have brought her along. I also did not believe what she was saying.

"It's totally working!" Tasha's laugh could definitely be described as a cackle. "Jamie likes me even more now, I swear. Remember how upset he was that night at the mall? By the time we get together, he'll be so grateful that there's no *way* he'll play around! I swear, if you ever want a boy eating out of the palm of your hand, then ignoring his texts and flirting with his best mate is *the* way to go!"

"Tasha, you're evil," her friend Hannah laughed.

"An evil genius," Livvy added. "The only girl in Lilyford who can tame Jamie Hart!"

"The hottest guy in Lilyford," Tasha sighed.

Ugh. I squirmed a bit. But the way Tasha sounded so... *gone* on my brother, I almost felt sorry for her.

It didn't last.

"I was starting to think you really fancied Liam, the way you were all over him, Tash!" Hannah said.

"As if I would ever be so obvious!" Tasha replied indignantly. "You know I've got way more class than that!"

They all walked off, laughing in a way that made me a tiny bit surprised not to see a witches' cauldron or a puff of green smoke where they'd been standing.

I wasn't sure what to think about what I'd just heard. On one hand, they had a point about my brother. He had a really bad reputation with girls. He kind of deserved to meet his match.

On the other hand, I knew how he felt about Tasha and I didn't like her thinking she could control him. He *was* my brother, after all. Plus, how dare she play Liam like that! Not to mention all the problems it had caused between me and Liam, and also, in a way, between me and Jasper. And the fact that it had threatened Liam and Jamie's friendship, however much Jamie liked to pretend I'd imagined their fight. It was all a bit complicated.

My feelings about Ameera, who had just arrived with Wendy, were much easier to understand. I wished she'd stop behaving like she held the secrets of the universe and was bursting to tell anyone who'd listen. I saw her sidling over to the DJ (a friend of Liam's who had set himself up on a coffee table with Liam's iPhone dock) and my first worry was that she was looking for access to the sound system or something, so that she could broadcast some kind of announcement about Jewel to the entire party. Or maybe she wanted to request an old track by The Red Sardonyx. She was forever playing their stuff on her phone these days, whenever Jewel wasn't around. I shot her several warning glances.

I also detected that Wendy, having thrown off the shackles of exam fortnight, was starting to get suspicious. She kept looking from me to Ameera and back, narrowing her eyes. Knowing Wendy, she was gearing up for a proper strop about me and Ameera obviously keeping secrets from her.

The party was filling up and simmering slowly, with the general feeling of impending doom. But the disaster waited for Jewel and Jasper to arrive, and even then it didn't strike instantly.

In fact, after the twins had been there for a few minutes and nothing bad had happened, I'd begun to breathe a huge sigh of relief and maybe even relax a little.

For starters, my fears about Ameera and the DJ had been way off-base. From where I was standing, it looked very much like what she was actually doing was chatting him up. Or maybe Mr DJ was a total stand-up comedian, so hilarious that she couldn't help throwing her head back with laughter and leaning closer every time he opened his mouth.

Either way, Ameera seemed way too busy to announce Jewel's secret. She couldn't even blurt out anything incriminating to Jewel herself, seeing as they were at opposite ends of the room. And Wendy had got so fed up with Ameera's flirting that she'd come over to speak to me instead.

Phew, phew and triple phew.

Wendy rolled her eyes in Ameera's direction and said, "Can you believe Ameera reckons the DJ looks like Taylor Lautner? And he's only Ravi, you know, the son of one of her mum's friends? Her mum would totally approve. Her sisters won't let her hear the end of it, if they find out." She laughed. "She's so going to regret this."

"Hmm," I said, resisting the temptation to add something like: *"As long as it keeps her occupied, I don't really care."*

"Oh, you're zero fun," said Wendy. She followed my gaze, which was very much wandering in the direction of Jasper, no matter how much I tried not to let it. He was shifting about nervously next to Jewel. He was wearing his usual black jeans and Converse, though this was teamed with a faded green band t-shirt instead of one from his usual black range. Woo, he'd dressed up for the party!

"OK, who's the smexy one?" Wendy craned her neck. "Julie's boyfriend?"

Why had both of my friends jumped to that highly dodgy conclusion? Jasper and Jewel did resemble each other a tiny bit, though maybe you'd have to know they're related to see it. And neither of them looked like a close relative of an international rock star – whatever one of those generally looks like.

"Her brother," I said as casually as I could manage, especially because Jasper chose that moment to look up, catch my eye and look away again. And my heart chose that moment to speed up in time with the superfast beat of the track Ameera's DJ friend, Ravi, was playing.

I tried to find something neutral to look at, but I ended up doing an impression of a shifty creature with multiple eyes and a guilt complex.

"Do you know him?" Wendy asked, and then she stage-whispered, "He's coming over!" She looked intrigued.

Meanwhile my heart increased its hip-hopping accompaniment to the Jennifer Lopez remix.

At that point, Liam and Jamie arrived from the direction of the kitchen, laden with drinks (Jamie) and a worried expression (Liam).

I glanced from Liam to Jasper. Jasper must have spotted Liam approaching me because he stopped by the patio doors and pretended to find something outside fascinating. Or maybe he really *did* find it fascinating – who knows? I told myself off for thinking it was all about me. Of course Jasper would prefer to stand close to the doors – he had a fear of closed spaces!

"Mate, seriously, stop stressing!" Jamie was saying to Liam as they neared us. "You've locked all your parents' breakables away, haven't you? What could possibly go wrong?"

"It's all in the attic room," Liam said. "It's not exactly locked, though – the handle's broken but it works from the outside. I've just been telling everyone not to go in there."

Jamie nodded. "*Well,* then! I'm sure they won't. Relax! Exams are over, your parents are in Spain, there's a houseful of gorgeous – Oh, hi, Measly. And, er, Wendy." He looked scared all of a sudden, like he thought Wendy might bite his head off. It made me smile. After all, she might. And he might deserve it.

"Hi, Jamie," Wendy said. "You OK?"

"F-fine," Jamie stammered.

"Sorry I had to rush off the other night." Wendy smiled serenely. "You didn't mind, did you? I asked Molly to explain."

I couldn't believe how amazingly cool my friend was being! I mean, I know she officially didn't fancy him anymore, but still.

They hadn't seen each other since that night at Paolo's Pizza Place, and I'm sure I'd be at least a *little* bit nervous talking to someone I'd dumped during a date. In fact...

"Hi, Molly," said Liam shyly. He studied the carpet under our feet, frowning at a cigarette butt that was lying there. "It's great to see you. Listen, sorry I'm a bit stressed tonight. I didn't exactly tell my parents I was having this party." He ran his hand through his hair. "But hey, I was wondering... Could we... Can I maybe talk to you... um, about something..."

I glanced around. Wendy and Jamie were making small talk about exams. Ameera and Ravi were still flirting with each other. Jasper was now standing in the garden and he'd been joined by Jewel. They seemed to be having some kind of intense conversation, judging by what I could see of Jewel's face. What I could see of Jasper made my stomach fizz.

"Molly...?" Liam said questioningly.

I turned my eyes back to Liam. I mumbled, "Yeah?" and then I wondered why I felt so different.

I tried glancing at the garden and back again. Jasper – butterflies. Liam – no butterflies. It was the oddest realization. *I didn't fancy Liam anymore!* It was the end of an era. Wow. How could this have happened?

"OK, so I wanted to ask you..." Liam said. "There's this thing next week..."

Luckily, he was distracted by a loud crashing sound coming from the kitchen. If he was about to ask me out again – and I had a feeling that's what he was building up to – then I'd use this time to think of a way of turning him down gently. He meant a lot to me and he had done for years. He was a great guy. He was my brother's best friend. He... had left the room in a total panic, with Jamie following him and yelling at him to calm down.

And now Jasper was coming over. Like he'd definitely waited for Liam to leave.

Jasper reached us. He wasn't smiling but he looked totally gorgeous anyway. "Molly," he said. "Hey."

I didn't reply. Those irrational feelings of annoyance suddenly swept over me again. Why hadn't he tried to see me again before now? Where did he get off, making me feel all guilty about having gone out with Liam just before our amazing kiss? Why did it even matter? It was Jasper I'd wanted to see that night, not Liam! It might have taken me a while to realize the truth, but there it was. There was no need for Jasper to have got all upset with me.

"My sister says I should talk to you," Jasper added in a low voice.

Oh, *great*. "Don't you have a mind of your own?" I oozed sarcasm. Well, *honestly*. I wouldn't dream of *ever* doing anything Jamie told me to do.

Wendy's eyes widened and darted between us like she was watching a tennis match.

"OK, forget it," Jasper bit back.

"Fine by me," I replied.

He glowered at me but didn't move away.

I glowered right back. Two could play the glowering game.

Wendy turned on the Bo family charm and the tone she uses on difficult customers when she's helping out in her mum's

Chinese restaurant. "I'm so sorry about Molly – she's not normally like this. Well, maybe sometimes." She considered it briefly. "Actually, she's quite often like this. It's Molly all over."

I turned my look on her.

"But not usually to hot... er, I mean, *complete* strangers."

"We're not strangers," Jasper said softly, making my stomach flip.

"Says who?" I retorted, but it came out less like the bark I intended and more like a whisper. What was up with *that*?

Wendy cast me a triumphant "I-knew-it" look, mixed with so much curiosity that she was practically jiggling on the spot.

"Molly?" she said.

"Huh," I replied, busy glowering again. Jasper glowered back. I felt like we could glower at each other forever. His glowering skills were amazing.

Wendy nodded firmly. "OK. You two are coming with me," she ordered. She marched out of the room, calling behind her, "Right now! Come on!"

What was she playing at? And yet Wendy in this mood was very difficult to disobey. Jasper and I finally broke eye contact and followed her into the hallway and up two flights of stairs. It seemed like we were headed for exactly the room that Liam had warned was out of bounds.

"Wendy, what are you doing?" I asked her.

"Ssh. I read about this in one of Ameera's magazines," she said. "It was about couples counselling. I'm finding a place you can have some alone time."

"Some *what*? Wendy!" I tugged at her sleeve but she shook

me off.

"Thank me later," she said, opening a small door at the top of the stairs. "Aha!" She flicked a switch, lighting up a small attic room that was absolutely crammed full of furniture, vases, lamps and what looked like every single breakable thing Liam could hide here during the party. It was piled up on top of a heap of dustier junk that was probably in its more permanent home.

"Perfect," said Wendy. "In you get, guys!"

It was weird how completely commanding her voice was. I walked into the room and Jasper followed me, looking bewildered as he blinked in the fluorescent lighting.

"OK," Wendy said. "Liam told me and Ameera absolutely not to come up here, and I think he's said the same to everyone, so you won't be disturbed." She fiddled with the door handle on the outside of the door as she spoke. "You two stay and sort things out! But if I don't see you back downstairs in ten minutes, I'm coming up to make sure you haven't killed each other, OK?" Her eyes sparkled wickedly, and she gave me a look that said *"tell me everything later, Molly, or die"* before she shut the door.

"Wendy, wait!" I shouted urgently.

"Talk to each other!" she called back, and the laugh in her dwindling voice made me want to kill her.

There was a silence.

I started to fill it, not bringing myself to look at Jasper. "I am *so* sorry about my friend! I mean she can be a bit weird, but I *really* don't know what's got into her tonight. I think Ameera must have given her too much inner confidence when she did her last makeover and – Jasper? OMG, are you OK?"

He'd shut his eyes and was taking shallow breaths, his body slammed tightly against the wall. He slid down into a sitting position, hunching over himself and trembling. It reminded me of the first time I'd been in a lift with him, the day I met him.

Now I wanted to kill Wendy even more. Of course Jasper wasn't OK! He was shut in a cramped room with no windows! Why on earth had Wendy thought it was a good idea to bring us up here? Not that she knew about his claustrophobia... or anything at all about him, for that matter. Why did I never tell my friends anything? Was this all *my* fault? I mean, maybe Wendy had meant well. She's always loved the idea of pairing her friends off – why else would she keep trying to get me to go out with her brother? So she must have seen the way I looked at Jasper and thought she was helping me and...

What was I *doing*, analysing all this instead of helping Jasper?!

I ran as quickly as I could to open the door.

And then I remembered what Liam had said about the handle being broken, and only working from the outside.

I rattled and kicked at the door for a while but it was no use – it was totally stuck. We were at the top of the house, and I could hear strains of the music that I knew was blaring downstairs. No one would hear me if I bashed at the door. My phone was in my pocket and I thought about calling someone like Ameera or even Jamie, but I wondered whether they'd believe me. And anyway, I needed a quicker solution, for Jasper's sake.

I flicked my eyes around the room and located a large skylight-style window on the right-hand slope of the roof. I tripped over a table leg and stumbled over a thousand other objects before I found a chair and manoeuvred it under the skylight, breathing a sigh of relief as I released the catch and it opened easily.

It must have been gone nine-thirty by this point but it still wasn't dark outside – I suppose we were coming up to the longest day. Natural light flooded the room and mixed with the fluorescent mall-like strip-light in the attic. I tilted the window as far as it would go, and so rapidly that I think I woke some pigeons roosting on the roof – there was this big flapping noise, a ton of cooing and blur of grey. I mumbled a quiet apology to the poor pigeons before I jumped off the chair and turned to Jasper.

"Is that any better?" I asked, wanting so desperately for him to say yes that I almost felt a bit panicky myself. "Does it help if you can see the sky?"

He opened his eyes slowly, gazed upwards and nodded. "Thanks," he mumbled. I nearly cheered at the fact that he was speaking, and therefore probably breathing more easily. "Molly? Could you... come over here?" he added in a small voice.

"Course!" I yelped, rushing to his side. Before I could think too much, I grabbed his hand and held it. "This helps, doesn't it?" I remembered that from what he'd said in the lift.

"Yeah," Jasper said softly. "Loads."

"OK, then..." I held on tighter. Jasper turned his head towards me. His expression was much calmer. I reached forward and instinctively touched his chest with my other hand, checking his heartbeat through his t-shirt. It didn't seem to have slowed. The opposite, maybe.

"Are you *sure* it's helping?" I asked. "Your breathing's still funny."

"I know," he said.

"So can I do anything else?" My brain chose that moment to beam in an image of us kissing in the lift. I shook it away. The guy was in the middle of a panic attack! Or at the end, hopefully – but still. How evil was I, thinking of turning it to my advantage? "Anything else to help you, I mean?" Be gone, evil thoughts!

He sighed. "Molly..." he said. He sounded sad.

"What?"

"Nothing. Nothing. I'm feeling better, honestly. I hope you didn't mind... calming me down. It's all just so *embarrassing*." Before I could reassure him, he took a deep breath and said, "I think I'm learning to cope now, though. Gradually, once I get myself under control." He looked at our joined hands. "I'm going to try letting go now, OK? See what happens?"

"Yeah, sure!" I released my grip on his hand and reminded myself not to feel disappointed. This was therapy, nothing more. "How's that?"

"Much better." He sneaked a little glance at me. "In some ways."

My butterflies fluttered. What did he mean by *that*?

He stood up and stretched as if he'd just woken from a long sleep. "You know what? I really do feel OK," he said, his voice full of wonder as he looked around the cramped room, then back at me. "I can even go for milliseconds at a time without peering at the sky! Honestly, Molly, I could never have done this a few weeks ago."

"My crazy friend wouldn't have shut us in here a few weeks ago," I said. I couldn't believe I didn't even know Jasper then, back when Wendy first decided she fancied my brother and all my troubles started. So much had changed since the day Wendy accused me of being a mindless "mall girl".

Jasper laughed. "Look," he said, his eyes lighting up, "they've got a keyboard!"

He was pointing to a red plastic toy piano that was on the floor, poking out from under a pile of battered picture books. It was sprinkled with stickers depicting Fireman Sam and a few other residents of Pontypandy.

"Jasper, you're the musician here," I said. "Tell me, is that thing *really* a keyboard?"

He smiled. "As long as we're stuck here, it'll do," he said. He pulled it out and pressed the "on" switch. Nothing happened. "Aw," he said, turning it over. "No batteries." He turned it back and sat back down on the floor with it, resting it in his lap. He started tapping at it silently. I watched the concentration in his face as his fingers sped over the small keys.

Suddenly the thing I wanted to do most in the whole world was kiss him. I was unsure whether he'd want that, though. A couple of minutes had passed now since he'd recovered from his panic attack. We were sitting so close that he could easily have made a move, but he hadn't. And neither had I. Would Wendy be disappointed if she came back to open the door, like she'd promised, and she found us playing with Liam's old toys like a couple of toddlers?

Jasper stopped tapping the keys and looked up. "Are you OK?" he asked me.

"Yeah, I..." I decided to go for it. What was the worst that could happen? Apart from being trapped in a room for ages with a boy who'd just rejected me, of course. Hmm. Even so. I took a deep breath and moved closer to him on the dusty floor. Then I chickened out. "I was wondering if you'd still teach me? To play the keyboard, I mean? You, er, said you would... that day when..."

His eyes slid over my lips. Ooh. OK, that was good.

"I'm not sure if I can after all," he said. "I've been really busy lately."

And that definitely *wasn't* good. I shifted away slightly. "Right, OK. No problem."

"No, I don't mean it like that," he said quickly. "I'd love to teach you. It's just that things have been increasingly weird at home and I've been taking over all of Mum's lessons as well as doing those big exams, and on top of that there's been..." He paused and gave a little laugh, as if he was laughing at himself. "Inner turmoil," he finished. He glanced at me.

"Oh," I said. Inner *what?*

"Though my sister calls it 'emo moping'." He tapped repeatedly at one key. "You know, Jewel told me she saw us in the elevator," he said through the tapping. "*That* night."

I wriggled with total awkwardness. "Why do you sometimes say 'elevator' and sometimes 'lift'?" I asked him. And where had *that* come from? I seemed to have an urgent need to change the subject whenever I thought about Jewel seeing me kissing Jasper in the lift.

"Do I?" he asked.

I nodded.

"Oh, maybe I do. I've never thought about it. Some of my family are in the States, and I lived there for a while too," he said. "I guess I've had a mixed upbringing. But not as much as my sister." He stopped tapping and fiddled with the Fireman Sam sticker instead.

As usual, I was dying to ask him more about his family. At the same time, I was cursing myself for accidentally bringing the subject up now that I knew things about him that I wasn't supposed to know. "Oh," I said, to stay on the safe side.

He looked at the ground, making me notice his gorgeous long lashes. "She also says she doesn't think you're going out with... the boy from the other night," he said. "I only told her about him a few minutes ago, when I saw him talking to you. Neither of us had any idea, when she dragged me out tonight, that she was bringing me to the house of the guy I thought you were seeing." He gave a wry smile. "The guy whose keyboard I'm playing right now."

"It could be his little brother's. Liam's more of a Postman Pat type," I joked. Then I made myself get back to the point. I didn't want to avoid it anymore. "Anyway, I'm not seeing Liam. I tried to tell you... I mean, I'd been out with him that night but I kind of went because Wendy was out with my brother, and I wanted to keep an eye on them." This was true, but I decided to stick even closer to the cringeworthy truth. "Not that I didn't like Liam, because I did, but..." I thought I'd better leave it there. What if I said the rest of it – *but not in the way I've just realized I feel about you* – and he laughed at me? My heart was thumping my ribcage so hard that I felt like thumping it right back.

Jasper still didn't meet my eyes. "OK. See, I'd... Well, I'd kind of tried to ask you out for that night. And you said you weren't sure but then you turned up at my front door and I thought... But then it was obvious you'd been out with him, so... Oh, forget it, it's not important."

"Jasper?"

He lifted his head at last. "Molly?"

There was a bit of a silence, filled only with the sound of a pigeon cooing loudly. It was probably the one I'd disturbed earlier, when I'd opened the skylight.

I said, "Can we just..." I gulped. "Can we forget what happened that night and... you know. Start again?"

A smile spread slowly on his face. "You mean...?"

I leaned in and kissed him.

Wow.

He put his arms around me, pulled me closer. And we kissed.

It wasn't really starting again. It was building on what happened before. It was awesome.

That pigeon from the skylight clearly thought so too. It started cooing louder and louder.

"Shut up, pigeon," I mumbled into Jasper's lips, but neither Jasper nor the bird paid any attention, and pretty soon I stopped noticing all the cooing myself.

If there were footsteps on the stairs then the pigeon noise

must have covered them. Or Jasper and I were so involved in each other that we wouldn't have noticed a herd of elephants approaching.

Either way, it was a total surprise when the door burst open.

My first thought was that Wendy had finally returned and I quickly reminded myself to kill her, no matter how well things had turned out. She shouldn't have done this to us in the first place! But instead I heard a boy's voice say, "Don't follow me, Jamie, I don't want anyone thinking they can come up here and – oh."

It was Liam, holding two champagne flutes that he was probably wanting to put out of harm's way.

I fought the urge to spring away from Jasper in shock, remembering what had happened after our kiss in the lift. Then I thought I should probably untangle myself at least a little bit, just out of politeness. I also wondered about *extra*-killing Wendy for not coming back for us like she'd said she would. Surely we'd been here longer than ten minutes? I looked up. Even though the pigeon was still cooing like mad out there somewhere, the sky was growing dark.

While I was thinking all this, Liam was staring at me. "Molly," he said at last. "And..." he looked at Jasper and back at me. "Um. Didn't you hear me ask everyone not to come up here?"

"It was an accident. We couldn't get out," I said, as if that explained why we'd clearly been snogging in Liam's forbidden attic.

"The handle's broken." Liam's voice was flat. He rested the champagne flutes on the nearest table. "Dad always leaves the door well open if he comes up here because he can't be bothered to fix it." He demonstrated by opening the door as wide as it would go. I saw Jamie standing on the stairs, scowling at Jasper with that "hands off my sister" look I'd seen him display before. Wendy was right behind him, looking shamefaced. "I tried to stop him!" she called up to me.

It sort of made things worse, really.

"You weren't supposed to be here," Liam said, shaking his head.

Meanwhile the cooing sound had grown louder and louder. It was accompanied by an urgent flapping that made me realize the pigeon wasn't on the roof after all. It was inside the room. It was perched on a chunky old television set, staring at us. It had probably been there a while.

"OMG, the bird must have got in when I opened the skylight," I muttered.

Liam leapt towards the pigeon. "Get out! Get out!" he shouted, and for a second, I thought he meant me and Jasper. Well, maybe he did, but the pigeon obviously took it personally because it flapped up in a swirl of feathers and headed... out of the attic door and into the house.

"Oh no! Oh no! It's in the house!" Liam yelled.

I detached myself from Jasper and stood up, shouting, "I'll catch it!" I had no idea how to catch a pigeon, of course. I just felt responsible, and like I should do something.

I ran down the stairs after Liam and the pigeon but they were both too fast for me. The pigeon flapped into the hallway, depositing signs of its fear all over the place. Feathers flew, bird-poo splatted and party-goers spilled their drinks in shock and yelped things like, *"What is it?"* and *"Gran says they're like flying rats!"* and *"We could catch something!"* and *"Urrrgh!"* and *"Get it out, get it out!"*

Tasha's voice was one of the loudest. She was standing in a corner of the room with Livvy and Hannah, and she was wailing, "It's designer! It's dry-clean only! My life is ruined!"

Meanwhile, Liam was panicking and running about, shouting, "Out! Please, pigeon! Out, out!"

The pigeon responded by flapping up to the ceiling, leaving a trail of white all over Liam's family's smart living-room furniture.

Jasper appeared at my side and put his arm around me. "He's scared. He just needs to see a way out," he said, his voice low and tickly in my ear, making my insides melt.

He let go of me, walked over to the patio doors and pulled at them until they were wide open. The bird flapped in his direction.

Jasper stepped out of the way and the pigeon flew out into the night sky, hopefully to find a better class of roof to roost on.

The stunned silence that followed the pigeon's departure only lasted a few seconds.

Then the room exploded into chatter and noise. A lot of it seemed to be moving towards Liam's front door. I realized that people were leaving the party in big groups, talking about other parties and places to go.

I looked at Jasper, who was standing next to me again. "How did you *do* that?" I asked him.

"I didn't do anything," he said. "I just opened the patio doors wider. Someone else would have done it if I hadn't."

I wasn't so sure – everyone else seemed way too concerned with avoiding pigeon poo, laughing at the people who'd got splatted, spilling drinks and deciding where to go next.

Jasper looked around and said, "Now where's my sister? Have you seen her at all since we came downstairs?"

"No. Why? You're not worried about her, are you?"

He frowned. "Maybe. A bit." He sighed. "Yeah, I am, actually, Molly. Listen, I can explain. Another time. I probably shouldn't have left her for so long. I didn't even think about it, while I was up there with you..." He went a bit red. "But I've got to look for her. Sorry." He stepped away. Then he retraced his steps. "Hey, can I have your number?" he asked. "Then I can call you tomorrow instead of turning up at your front door like I sometimes do! Not that I've been getting any time to do anything like that lately."

"But aren't you coming back later? Where do you think Jewel's gone?"

Jasper just replied, "Please?"

So I told him and he tapped the number into his phone, his fingers moving as quickly as they had on the little keyboard. He was so gorgeous. And he was kissing me again. But it was a quick kiss and then he was gone, and I was alone in a rapidly emptying room, watching my ex-crush run around with a wad of paper towels and a bottle of cleaning fluid while my brother and Wendy followed him, making reassuring noises and telling him they were sure his parents would spare his life.

I walked over. "Liam," I said. "Can I help? I feel like it's all my fault."

He didn't say anything but I thought I saw him grit his teeth. He shook his head and edged away, cleaning as he went.

Wendy gave me a sympathetic look but Jamie said, "It *is* all your fault, Molly! You've ruined the whole party! What were you even thinking, going up there? And with... with..." He glanced at Liam, checking he'd moved out of earshot. "That music guy!" He lowered his voice to a whisper. "Liam's gutted! He was planning to ask you out again tonight, you know. I *told* him it wasn't a good idea!"

Wendy said, "Oh. Liam likes Molly?"

"Liam *liked* Molly." Jamie sighed. "Right now I think he'd be happy if he never saw her again in his life." He frowned at me. "I know I said hanging around with you would put him off you, Measly, but I didn't expect you to do it in such style." His tone was jokey but he didn't smile.

"But I..." I began.

"I suggested they should go up there, J," Wendy said generously.

Hold on, I suddenly thought. *"J"*?

"But *she* opened the window and let the bird in, didn't she?" Jamie insisted. "And she's the one who was in there with her musical boyfriend."

"His name's Jasper," I pointed out, mostly because Wendy and Jamie seemed to have forgotten I was standing right there.

"What do you know about him, anyway?" Wendy asked Jamie. "I talked to Ameera earlier and she just giggled for ages about how his name was Jasper and she'd been planning to go after him herself but never mind, good for Molly, and at least she'd still get 'special invitations'. I have no idea what that means, but it's typical of the strange things Ameera's been saying lately. So then I thought of talking to Jasper's sister but she must have left really early."

"I didn't even know the music guy had a sister," Jamie said.

"His name's Jasper," I repeated, but they both ignored me again.

I suddenly realized how close Jamie was standing to Wendy. And I remembered that she'd been behind him on the stairs earlier. And now.... they were holding hands. Wendy and Jamie were actually holding hands. Then Jamie whispered something to her. *Whispered!* Jamie was whispering to Wendy!

Jamie suddenly seemed to remember I was there. "I'm going to talk to Liam a sec, but as soon as I'm sure he's OK, I'm taking you home, Measly. And I am *never* letting you anywhere near my friends ever again!"

I was so stunned that I couldn't reply. I didn't even say, "What about *you* and *my* friends!"

"Wendy!" I gasped when I was sure he'd gone. I remembered that I still hadn't killed her for locking me in the room with Jasper, but I was in too much shock about the Jamie thing now. "What's going on?"

"Where?" she asked innocently. "Oh! You mean me and Jamie? Don't worry about that. I haven't changed my mind about him. I stand by what I said the other night! It's nothing serious, Molly. Just fun, I promise. He seemed interested, if a bit scared of me. And Ameera was with Ravi so I thought, what the heck, exams are over! Live a little!" She laughed. "I know he's not intellectually my match, but physically, you know – phwoar! Oh, sorry. He's your brother."

I shook my head at her. I could not *believe* the way things had gone in the space of a few hours.

I surveyed the room. How could a small bird leave the kind of mess you'd expect from a rampaging bull?

And had I really hurt Liam as much as Jamie said I had?

Not to mention having a part in wrecking his house, ruining his party and getting him into trouble with his parents.

All things considered and apart from those few moments with Jasper, it has been a *nightmare* of a night.

Saturday 18th June

Hanging around at the Hart residence, 5th floor, The Lilies eco-mall, Lilyford

Spent half of the day lying on my bed contemplating life and pigeons and feeling bad about Liam. There was also quite a bit of daydreaming about kissing Jasper.

Spent the other half of the day chatting to my friends on the phone and on the laptop.

First Ameera called and said sorry she wasn't going round the mall with me today but she was with Ravi in the food court right now and they were "just friends, honestly" because "in the cold light of day he was no Taylor Lautner after all". Then she talked about Jasper, told me I was a "dark horse" and asked me if I was thrilled that I was going to be linked to a famous person, leading to fame and fortune of my own. I told her it wasn't like that but I don't think she was listening. Ravi came back with some drinks and she said she'd call me later and hung up.

Jasper called immediately afterwards, meaning that I spent a few minutes feeling guilty about having snooped in his flat and knowing his secrets. But he was being so lovely that those thoughts soon left my mind. Among other things, he told me that he'd found Jewel back at The Lilies and there hadn't been anything to worry about after all. He didn't tell me any more about why he'd been worrying in the first place, though. He said he couldn't wait for things to calm down at home because maybe we could go somewhere together, and then he had to rush off, too. When he hung up, I had to stop myself hugging the phone like a love-crazed loon.

A bit later, Wendy and I chatted on Facebook for ages. She didn't mention Jamie, so neither did I. She asked about Jasper, but I didn't tell her much. When I thought about the fact that we knew stuff she didn't, I felt terrible. Maybe Ameera and I should tell her what we know. I decided to ask Ameera what she thought about that. Then I remembered that I was supposed to be trying to find out Jewel's reason for keeping her family secret. I looked for her on Facebook but there was no sign of her under any of the name combinations I tried. Weird. I was sure she'd mentioned reading our school's page in the past.

Jamie came home from work. We bumped into each other in the kitchen and he scowled at me a bit more about last night before he relented and mumbled, "You know, I'm sort of relieved it didn't work out between you and Liam, Measly. It might have been better if you hadn't trashed his house, though." He gave a small smile.

"What about you and Wendy, then?" I asked, since we were getting personal.

He looked confused. "I like her. Though she scares me a bit. I don't think she's all that interested in me, to be honest. I'm not quite sure what happened last night."

I rolled my eyes. *Wendy* happened. "And Tasha?" I asked. I remembered what I'd overheard at the party and wondered whether to tell him, now that he was being nice to me. I decided to test the waters. "You know, I really don't think she fancies Liam after all."

"Hmm," Jamie said. "Actually, I sort of went off her a bit last night. It was weird. I mean, I still fancy her, but the way she went on and on about her designer jacket, you know... Whereas Wendy looked just as great and she didn't seem to care."

Wow. That's possibly the closest my brother's ever come to seeing beyond a girl's stunning looks. Maybe Nan's right and he's actually going to grow up one day.

Mum came in so we stopped discussing our love lives. She seemed even more distracted than usual as she threw some dinner together and rushed out without telling either of us where she was going. Again.

Sunday 19th June
After a day at Dad's

Had a big Father's Day outing to a Chinese all-you-can-eat buffet place with Dad, Nan and Jamie. Wendy walked past with her mum and they looked through the window and spotted us. Wendy waved and her mother frowned. I'm sure Mrs Bo now approves of us even less – we were in a rival restaurant and Wendy's mum calls buffets "gimmicky and cheap" anyway. I can't believe Wendy and Jamie are now possibly back on the "star-crossed lovers" track that Wendy was so fond of a few weeks ago.

Jasper called me tonight and when I mentioned Father's Day, he went all quiet and totally changed the subject. I think I'm going to have to admit to him that I know. Soon. Maybe.

Monday 20th June

After a day at West Lilyford Community College

School has been full of preparation for next week's work experience, combined with "orientation" stuff for next year, "the most important year of our school lives" etc, etc. Yawn. I'm just glad exams are over for the next six months.

I was really nervous when I met Jewel this morning for our walk to school, but she didn't really say all that much about Jasper. She did smile kind of knowingly when she said, "My brother seems a lot happier all of a sudden." But I just smiled back at her and ignored the way that thought made my heart beat faster.

I asked her what had happened to her at the party and she said she'd just decided to go home early and she hadn't bothered telling Jasper because she thought he was "busy" and wouldn't mind. (There was another knowing smile there.) "Seems I missed all the fun," she joked, so then I described the pigeon incident and we fell about laughing at the whole disastrous night. I didn't talk about how the pigeon got into the house in the first place, though.

The weirdest thing about my day was getting home and finding Mum in the living room, slumped in front of the tennis. It's her favourite sport, so that wasn't unusual in itself. But Mum should not have been home from work yet.

"Mum, have you taken time off to watch Wimbledon?" I asked her.

"What? Oh. No. No." She frowned. "Listen, Molly, have the teachers said anything to you at school?"

Ooh, she was behaving oddly. "About what?" I asked. "You know what teachers are like. Blab blab blab. Can you narrow it down a bit?"

"Oh! Yes, sorry, I didn't say. I mean about next week. Your work experience."

Still strange. We'd arranged it all months ago! I was all set to go to Mum's work. I thought a bit. "They made a fuss a few weeks ago about some paperwork," I remembered. "Some admin mix-up that meant they didn't have the right stuff. I think it all got sorted out."

She nodded. "Well, good. Let me know if it isn't, OK? And I should... I should chat to you about something soon." She looked at the time display on the digibox. "Another day! I have to get ready now. I'm going out." She sprang up and headed for the door.

"Mum?"

She stopped in the doorway and turned round.

"Is everything all right?"

"I'll tell you soon, Molly, OK? I promise."

So then I felt terrible for ever worrying that she had a new man and that he was causing her weird behaviour. Because this seemed way scarier than that.

I called Jasper but he was in the middle of a lesson and couldn't talk, and then I realized that he might not be the best person to share family worries with anyway. It was hard to imagine that the son of a rock star could seemingly have so many problems, and also end up working so hard through his study leave. Ameera would be utterly disappointed if she knew how unglamorous his life actually appeared to be.

I had another wave of guilt about the way Ameera and I knew the secret of Jasper's background. Then somehow I rode that wave, switched on the laptop and searched for Zircon and The Red Sardonyx, wondering why I hadn't thought to do that before. I found loads of band pictures and discographies but nothing much about Alan Stone's personal life, except what I already knew or suspected from what Ameera had said. Wikipedia wrote that he was "now divorced from teen bride Katie Brady", and that sixteen years ago they'd had "twin babies kept out of the public eye at then-wife Katie's insistence". It didn't look like the page had been updated much for the past few years, either. Maybe the hardcore fans of The Red Sardonyx were all a bit too old for that kind of thing. There were some news articles about Zircon's recent car accident, but they didn't give much away either.

After that, I felt even more guilty for trying to cyber-stalk

Jasper instead of actually talking to him. I found Ameera and Wendy online and chatted to them for ages about nothing much at all, until I felt better about myself.

I really need to sort this all out. Somehow.

Tuesday 21st June

After another day at West Lilyford Community College

Finally found out what's going on with Mum. I achieved this by forcing Jamie to pay attention to my concerns for a change. And I achieved *that* by switching off his computer and refusing to leave his room until he'd listened to me. Then we teamed up to catch Mum before she slipped off anywhere, and we sat her down and questioned her.

So here it is.

She's been made redundant – i.e. sacked from work because they're "downsizing". She's actually still on full pay at the moment and for quite a bit longer, but they "let her go" just over a month ago, and she's been desperately looking for something else ever since. She told us her main idea is to use her severance pay to manage a beauty shop. That's why she's been trying out all kinds of samples and visiting potential rivals in the mall to look at price lists and to consider the staff she'd need to hire.

She also told us she's been working evenings, Saturday mornings and other odd times behind the scenes at the mall's multiplex, "just to keep my hand in with work".

Wow.

I asked Mum when she'd been planning on telling us any of this and she apologized a lot and mumbled things about not disturbing our important exams and – though she did smirk a bit here – complicated social lives.

Then Jamie – *Jamie,* mind you – told Mum that was ridiculous and she should tell us stuff because we might be able to help. He even suggested she should tell Dad, which I'm sure was slightly crossing the line.

Mum looked horrified before she recovered and reassured us that things would work out. She said her biggest worry recently had been about my work experience, but she was relieved to hear it was all going ahead despite the paperwork glitches. She thought those had probably happened because she was exactly the person responsible for sorting out that kind of thing. "I know all about public liability insurance," she declared.

"And that's why we love you," Jamie said before I attacked him with a sofa cushion.

Oddly enough, our ensuing cushion-battle seemed to put a big smile on Mum's face. Normally she'd have had such a go at us. Maybe losing her job isn't all bad.

Wednesday 22nd June

After yet another day at West Lilyford Community College

I've been thinking about it, though. Do I really want to go and work for the firm that caused Mum all this worry and upset? On the plus side, it's a cosy office-based job, unlike some of the placements people in our year have got – ones that sound like totally scary hard work. Also there's the fact that Mum's old law firm have connections to Art Boy and the mural project, and I'm still really curious about all that, not to mention the way he also knows about Jewel. Maybe I could ask some questions and find out a bit more about Art Boy.

On the minus side, they sacked my mum!

I suppose I could go in and pretend to be nice but "accidentally" put salt in people's tea and lose their important documents and stuff. I've seen TV shows where unpaid interns do things like that for revenge.

I mentioned my thoughts to Mum and she said, "Molly, don't be so dramatic. Just go and learn what you can. It's an opportunity." Then she smiled a bit and added, "And yes, I wouldn't mind hearing some stories of how badly they're coping without me. In fact, I'm positively looking forward to it."

I talked about it to Jasper on the phone later, too. He went quiet for a while and then he said, "You know, we could use some extra help at the music school. I nearly asked Jewel but she told me she loves the placement the school have given her, weirdly enough. But maybe you could change your placement and come and work with me? Technically you'd be working for Mum, I suppose, but until she feels better it's mostly just me. Unless you can't because we need special paperwork, or something?"

Ooh. A whole week of working with Jasper, when we hadn't even managed to get together since Friday? Plus bonuses like the music itself, and getting to hear Jasper play on a proper keyboard with sound and without stickers all over it?

"Mum knows all about public liability insurance," I told him.

My brain was ticking.

Thursday 23rd June

After a fourth day (this week alone!) at West Lilyford Community College

My brain ticked all morning at school, to the point where I spilled its contents out to Wendy and Ameera at lunchtime. To put it less disgustingly, I told them about Mum's job situation and my reservations about working for the Mum-sacking meanies at the law firm.

Before I could even mention Jasper's offer of an alternative placement, Wendy started fizzing with excitement.

"Ooh! Come and work with me in Mum's restaurant!" she said. "Please please please. Please. I'm sure they can have two work experience people, and then I might actually enjoy it. Think of the fun we'd have!"

So then I didn't talk about working at the music school after all. What if Wendy and Ameera thought I was dumping them again, for Jasper this time? I did not want a repeat of the whole falling-out trauma from before. Especially when I didn't even know if it was possible to change my work placement anyway.

"The school probably won't let me go anywhere else. It's been arranged for months," I said, half hoping Wendy would tell me I was wrong.

She did! "They will, Molly, honestly! When Harry was in Year 10 loads of his mates changed their placements, even in the middle of the week! Just tell Mr Clark that there are special circumstances – you know what he's like about solidarity, evil multinationals and workers' rights."

She was right. Mr Clark taught history as well as being a

careers adviser, and he was always the first to call for strike action, sometimes even among the students. He wasn't very popular with the Head Teacher.

"Besides, if you come and work at the China Palace you can help Mum to realize that the Hart family are not the sworn enemy of the Bo family," she added dramatically. Her face clouded over with a daydream. "Or that they *are*, which would possibly be more romantic for me and Jamie."

"I thought it wasn't serious between you and Jamie," I said.

"It isn't," she agreed. "But it can still be romantic, can't it?"

There is no hope for my friend Wendy.

There might be hope for me to change my placement, though. We each have a five minute slot tomorrow with Mr Clark to discuss next week's placement. The time is now.

Argh! What should I do...?!

Friday 24th June, afternoon
After some confusion at the Careers Resource Centre, West Lilyford Community College

Well. That wasn't half as easy as Wendy had suggested it would be. (Mustn't think about Wendy and how upset she's going to be when she hears what I've done. Argh!)

First Mr Clark sat listening to me for ages, interspersed with his occasional mutterings of, "Hmm, yes, I see."

He probably didn't see, though. Or not all that clearly, anyway. He'd taken off his extremely thick glasses and he was rubbing at them with a grubby-looking cloth. It was making me nervous, which was making me blabber. And the more I blabbered, the more he cleaned. We were stuck in a blabbering/cleaning loop. It couldn't possibly end well.

Finally I managed to stop talking, with the result that he put his glasses back on. Phew.

Except that then he stared at me for a very long time.

I wriggled under his gaze, and I was just getting ready to begin the blabbering again when he spoke.

"OK, let's get this straight," he said. "Essentially you're telling me that you want to cancel your prestigious work placement in one of Lilyford's most respectable law practices, and spend the week with your boyfriend instead?"

OMG, total communication *fail* or what?!

"No, no! That's not what I meant." I tried to remember what Wendy had told me. "I have special circumstances!" Yes, that was it. "Like I told you, the law people have sacked my mum! *Sacked my mum!*" Repetition would surely help? "I can't work for them in these... *special circumstances*. You see."

He'd taken his glasses off again and the cloth was poised. "I do see," he said, which had to be a total lie at the time that he said it. "How does your mother feel about this?"

"I... er... haven't told her," I admitted. Well, I'd only decided five minutes ago, after all.

He rubbed at his glasses again. "Hmm. And your boyfriend? Can he definitely secure you this alternative placement you seem to think he's offering?"

"He's... he's not my boyfriend." Or was he? Maybe he was. What a thrilling thought! Maybe Jasper *was* my boyfriend! Even though I hadn't seen him since last Friday, which was so long ago that it already all felt like a dream. A wonderful dream filled with kisses in the attic, despite the interruption by Liam and resulting pigeon nightmare. I imagined spending a whole week with Jasper. Seeing him every day. Kissing him every day...

"Molly?"

I blinked several times. What was this bespectacled middle-aged man doing in my awesome daydream? "Yes?"

"Oh, good. I thought you'd left us for a moment then." Mr Clark laughed. He was relatively cool, but he still sounded like a teacher. "So you're saying this boy can offer you a work placement in his mother's music school?"

"Er... yes," I said. At last, we seemed to be getting somewhere!

"And does it interest you? This placement?"

"He really does!" Oops. "Um, I mean, *it* really does."

"OK."

"OK?" I beamed. "You mean I can do it? Spend the week with Jas– Learning about the fascinating inner workings of a music school?"

"No, I mean, OK, I'll look into the possibility." He looked at his watch. "You've really left it quite last-minute, Molly, so I can't promise anything. And I'll need to speak to your mother. Is that all right?"

"Yes! Of course!" No! No! Mum would not be happy about this. She'd been looking forward to reports of the way her old workplace was collapsing without her.

"I'll also need to speak at some length to your potential employer at the music school."

"To Jasper?" I asked, trying not to die on the spot at the

thought.

"Jasper's the one who's just finished his GCSEs and has this amazing musical talent that has inspired you to be interested in a career in the music industry? Your boyfriend?"

Wow, I didn't remember saying any of that. I really had blabbered on earlier. "Yes," I said, not correcting the "boyfriend" thing this time, if he was going to insist. I gripped the edges of my chair to stop myself floating back into dreamland.

"Well, no, then," Mr Clark said patiently. "I'll need to speak to an adult. The person who's actually in charge of the school. There's legal ground to cover, and paperwork to be done. I'd also have to arrange a visit for Thursday – I do the rounds of all the placements, seeing what you're up to. Will that be a problem?"

I gulped, thinking of Jasper's strange family situation and all the secrets he was always keeping about it. "No!" I squeaked. "No problem at all."

"Good. I have appointments with members of your year-group for the rest of the afternoon and then I should have time to make some calls. Come back at the end of the school day with the details and I'll see what I can do."

Oh.

Help.

Instead of going back to the lesson I was supposed to be in, I texted Jasper from outside the Careers Resource Centre. Amazingly, he replied straight away. He said he was at home, doing "nothing much for a change!" After several back-and-forth texts, I even managed to get as far as telling him why exactly I was texting in the first place. My heart was in my mouth waiting for a reply to that one. What if he said, "Oh, I was only joking about the placement. LOL!"

But he didn't. He said, "Srsly? Awesome! x"

I stared at the "x" for ages. Then I wrote back explaining that Mr Clark needed to speak to Jasper's mum. Eek. I put an "x" of my own on the end of the message, if that was the stage we'd reached in our relationship. (Wow.)

There was a long pause after that. I don't think he was dwelling on my "x", though. He was more likely to be thinking about letting me in on family secrets. At least one of which I already knew. But Jasper didn't know I knew, or *how* I knew. Argh! I finally get together with an amazing guy who seems to like me back, and things are *still* difficult!

Eventually, Jasper replied. "OK. Will txt Jewel and explain. Maybe she can go with you to see yr teacher? Call u later. xx"

The fact that he'd already doubled the number of kisses almost distracted me from my worrying.

I'm worrying now, though.

A ton of worry later

On the plus side, it is sorted! I am going to work with Jasper next week. Woo. Also, hoo.

It's kind of hard to get too excited when I think I've lost my friends again, though. And I mean all of them. Maybe even Jewel this time. Plus Mum's annoyed, and Jamie's in a grump.

Why is life so HARD?!!!

So I caught up with Jewel when she came out of the lesson I was supposed to be in and I told her to check her phone. I thought she'd better hear my news from Jasper first. So she did, and I thought she looked a bit surprised. She confirmed this when she said, "Wow, Molly, I don't believe this. What have you done to my brother?"

"What? Me? Nothing!" I yelped.

She laughed and said, "Relax. I don't mean it in a bad way. I mean, wow. He's actually happy for you to come into our apartment, after everything he's been making me promise for weeks and weeks now!"

I gulped. "He is?"

"Yes." She waved her phone at me. "If he wants you to do admin for the music school, well, that's where it is. The office is in our apartment. Mum wanted to start doing the actual lessons up there, too, but she and Jasper were busy setting it up when –" She stopped herself. "Stuff happened. And then Jasper couldn't persuade Mum to... make the place suitable for visitors. So the lessons have stayed down in the mall for now, in a side room at the music shop. But the administration is definitely at our place."

"Oh." I said. Wow. Jasper hadn't mentioned any of that.

"You've been inside already, of course."

I stared at her as my heart pounded. Had she seen me and Ameera after all?

"Don't you remember? That day when you first met Jasper, after the lift got stuck and Jasper was too shaken up to worry about you following him in. You were looking at our walls. At Mum's shrine." She frowned at the phone. "I probably shouldn't have said that. I think I need to speak to my brother."

The bell rang.

"But you'll do it, right?" I asked her. "You'll speak to Mr Clark with me and give him your home number and stuff?"

Jewel shrugged. "If Jasper says it's OK. I'll ring him in the next break."

Honestly, they were the strangest brother and sister I'd ever met. They always seemed to be worrying about each other and following each other's instructions. I couldn't imagine being like that with Jamie in a million years. I wondered if it was a twin thing, or maybe a celebrity child thing. Or maybe just the result of not growing up together. Jewel had once told me they hadn't. Maybe it made them look out for each other more.

We both had ICT next – even though all our lessons had now merged into a mass of "preparation" for Year 11 – so we walked down the corridor to the labs, and bumped almost immediately into a hyper-excited Wendy, with Ameera in tow.

Oh no. I was not ready for this.

"So did you ask Mr Clark about changing your placement?" Wendy asked immediately, gripping my sleeve and practically jumping up and down.

"I bet she didn't," Ameera teased. "Bet she chickened out and she's going to the boring old law firm."

"She's not," Jewel said, sticking up for me. I knew Ameera wasn't being mean, but I didn't think Jewel had ever really forgiven her for that day when she called us both "mall girls", after she found out I was seeing Jewel and Art Boy instead of going to Wendy's party. It was nice of Jewel, but also – noooo!

"Seriously!" Ameera looked impressed. "You actually asked

him, Molz?"

Before I could say anything, Jewel answered for me – again. Double-noooo! "Yes, she did. And she's almost got the go-ahead to work with Jasper at the music school next week! They just need to make some phone calls."

Wendy's excitement vanished instantly. "Wait. She's – what?"

Ameera's eyes narrowed, just like they had that day at the mall. Argh! This could not possibly have worked out any worse. I hadn't had a chance to explain anything, and now I couldn't seem to speak at all.

"So you didn't even ask about working with Wendy at the restaurant?" Ameera asked. She looked at Jewel. "All because of her and her brother?"

"Jamie and I are supposed to be star-crossed lovers," Wendy mumbled in shock. "I needed you there to remind my mother that our family are at war with yours!"

Jewel looked from Wendy to Ameera to me.

"Come on, Wendy," Ameera said, pulling her away to their next lesson. She didn't look at me as they walked off. Jewel sighed. "Did I put my foot in it again? Like that day at the mall with Ameera?"

I hung my head. What could I say?

"Oh, who cares?" she said, in her typical Jewel way. "Though Molly, you know, I respect that you're a very private person – I am too – but I wish you'd *warn* me about these things!" She shook her head. "I can't believe Wendy and Ameera are mad at me again. I thought they were starting to like me – especially Ameera."

I sighed. "It's not you they're angry with," I told her.

"I wouldn't be so sure. I'm the outsider here." She sighed. "Never mind. Come on."

Jewel was OK with me during the lesson, and she came to see Mr Clark and stood around while he made phone calls and asked her questions about the music school. But she seemed guarded – more than usual, that is – and I couldn't help thinking that something had changed between us. Which was just *great* when I was about to spend a week at her place. And I had no other remaining friends, once again.

Then I went home to listen to the ravings of Mum, who'd been polite on the phone to Mr Clark and had saved up all her annoyance for my return.

"Honestly, Molly, I'm glad you're suddenly into music, but you could have talked to me about it first!" she ranted. "I felt like such a fool when your teacher called! And, you know, I bumped into the receptionist buying a sandwich this lunch time and let her tell me all about the jobs they'd prepared for you at the law firm. Which, I have to say, sound pretty good for a work experience placement! Last year's kid just made tea, but this year they were actually planning to let you loose on the in-house magazine. They wanted you to interview that young man who's doing the mural in the mall!" She sniffed. "Probably because they're drastically short-staffed now. After spending all their money sponsoring a ridiculous art project instead of paying my salary."

Art Boy? They were going to get me to interview Art Boy? But I would have loved to do that!

Meanwhile, Mum was talking herself down. "Actually, Molly, maybe you have done the right thing after all. Thank you."

I couldn't believe she was saying that just as I was starting to think she had a point.

"But you still should have told me first!" she added, switching on Wimbledon and turning her attention to Andy Murray. "So I'm annoyed with you in any case."

"Me too," said Jamie, who'd listened to the whole thing while making grumpy faces from the doorway. "I don't trust that guy!"

"No one asked you, *big brother*!" I told him. I pushed roughly past him and went to my room, where I logged into Facebook and watched Wendy and Ameera exchanging silly messages with each other. I didn't even try to join in. I was starting to feel pretty annoyed with *myself*, to be honest, so everyone else could just get in line.

Saturday 25th June, late
Sadness at the Hart residence, 5th floor, The Lilies eco-mall, Lilyford

Totally mixed day. I spent the morning moping, listening to Adele and staring at my blank phone. There was no call from Ameera asking to crawl the mall with me. Of course.

I texted Jasper but he wrote back that he had a crazy day ahead and he'd call later.

I didn't wait by the phone or anything, because waiting by a phone for a boy is deeply wrong and Nan told me this as soon as I was old enough to cajole Mum into giving me her old mobile for the first time. Though I'm not sure whether this rule applies to the twenty-first century, seeing as my phone is always in the bag I carry so I'm usually by the phone anyway. But he didn't call. I'm just saying.

Maybe I shouldn't have changed my work placement.

Argh.

Some bits of today were also strangely OK. For example, Mum came home in a good mood and lavished me with foodie treats, saying that she had details of a new business contact and her plans for future mall domination were going better than expected.

Also, Wendy came round in the evening to go out with Jamie. Awkward. At least he answered the door, so it wasn't like she had a chance to blank me too obviously. When I heard her voice, I took a deep breath, poked my head out of my bedroom and waved tentatively at her. She was on her way out – holding Jamie's hand! – but she grinned at me and raised her eyebrows in Jamie's direction. It was almost as if she wasn't *completely* in a mood with me.

It was probably an act, though, because she was going out with my brother and she had to be polite to me when he was around.

I spent the evening watching the Glastonbury Festival on television and wishing I was in a muddy field surrounded by great musicians. And friends.

Sunday 26th June
After a day at Dad's

Another strange day. Tried to watch more Glastonbury at Dad's but Jamie was in blabbermouth mode and could not seem to shut up.

First he totally told Mum's secret to Dad and Nan, going on about how she'd lost her job and had all these plans she hadn't even told us about. It's the most I've heard Jamie say to Dad for weeks, and I didn't see why he had to start talking now.

When I took Jamie aside and hissed this at him, he said, "It's not like she can keep it hidden forever, is it? And what if Dad can help?"

I rolled my eyes. "As if Mum would ever let him," I pointed out.

Anyway, that wasn't as bad as what Jamie did later, which was to tell Dad about how I'd changed my work placement. He also added, "And she only did it to be with her boyfriend. Who I don't trust at all."

I glared at him. "I did not! I did it out of support for Mum! Which is more than anything you ever do, you... you *traitor*!"

"Break it up, kids!" Dad said good-naturedly, though really I think he was grateful for an excuse to avoid the fact that Jamie had just told him I had a boyfriend. Dad never, ever talks about that kind of thing to me. He much prefers laughing about it with Jamie, and he hadn't even done *that* for a while. "I'm sure Molly's work experience will be valuable wherever she goes," he added.

Nan got a bit hung up on the "boyfriend" thing, though. She waited until it was just the two of us and she said, "Are you still keeping that diary, Molly?"

"Yes," I admitted.

"Good. I hope it's helping. Because I know things can get complicated when you get... romantically involved with people."

"Nan!" I cringed.

She gave me a look. "Fine, I'll stop. But first tell me this: is there any reason why Jamie might be right about your boyfriend being untrustworthy?"

"No. Jamie's just being a pain," I said.

I hoped.

Jasper didn't call, and I didn't call him because I didn't want to look desperate. I only wish this would stop me *feeling* desperate.

Anyway, I'm seeing him tomorrow, on my first day of work.

Monday 27th June

After my first day at "work" at Jasper and Jewel's house

When teachers go on about school being preparation for the world of work, I had no idea they actually meant that a working day could be as boring as a day of school, only with fewer mates to talk to and longer hours. On the plus side, there was also more tea and less homework.

Additionally, in this particular workplace, there was Jasper – or rather, the promise of Jasper and a few fleeting glances here and there, while he wasn't downstairs at the music shop or taking lessons. Apparently, he helped in the shop in exchange for use of their room, so even when the music school was quiet, Jasper was busy. I couldn't believe Jasper had been doing all this as well as taking exams and having the occasional night out. No wonder he hadn't always managed to phone me when he said he would.

The day started off well. And intriguingly. When the lift arrived on Level 6, Jewel was standing there waiting to get in. I realized that I didn't even know what her work placement was. So I asked her and she said, "You'll never believe it. I'm going to school!"

"School? *Our* school?"

She nodded.

"You're kidding! On our week off?" I caught myself. "Er, I mean, our week of working really hard for *your mum*, in my case! Are you going to be a teacher?"

She laughed. "No, thanks! Well, not that they'd let me. I'm in the Learning Resource Centre, shelving books and stuff. It's my dream job!"

"You're weird," I said, though I didn't really think so. I'd really enjoyed hanging around with Jewel in the library back when Ameera and Wendy weren't talking to me. (The *last* time they weren't talking to me, that is. What is *wrong* with my *life*?!)

Jewel definitely seemed to be fine with me, anyway. She'd lost that strange edge she'd had on Friday at school. Maybe she'd got used to the idea of me working in her flat?

"You don't know the half of it," she said, pressing the "lift call" button to hold the doors. "Wait till you find out all about my family." She went a bit quiet. "Me and Jasper and Mum have talked about it this weekend, and we've all decided it's OK to tell you." She looked all serious. "And Molly, sorry I haven't said anything before. I didn't want to keep secrets from you, I swear, but Jasper decided it was for the best and he persuaded me to see it his way. Though changing my first name at school was *my* idea and Jasper thought it wouldn't work. In fact, he thought I shouldn't go to a normal school at all, but I really wanted to, and I'm glad I did, and... Argh, the time! Sorry, I have to go!"

I watched her bound into the lift and I thought, *yay!* Jasper was going to tell me the stuff I already know about his family, and possibly more, and I wouldn't have to pretend I didn't know, or ever admit how exactly I found out.

Then I replaced these thoughts with nerves about the fact that I hadn't actually seen Jasper since the night we kissed. What if he'd changed his mind about me and now we were stuck together for a week? Actually, what if *I'd* changed my mind about *him*? For a second, as I rang the bell, I couldn't even remember what he looked like.

And then he answered the door and it all came back to me. He was in his usual black jeans, Converse and band t-shirt, with his scruffy hair, dark eyes and... he was grinning at me like he was over the moon at seeing me. He was just totally Jasper. Wow.

"Hey, Molly," he said, sounding a bit nervous. "I can't believe you're here."

"I know. Isn't it awesome?"

"Yeah. Hi. Listen, I'm sorry I didn't call at the weekend." He frowned. "I meant to, but I kept waiting to have enough time for a proper chat and it never seemed to happen. You'll see what I mean when you experience the chaos I live in." He opened the door wide, and I tried not to think about the day I'd sneaked in with Ameera. "Come in."

And that's when I started to find out all about Jasper and Jewel's family.

But right now I'm exhausted from a day of sitting at a desk doing nothing except occasionally answering the phone and pretending I know what I'm talking about when people enquire about music lessons. I've also mastered the skills of printing out forms, sorting through a big messy pile of receipts and yearning for five o'clock. More tomorrow.

Tuesday 28th June
After my second day at "work" at Jasper and Jewel's house

Another fun-packed day at the world of work. I sorted through a mountain of receipts, filled in a spreadsheet, answered the phone three times more than I did yesterday and I changed a printer cartridge. I also saw Jasper four times, kissed him twice and made us both three cups of tea.

Yawn. But still marginally better than certain lessons at school, though the Jasper factor does bump it up a bit.

Wednesday 29th June
After my third day at "work" at Jasper and Jewel's house

Same as yesterday, but with zero printer cartridge changes and one extra kiss. I possibly have the best job in the world, apart from the really boring bits.

You know, though, I still haven't written down all the stuff I found out about Jasper's family. Is it because Jasper has sworn me to absolute secrecy and I'm scared someone's going to see this? Because I doubt they ever will, so that's just silly.

Or maybe I could change the names I use here or something. Then, even if people read this, they'll never know whether Jasper and Jewel are really named after gems or whether they're actually named after... I don't know. Fruit, or something equally A-list.

Anyway. Here is the short version. Jasper told me a much longer one, and not all at once. And there was the occasional bit of kissing in between sections. I'll skip that too.

The twins' mother is Katie Brady, the "teen bride" I read about on Wikipedia. She actually met Zircon at one of his gigs in England – he's a *lot* older than her – and apparently he was charmed by the fact that she didn't like The Red Sardonyx at all and she told him so. She was just there with a friend who was such a fan that they gatecrashed backstage (and this person is no longer a friend, out of sheer jealousy).

So eighteen-year-old Katie met Zircon, married him and had twins – a boy called Jasper and girl called Jewel. Katie was really insistent about keeping the kids out of the public eye because she hated that kind of thing herself. She was starting to become a fan of The Red Sardonyx after all, though – in fact, so much so that she was building up huge collections of photos, gold disks, gig programmes and newspaper clippings. Jasper told me the memorabilia completely covered the Los Angeles house he originally lived in, which I can believe because every corner of their flat at The Lilies is now crammed with this stuff, and the office I work in practically has The Red Sardonyx wallpaper.

Jasper said it was his decision to avoid letting visitors into this flat, and he made Jewel promise too. "It's kind of hard to explain away," he said. "The pictures with Jewel in them, I mean. It didn't matter so much before Jewel lived with us – I just used to say Mum was a huge fan. But now people might recognize my sister." He sighed. "I was in the middle of persuading Mum to take those pictures down for when she does her music lessons up here. But that was before… I'll get to that." So then he told me that his dad was on tour a lot when he and Jewel were little. Their parents' marriage started falling apart when the twins were about eight. By this point, Jasper was a musical whiz who refused to play in front of an audience, and Jewel was a child star, modelling in various US ad campaigns. She never used her real name or heritage to get ahead. (Here Jasper pointed to the poster-sized photo of ringlet-haired Jewel gazing in wonder. It was the one Ameera and I had spotted. Eek.) Jasper said that Jewel begged and begged her mum to take her to auditions and things because she loved modelling, and Katie relented but didn't approve. He frowned a lot when he told me. It was obvious whose side Jasper was on. Talking of sides, when Zircon and Katie split up, Katie had to move back to England. Jewel was in the middle of an ad campaign in the US and they agreed to let her stay with her dad for a while. So Katie left Jewel with her dad, and she and Jasper flew back together.

But the "while" got longer and longer, with new modelling contracts, interspersed with several boarding schools for Jewel on both sides of the pond. In the meantime, Katie was really struggling financially. "Mum wouldn't accept a thing from him,"

Jasper told me. "She still loves him and I swear she thought he'd come back to her so she didn't want to... sue or anything. She started teaching and stuff, to support me. But she also started falling apart. She's been fighting terrible bouts of depression for years. That's what's wrong right now. And now I guess *I'm* supporting *her*, as much as I can." He sighed. "Though it's all *his* fault this time. When Jewel told us the news, that he'd secretly married again at his hospital bed after the crash... Well, I can't believe he's got the nerve to write and tell me he wants to see me!"

I thought about the day Jasper was kicking at the fountain, which must have been the day he'd heard from Jewel that their dad was recovering and she was coming home.

"Are you still really angry with your dad, then?" I asked – not that I needed to. He obviously was. I think I just wanted him to know I was listening.

Jasper frowned. "Yes. I don't know. Maybe it's not rational. But my life changed forever that day when we got on the plane to England without him. And especially without my sister. When the flight attendant shut the plane door, it felt like they were locking me away, or something." His eyes filled with confusion at the memory. "And I had my first panic attack. It was horrible." He sighed. "Maybe it's not his fault they broke up. Mum says it's just life. It doesn't stop her missing Jewel – and him – like crazy, though. At least we have Jewel back now, at last. I missed her loads too."

"What happened there?"

He actually smiled a bit. "We hit our teens and Jewel started going off the rails. Dad's team were finding it harder and harder to keep her out of the media, and by then even Dad could see that she needed to avoid it. Eventually, even *Jewel* could see it! A couple of months ago she rang and told us she didn't want to be the next Lindsay Lohan and would we save her?" He grinned. "We were living in a tiny place not too far from Lilyford – you know, in the town where I still go to school. There was no space for Jewel in our flat so, for once, Mum agreed to let Dad find a place for us nearby. And he came up with this one, through some friend of his. Then Jewel arrived and insisted on enrolling at a normal school, even though I warned her she'd never manage to stay anonymous, despite using fake names and a fake profile on Facebook and all that stuff. There are people who know the truth, you know, and want to use it for their own gain." He gave me a look. "Please don't tell anyone. I trust you."

"Sure," I said, without thinking. My mind was racing. "But what about you? Don't you have to use a fake name or hide your identity or anything?"

He shook his head. "I've been out of the limelight all my life. Plus my last name is Brady, unlike Jewel – I changed it a few years ago. No one even seems to remember that Zircon had a son. But Jewel has been *this* close to getting really negative publicity, and... I just worry about her so much!"

Wow. "She's done a pretty good job of blending in at school," I told him.

"She wants to be an actress." Jasper sighed like he couldn't believe his sister.

I thought about it. "Actually, she's probably done a bit *too* well. She's always off in the library and stuff. It's not normal."

He smiled. "I don't think that part's acting. It's the reason she wanted us to help her. She didn't want to be a wasted starlet. She's not really so interested in the social side of school – she's done all that."

I looked at him. He seemed to love his sister *so* much. He'd been looking out for her, looking after her. It was so... sweet. I wondered if me and Jamie could ever be like that, and then I wondered whether maybe we had been, a bit, in our own way. With the obvious limitations of the fact that Jamie was *seriously* annoying.

So that's the full, thrillingly rock-and-roll story. Though I bet it's hard to live with for Jewel and Jasper – especially Jasper, who seems to have taken all the responsibility for everyone including his sister. That makes it way less thrilling.

I mentioned this to Jasper and he replied, "Jewel looks after herself. And I worry about her. That's how it goes. But Mum..."

He told me about how Katie hasn't been out of bed since she and Jasper got the news from Jewel about the secret marriage, just before Jewel got back from Los Angeles. Jasper says he's seen her like this before and he needs to get her to a doctor for antidepressants, but she's refusing to go. Jasper had to wake her up specially so that she could speak to Mr Clark the other day. He was really happy that she'd managed it for him.

I reminded Jasper about Mr Clark's inspection tomorrow. I knew Mr Clark would want to see Jasper's mum, my employer.

Jasper frowned and said, "Oh."

Help.

Thursday 30th June

After the inspection

I managed to persuade Jasper to let me talk to his mum. I bought flowers – I remembered how Jewel had told me she liked them before. I also brought Jewel. I spoke to her last night and asked her to do this with me before she left for work (at school!) this morning, and she agreed. So we went in and talked to her for a while, and I explained everything and Jewel and I smiled a lot and hoped for the best.

Katie Brady was thin and pale and sort of vaguely glamorous despite clearly being pretty ill right now. I could picture her being Jewel and Jasper's mum, anyway. She had the same charisma as her children.

Then Jewel went to work and her mum threw on some of her boho-chic clothes and we all went down to the room at the side of the music shop, where Jasper said it was best to have the inspection. It was Katie's first time out of the house for weeks but she put on a brave face and was a total star.

And we did it! Success! It probably helped that Mr Clark had accidentally sat on his glasses the night before and cracked them all over. He was on his way to getting them repaired in the mall when he "dropped by", as he put it. He said "good, good" for about a minute and left in a hurry.

After Mr Clark had gone, Jasper's mum said, "That went well, don't you think?"

Jasper and I nodded.

Then she said, "You know, I think pretending to be fine has made me feel a tiny bit better. I think I might visit that doctor you've been nagging me to see for the past few months, Jasper."

"It's only been a few *weeks*," Jasper said quietly, but I could tell it felt like more to him.

After work, when we were out together, Jasper squeezed my hand and said, "Molly, thanks for helping out with Mum."

"I didn't do anything," I said.

The look he gave me said, *"I'm not so sure about that."*

We wandered around the mall until we found ourselves by the giant lily statue, the one where we used to meet. And when Jasper pulled me over to the fountain where I'd sat with him so many times before, I leaned into him and we kissed until my head was spinning and I felt like I was actually *in* the fountain, in a watery world with just me and Jasper in it.

Wow, wow, wow.

Friday 1st July

After my last day with Jasper, ever ever ever

And then it all went horribly wrong.

It had been a normal day at work, and I was a bit sad that it was my last. Jasper's mum was around a lot more and really seemed to have improved, but she still wasn't up to working, of course. So Jasper was doing his usual running about, helping at the music shop and taking a few lessons in the side room. I realized that I hadn't actually managed to hear him play any music because I was supposed to stay up here and answer the phones. I decided to ask him whether I could listen to him play something another time. Soon.

When it got to about five o'clock, the end of my working

day, and Jasper still hadn't surfaced, his mum said, "Molly, you might as well go now. And thanks for working here!" She shook her head as if she couldn't quite believe she'd had a work experience girl in her flat for a week.

I left, thinking what a strange week it had been and how weird it would be to go back to school next week. I was sort of looking forward to normality and missing this already, all at the same time.

I took the stairs just in case Jasper was on his way up, and sure enough I met him on the first floor. We kissed for ages in the stairwell nearest the food court, which is actually a well-known snogging place at The Lilies, in joint first place with the stairwell at Service Entrance B. I'd seen so many couples from school meet up here – not that I'd looked, but you couldn't avoid them, really. I remembered what a nightmare it had been when I'd seen Jamie with a random girl, and Wendy had got upset with me for not telling her. I could never have imagined he'd actually end up going out with Wendy. Or that I'd end up kissing Jasper here! After a while, Jasper suggested getting something to eat, so we headed into the food court, holding hands. So far so wonderful.

I saw Ameera before she saw me. She was sitting at a green table with one of her sisters – Rukshana, I thought. They were chatting and laughing and generally looking happy. I wasn't sure what to do – would she blank me if I said hello? But she glanced up and waved me and Jasper over.

"Molly, have you had a good week? I mean, have you *two* had a good week?" She looked from me to Jasper and smirked a bit. "Sorry I haven't texted but we went away for the weekend and then I've been crazy busy at Rukshana's work. It was ace, though. I broke the printer twice and bought tons of lattes."

Rukshana laughed and said, "That's my little sister – Employee of the Month!"

I smiled. Jasper offered to get us all drinks so we put in an order and watched him head for one of the kiosks.

"Buff," Ameera commented, and I pretend-hit her arm and said, "Hands off!"

Rukshana rolled her eyes as if to say "kids!" though she was only about four years older than us.

It occurred to me that Ameera was being really normal with me. "So, hey," I said to her. "You've just been busy?"

"Pretty much, yeah," Ameera agreed.

"You mean you weren't annoyed with me about not working at Wendy's restaurant?"

Ameera looked sheepish. "Well, yeah, I was a bit. But Wendy said she didn't blame you, because she didn't want to work there either. And we both still feel a bit bad about last time we fell out. And also I thought about the whole celebrity thing and, well, I wouldn't turn down the chance to work for Zircon's son myself! Not to mention actually going out with the son of a rock star, you lucky... Oh." She went quiet and her eyes widened.

"Oh?" I said. "Why oh?"

Rukshana raised her eyebrows at someone standing close behind me. Within earshot.

I turned. It was Jasper. And he was looking shocked. Like he'd heard.

"They don't have wheatgrass drinks," he said to Ameera.

His voice was a monotone. "I couldn't get your attention to ask if you wanted something else."

"Oh," said Ameera.

He turned to me, and still in that strange voice he said, "Molly, how does she know about my family?" What he actually meant was clear. *Molly, have you told your friends when I expressly told you not to, and I trusted you?*

So he'd heard. I went hot all over. I didn't know what to say.

Ameera stepped in to defend me. And I immediately wished she hadn't.

"Molly didn't tell me," she said quickly. Her brain was clearly switched off because she added, "I saw the pictures of Zircon with your sister in your flat and it was obvious."

"When did you come to the flat?" Jasper asked. "Did my sister let you in?"

"Yes," said Ameera, but at the same time, I said, "No."

I didn't want to lie to him. Any more than I already had by not telling him this.

"No," I repeated in the silence. "We sneaked in one day..."

"There was a letter by the door!" Ameera chirped. "It blew on the floor and we picked it up!"

I wished she'd shut up. Rukshana must have noticed because she nudged Ameera and pulled her away, mouthing something like "leave them to it".

They didn't go very far – I think they could still hear us – but they were far enough to stop Ameera chipping in. Not that it made any difference. I couldn't explain, because there was no explanation.

"You saw my letter?" Jasper asked. "The one from Dad, the one I've been stressing about for ages? I kept deliberately knocking it on the floor and Jewel kept propping it up by the door again, until she practically shoved it under my nose and forced me to read it." He looked stunned. "Did you read it before *I* did? And before I'd told you anything about my family?"

"No! No, I didn't read it at all! We didn't touch anything, I promise. We just looked at the pictures on the wall, and Ameera recognized Zircon and –"

"Is that when you decided you were interested in me?" He lowered his voice, though the shoppers around us weren't paying the slightest bit of attention. "When you found out who my dad is? Was that why you changed your mind about seeing me that night when you were out with the other guy?"

"No!"

"I can't believe this is exactly what I've been warning Jewel about all this time. I've been so worried about anyone showing an interest in her for the wrong reasons that I was driving her crazy. She left that party early the other night because she'd had enough of my questions. She left to get away from me! And all that time, it was happening to me instead." His phone went off and he took it out of his pocket in a daze.

"Jasper, seriously, it wasn't – *isn't* – like that. I..."

He looked at his phone and a look of panic crossed his face.

"What's wrong? Jasper?"

"Paparazzi!" he exclaimed. "Jewel says they're following her near service entrance D. This hasn't happened to her since she moved to Lilyford! Or ever, actually, in this country, and not that often in the States, either, because she kept moving. We've all worked so hard to stop this kind of thing. Someone must have called them. Someone who knows." He wouldn't meet my eyes. "I've got to go, Molly. Bye. And, um, sorry. About us."

It felt like he'd just said, *"Have a nice life."*

Ouch. Ouch. Ouch.

I stood there for a while and didn't even notice when Ameera came back. Not until she started apologizing so much that she was almost grovelling at my feet.

"Don't worry," I said. "He's gone. It's over. He finished with me." I felt like I was telling myself. I remembered something. "Hey, Ameera, didn't I ask you not to say anything to Rukshana?" As if it mattered now, anyway.

"But she's my sister," Ameera whined. "We talk about everything. And besides, I was bursting to tell *someone*." Then she started saying sorry again.

Rukshana interrupted. "I heard what he said about paps," she said. "And I bet you it's that art guy who's behind it. You should hear the things he's been yakking about to my friends, trying to impress them. He told them he was going to be interviewed for a magazine, and then my friend found out that it was just some local company getting a work experience girl to write something for their in-house newsletter. And then even *that* didn't happen! He's increasingly desperate for publicity. And he seems to know about your friends."

"That art guy?" I repeated, dazed.

"Yes. The one with the mural project. Isn't he around every Friday night? Go and talk to him. Maybe you can sort things out," Rukshana said. "Please, for my sake. I can't stand listening to my little sister whingeing like this. Besides, you and Zircon's son looked really cute together."

A bit later

The giant clock outside the jeweller's showed me it was past six o'clock, and I knew that was the time of Art Boy's regular Friday meetings. Maybe Rukshana was right. I could talk to Art Boy – ask him what he knew about the Stone/Brady family and confront him with Rukshana's suspicions. Perhaps he could somehow clear my name, at least a little. And maybe I could ask him to stop whatever he was doing to upset Jasper's family. Jasper might never trust me again, but maybe I could make things better for Jewel, and for all of them.

It had to be worth a try. Maybe. Or not.

I walked past the skating rink, where I spotted Jamie and Liam with a crowd of people – including Wendy and, incredibly, Tasha and her friends. They were all mucking about, pushing each other over, screeching and generally having fun. They'd obviously gone out mega early and were probably headed to some party or other in a couple of hours. I wished I was one of them.

I thought about joining them – I'd learnt by now that Jamie would welcome me at first and grumble about it later – but I couldn't face it. I knew I'd totally ruined things with Liam. I'd blown my chance of an easy-going, friendly kind of relationship with a normal, down-to-earth boy. Instead, I'd fallen deeply for the dark intensity of Jasper – and totally wrecked that, too.

I didn't turn towards home and Service Entrance D, where Art Boy would be. I was almost on auto-pilot as I took a detour. And before I knew it, I was sitting by the giant lily statue, in the part of the mall that belonged to me and Jasper. I sat there thinking about him and struggling to stop my eyes matching the watery output of the fountain itself.

I was about to give up and let the tears flow when I heard a boy's voice.

"Molly?" he said.

I looked up as he sat down next to me.

It was Liam.

"Hey. I saw you walk past, and you looked upset, so I told Jamie I'd check... Are you OK?"

I brushed at my eyes, which probably didn't help me look OK, but the alternative, fountain-eyed look would have been way worse. "Yeah, great," I said, but my voice wobbled with a distinct lack of greatness. I also might have let out the tiniest sob. I hadn't meant to, but the sound had obviously been lurking in the back of my throat, waiting to pounce as soon as I spoke.

"What's wrong? Or shouldn't I ask? I won't ask," he decided all by himself. He was so *nice*. He'd always been like this, and I'd known him a long time. "Just... I hope you're OK."

"Thanks," I said. It was weird how I felt a bit calmer already. "And sorry about your party," I remembered. It seemed like so long ago. "And, er, what happened there."

He gave a rueful smile. "Oh. Yeah. It's OK – I lived. So that guy you were with, in my attic... Jamie says he doesn't trust him. Is he... Is he the reason you're...?"

I nodded slightly. I nearly added something like "he dumped me", but Liam was really not the person to have this conversation with. Besides, I was sure it was written all over my face.

But Jasper wasn't the reason I was so upset. Not exactly. It was the realization that *I* was the one who couldn't be trusted – not Jasper. I was the mindless "mall girl" follower that Wendy had accused me of being all those weeks ago. It was not a happy thought.

"I'm sorry. I said I wasn't asking." Liam rubbed his hands on his jeans. "Anyway, don't worry about the pigeon thing. Mum didn't even ground me for a full week for the party, she's so distracted these days." He hesitated. "Can you keep a secret?"

"No," I replied honestly. "Probably not."

He laughed. "Well, I'll tell you anyway. It will be pretty obvious soon."

The tiniest beam of curiosity shone through my fog of misery. "Why? What is it?"

"You know how my parents have been going to Spain a lot lately?"

I nodded again.

"Well, we're moving. To Spain, I mean. For good. My parents have been out there with my little bro, getting a place to live and a café to run, though Mum's popped home for a few days. I was going to stay here until the end of term but there's not really much going on at school now that my exams have finished, and Mum wants me to go back with her this time."

"Because of the party?"

"Yeah, maybe. They're finding tenants for the house and it

needs to be perfect. Not..."

"Covered in pigeon poo?"

"Yeah." Liam paused. "Jamie's going to visit in the summer."

"Seriously?" Typical Jamie! "He hasn't said anything to me about that!"

"That's probably because he only decided about an hour ago, when I told him what I've just told you." He sighed. "It's going to be weird leaving Lilyford and all my friends and... you." He gave a little cough. "Anyway, I'm mostly telling you because, if you did want to talk about whatever's bothering you, then, you know. I'll take your secrets with me. So they'd definitely stay secret." He smiled.

I came very close to smiling back. Should I talk to him about Jasper? It wasn't exactly the kind of thing you discussed with the boy you've fancied for as long as you can remember.

"I don't know. I just feel like... sitting here," I said.

"OK." He looked away and kind of shut his eyes for a second. Then turned back and put his arm around me.

"I don't mean to... you know." he said quickly. "I just thought you needed a friendly hug."

"Thanks," I said. Well, it sounded reasonable. I leaned my head onto his shoulder, resting my cheek on the soft cotton of his t-shirt. It was so comforting. We sat there together, the sound of rushing water filling the air around us.

After a while, he tightened his hold on me and started gently stroking my hair. My stomach fluttered at his touch. The thought crossed my mind that what was happening now was probably moving a tiny bit away from "friendly".

I think he knew it too. "Maybe I should go," he murmured.

I thought maybe *I* should go – I should find Art Boy, I should work at sorting things out – but I answered, "I don't want you to go."

"Great," he said softly.

I didn't know *what* I wanted anymore.

Back in a minute. Everything's gone blurry.

Friday 1st July

After my last day with Jasper, ever ever ever, continued

OK. So... yeah.

For years, I've been dreaming of a chance to kiss Liam. He was my first crush and my ideal boy: kind, gorgeous and... well, always there. I saw him a lot because of Jamie. And because I constantly sneaked glances at him at school. When Ameera was busy ogling pictures of boy band stars from her big sister's magazines and she and Wendy giggled over them at lunch time, I joined in. But secretly I was scanning the canteen for Liam, thinking: *those guys have nothing on my brother's best mate.*

Sometimes I dreamed of him *literally*, including a wonderfully vivid one where Liam and I walked home from school together even though we live at opposite ends of town. It started pouring with rain and we ran under a bus shelter and were extremely close to snogging when some random interfering woman shouted, "Molly! Get up! Now!" The woman turned out to be Mum, looming over my bed and telling me I'd be late for school.

Anyway, the point is, I never really thought it would happen for me and Liam. Not even in my wildest, rainiest dreams.

Yet here I was, sitting by the wet wilds of The Lilies fountain, resting my head on Liam's shoulder as he held me tightly and stroked my hair. And after I told him to stay, he moved his hand to my face, softly running his thumb across my cheek, brushing away the track marks of a tear that had annoyingly escaped earlier. I lifted my head and he shifted, facing me. My stomach fizzed at his closeness and I had a fleeting thought that this shouldn't be happening, not when I was so upset about Jasper. So I pulled away a bit, but when I did, Liam's eyes locked on mine and... well, I reached for him.

And I kissed him.

What else could I do? It was Liam. Liam and me – together at last. The boy of my dreams.

"Molly...?" he murmured. It was a question. He was asking whether it was OK to kiss me, I think, but whatever it was, I didn't want to answer. I just wanted to keep my lips pressed on his.

He gave a small sigh, relaxing as he returned my kiss. The sound of rushing water surrounded us as I wrapped my arms around him. I felt... I don't know. Reckless, maybe? I was grasping at him, gluing myself to him, desperately trying not to think about the fact that he wasn't Jasper. *He wasn't Jasper!* It was no good – I couldn't make that thought go away. But Liam was here... and doing this was wrong – I knew it – but it didn't stop me, or not immediately.

When I did break away, a horrible lump of self-loathing settled in the pit of my stomach.

He was gazing at me, his eyes filled with confusion and a

hint of happiness. "Hey, Molly," he said.

Oh no. Jamie's words from a few weeks ago echoed in my head. *"Liam likes you, Molly. He* really *likes you, though I have no idea why, personally."* Good point, big brother. I wasn't too sure I even liked *myself* right at that moment. What had I just done? And to such a nice guy? When all I was thinking was: *Jasper dumped me! Jasper hates me! Jasper Jasper Jasper.* I was a terrible, terrible person.

"Um," I said. "Liam. I..."

The smile disappeared. He looked really nervous. He'd always been quite shy, I realized. He's generally kind of in Jamie's shadow. In fact, I can't even remember him having had a girlfriend, not for longer than a week or so anyway, and even those girls were kind of an overspill from Jamie's admirers. He's really fit so I guess it must be all about an inexplicable lack of confidence. That's probably also the reason he'd found full-on Tasha so hard to deal with, back when we went to Paolo's Pizza Place together.

"Yeah?" he mumbled.

"I am *so* sorry," I said. I poured my heart and soul into the "so".

I think it was pretty obvious what I meant but, weirdly enough, he didn't move away. He kept his arms around me, casting his eyes downwards for a bit as if he was gathering courage. When he looked up, he said, "Molly, you know..." His voice was really low. "I've always liked you."

Always? Why didn't he tell me before? Before Jasper... If nothing had ever happened between me and Jasper, would things have been different?

"I've always liked you too," I admitted, almost whispering. But that wasn't the right thing to say, and especially not the way I'd just said it! Honestly, why doesn't anyone teach you how to behave in situations like this? School could really do with offering a GCSE in "Dealing With Crushes" as well as all that maths and science they're so keen on.

"But..." I tried. I couldn't think of anything to add.

After a silence he finished my sentence for me. "But the timing's all wrong, isn't it?"

I nodded. That was one way of putting it.

"Look, I shouldn't have..."

"No, but *I*..."

Sooner or later, one of us was going to finish another sentence. It had to happen.

Liam beat me to it. "Listen, Molly, I'm leaving for Spain next week."

"Next week? So soon?" Hmm, I wasn't exactly behaving like someone who deeply regretted what she'd just done. This was confusing. If I was going to have a meaningless comfort-kiss with someone, why had I picked the boy I'd had a crush on for years? A boy who really did seem to like me back.

"Yeah, 'fraid so." He shrugged. "But not forever. Mum has to pop back for various house things, and we still need to pack our stuff. And Jamie's visiting in a few weeks and you could... you could visit too... if you wanted to. At a better time."

"Liam, I..." It was no use. I wasn't going to finish that sentence either. Because *"Liam, this was a big mistake and I don't think we should see each other at all"* sounded all wrong, especially when I was still in his arms and making no move away from him.

Or not until a loud, shocked male voice rang in my ear, anyway.

"Molly! Liam! WHAT is going on?"

We broke apart at last. Liam shifted away and I swung my legs around, turning to face the voice.

It was Jamie. He was glaring at us even more fiercely than he had when Liam found me with Jasper in his attic. In fact, I'm not sure that I'd ever seen him look this angry. And, even though Jamie is usually a very laid-back person, that's still saying something.

Strangely, it seemed to be his friend he was mad at and not me. "Liam," he said tightly, "I thought you said you were checking that Molly was OK?"

I sprang to Liam's defence. "He was!" Well, he *was*. It was me who had taken it one step further. I think.

"That's not what it looked like from over there!" Jamie said.

Liam looked embarrassed. Well, I wasn't surprised. This was seriously embarrassing.

"Jamie, stop it," I said. "So what if... I mean, so what? What's it to you, anyway?"

The wind left Jamie's sails a bit. "So... I don't know, Measly. Maybe I don't want to see my little sister getting hurt."

Oh, honestly! He'd picked a fine time to practise his new-found, protective big brother routine again. I nearly said something like, "Not *all* boys are like you, Jamie!" Or, "I think Liam's the one getting hurt here, thanks very much." But –

and it's probably just as well, really – I didn't get the chance to say anything, because Wendy arrived, tailing after Jamie and looking indignant.

"Jamie! Molly! WHAT is going on?" she asked.

It was about time someone came up with a more original question. My head pounded. Oh, I could NOT be bothered with this. I'd let Jasper down big-time – no, worse than that – I had let *myself* down – and probably Liam too – and now I had to deal with *this*?

"Wendy, it's like this," I stated. "Jasper dumped me, Liam came to see if I was OK and I snogged him by mistake. That's all." I just didn't care anymore. Did. Not. Care.

Except maybe about Liam, who was staring at his phone, clearly finding it fascinating. "And I'm sorry," I said in his direction. He gave a tiny shrug and started tapping out a text or something.

"You did what?" Wendy said, all horrified. Like it mattered to *her*! "How do you snog someone *by mistake*? So Molly, you totally ditched me last week to spend time with Mystery Boy and then... and then you're off with Jamie's friend instead? I don't believe you! You... you total *mall girl*!"

"Hey," said Jamie calmly. He seemed to have chilled out right around the time I said the word "mistake". "Cool it, Wendy. That's my sister you're talking to."

"She *is* a mall girl!" Wendy steamed. "It's what Mum says! No soul, just like the mall itself!"

I snapped. "OMG, Wendy, I know I've made mistakes, but that is *ridiculous*!" I glared at her. "And actually I am *sick* of worrying about you getting upset with me and de-friending me every other week! A proper friend would try to understand! I don't need friends like you *at all*!" I looked at Jamie and back at her. "You're not so perfect anyway! You're just using Jamie, for a start!"

Wendy glared at me. "What do you mean?"

"You told me you were only after him for his body!" Oops. I probably shouldn't have said that in front of Jamie, no matter how angry I was with Wendy.

Her eyes filled with horror. "Molly!"

"Well, you did," I mumbled. "And you know what? Right now I don't *care* if you never talk to me again."

"Wait till I tell Ameera about this!" Wendy huffed.

"Oh, and here you go again, trying to turn Ameera against me!"

"*Ameera* is loyal to her friends."

"OK! Great!" I was gathering steam again. "Tell her! And while you're at it, Wendy, why don't you ask her about how she accidentally broke up me and Jasper? How she blurted out a secret – something Ameera and I knew weeks ago, but didn't tell you about?"

Wendy swayed a bit. "Ameera wouldn't keep secrets from me."

"Oh no? Ask her! And don't bother calling me to say you're sorry. I'm completely sick of *both* of you. So much for my so-called friends!"

Jamie said, "Molly, that's enough." He sounded so, well, *mature*. It was weird. He turned to Wendy. "Isn't your brother picking you up soon? For that family thing you were going to?"

Wendy looked dazed. "He's waiting for me now. That's what I came to tell you."

"Great. I'll give you a call later. Liam, mate, I'm taking my sister home and I'll see you tomorrow at work."

He slung an arm over my shoulder and steered me away. I fought the urge to complain and say I'd leave when I wanted to, thanks very much. Mostly because when I wanted to leave was *right now*.

Jamie and I walked in silence for a minute or so. He let go of me as soon as he realized I wasn't going to make a run for it. Then he said, "So, that was interesting."

"Yeah," I mumbled. "It had its moments."

We passed several closed shops. Two security guards nodded at us.

"I think you might have properly broken Liam's heart this time," Jamie added. "Instead of just ruining his party."

"*Me?*" Like I was the heart-breaker type!

"Of course you. Liam's crazy about you. I did warn you." He rolled his eyes. "And guess who's going to have to pick up the pieces, out in the bars of sunny Spain?" He made a pretend-sad face as summery partying potential flickered in his eyes. "Anyway, what about the music guy?"

"Jasper?"

"Whatever his name is. Did he really finish with you? Why? You two were all over each other, last I saw." He held up clenched fists. "If you want me to get him, I could..." he trailed off.

I looked at my brother. He was frowning. "What *could* you

do, Jamie?" I said. "Scowl at him?"

"I thought I might glare a bit too. No one upsets my little sister and gets away with it."

"That's nice of you, Jamie," I said with only a tiny bit of sarcasm. "But Jasper's annoyed enough with me as it is, without me setting my growly brother on him. Anyway, what's with all this sudden protectiveness lately?"

"I don't know," he admitted. "I think I'm getting soft. It started when Tasha made me realize how horrible all that not-texting stuff could be, and I decided to stop messing girls around. And right now it's probably Wendy's influence."

"*Wendy* is turning you soft? Did you *hear* her back then? And it's not the first time she's gone off on one like that, either. She did it on the school's Facebook page a few weeks ago!" Back when my life started falling apart.

"Wendy's so... fiery." His face went dreamy for a second before he hastily added. "She needs to be more respectful to my little sister, obviously. But I really like her, Molly. Shame she's only after me for my body." He looked at me and grinned.

I groaned. Why had I said that? "Oh no, Jamie, don't let that go to your head!"

"I'll have you know it's kind of hurtful, actually," he said seriously. "It's a good thing I don't believe her." He thought a bit and the dreaminess crept back. "Or maybe it was true at first, but I think I might be winning her over."

"Only because she loves the fact that her mother wouldn't approve, *mall boy*," I said, but I was smiling now too. It was sort of nice talking to my brother like this after everything I'd been through today. Even if it meant future awkwardness with him seeing my ex-friend. "So does this mean you're really over Tasha?"

He shrugged. "It took her an hour to get over breaking a nail earlier tonight. But she kept glancing over at me. You know, I think she might have been playing games with me all along." He sighed. "So I'm not saying never, Molly, but right now I'm happy with Wendy. And I think Tasha needs to grow up a bit."

I howled with laughter at Jamie – *Jamie!!!* – saying that about *anyone*. In fact, I only stopped laughing because we'd reached Service Entrance D and everything looked different.

Art boy and his gang of arty helpers weren't there, which was weird in itself. I'm pretty sure we were still within their normal meeting time, and I'd been planning on coming here and having a little talk with Art Boy about spreading Jewel-related rumours. Maybe it was just as well I hadn't tried it. Although perhaps what I'd done instead wasn't strictly ideal.

But the absence of Art Boy wasn't what made me stop in my tracks. It was this...

In the space where the mural project had been taking shape there was a mountain of scaffolding covered in a huge grey tarpaulin. And across that hung a banner.

"LILYFORD SPECIAL EVENT!" it said in huge letters. "Zircon from The Red Sardonyx to unveil the new mural at The Lilies, Friday 15th July!"

Wow! Zircon was coming to Lilyford. To our mall. In exactly two weeks' time.

What would Jasper think of that? I couldn't help worrying.

I pulled my phone out of my bag and stared at it. As if Jasper would have texted me, after what had happened earlier.

He hadn't, of course. But I had missed one text from an unknown number, sent about three minutes ago. I must have been too busy talking to Jamie to hear the alert. I opened the message.

"Just so you have my number," it said. "No hard feelings, OK? L x"

OMG. "Jamie, did you give Liam my number?" I asked.

"What? Oh, yeah, that night when we all went out, he asked for it because he thought he might be late. I didn't think you'd mind." He sounded a bit stunned. "Measly, why on earth would a mega-star from a legendary rock band come to *Lilyford*?"

Saturday 2nd July
Hiding at the Hart residence, 5th floor, The Lilies eco-mall, Lilyford

I spent so much of the night stressing about Jasper – and Liam and Wendy and Ameera and Jewel and, well, every single friend I've ever had – that I almost forgot about the banner. I remembered Jasper rushing off to Jewel's paparazzi emergency, but I hadn't seen any evidence of it myself, of course. So I didn't really think about what the consequences would be.

What happened next was that Lilyford exploded into The Red Sardonyx fever. Overnight, pictures of Zircon and his band were everywhere. Old tracks by The Red Sardonyx blasted from every boutique and non-chain store in The Lilies, creating a total rock cacophony for all the Saturday shoppers walking past. The local papers and radio seemed to be loving every minute of it.

The pictures of Jewel trying to escape the cameras at Service

Entrance D quickly made it to the national press, too. *"Sparkling Teen Starlet LIVES to SHOP!"* was one of the kinder headlines. Basically, every paper latched on to the fact that Jewel was a) the daughter of a rock star, b) an ex-model and c) lived in a mall. The journalists almost reminded me of Wendy as they went on about The Lilies and what an exclusive, expensive place it was to live in, making anyone resident there automatically some kind of celebrity brat. Obviously no one had told them about the "affordable residential units". Although, judging by the way Mum had been worrying and Jasper's mum had said they needed help from Zircon for the rent, maybe the "affordable" thing was a bit of a lie, anyway.

The Lilies' administration laid on more security guards by the doors to our wing, added an extra lock on the stairway doors and issued a new special code for the lift, but it didn't stop the paparazzi congregating outside our fortress. Jamie had to walk through a crowd of photographers when he left the lift to start his shift at the food court on Level 1. He told me later that it was the strangest thing that had ever happened to him – walking out into flashing cameras and people shouting questions at him about the residents of Level 6. Up until this morning, he hadn't even realized that the new girl he'd seen me hang around with sometimes was Jasper's sister Jewel. (And no one was calling her "Julie" now, I noticed.)

I watched some of the media frenzy from the kitchen balcony and I worried. How would Jasper be handling all this? There was no sign of him in the papers, except one small mention of "Zircon and Katie's twin babies, now teens". I wondered about Jasper's mother too – she seemed so fragile, and this couldn't be helping. I knew Jasper must be hating it – and blaming it all on me. The more I thought about that, the less I could stand it. I wished I could talk to someone about it, but Mum was at her Saturday job (!) and Jamie was at his... and here I paused for a second to marvel at the fact that I'd even *considered* talking to Jamie. Wow, things had really changed between us in the past few weeks.

Ameera had texted me about a hundred times, and even Wendy had texted twice, but I hadn't opened any of the messages. I meant what I'd said to Wendy last night. I was better off without her… and Ameera. Neither of them had been good friends to me, not for ages – just as Jewel had suggested when I first met her, I realized.

Jewel. Could I maybe talk to her? Would she be on speaking terms with me after what had happened with Jasper? Would he have told her that he thought I was the one behind the sudden burst of paparazzi? Though the absolute truth was bad enough – the fact that Ameera and I had snooped in their flat and found out about Zircon before Jasper and his family had been ready to tell me. What would Jewel make of that? Would she listen to my side of things? She always seemed so chilled with everyone! Except for that time at Art Boy's private view when she saw the cameras... and got really annoyed with Art Boy, probably because she thought he'd called them. Oh.

Well, I didn't care. I could take it. I was no spineless "mall girl", whatever Wendy might think. I was going to try and talk to Jewel, who'd been my only friend through so many other ups and downs recently.

With my heart in my mouth, I rang the familiar bell, trying not to think about the fact that I'd worked in this flat for a week. Or that I'd kissed Jasper there so many times. What if he answered the door?

But he didn't. Jewel did, and she smiled at me. Phew.

"Molly!" she announced. "Come in, come in! It's a jungle out there!"

I walked into the Zircon-lined flat and followed her into the kitchen where she offered me a latte. She set about preparing two drinks, chattering on about escaping the media last night, and how Jasper had raced down and aided her escape into the lift which was "so brave of him – you know what he's like with elevators". She added, "He's been so much better since he met you, though."

I was distracted from pining about Jasper by the fact that there was something really strange about her voice.

"Jewel?" I said as she handed me one of the lattes she'd made with their special machine. "You sound different."

She laughed. "Oh, man, I totally forgot! It's been so crazy."

"Forgot what?"

"The accent! I forgot to do the British accent that I always do around you!" She looked worried. "Oh, I'm sorry, Molly, I didn't do it to deceive you! It was just what I did at school – and everywhere, really – and even after we told you about our family, it was easier to keep it going so that I didn't forget at odd moments, or anything." She sounded so... American. Like someone out of a glossy TV show, like 90210 or something. "I can't believe I forgot just now! Well, I might as well drop it altogether now, don't you think? *Everywhere,* I mean. My secret's fully out! Julie's totally gone. I am Jewel Stone, daughter of Zircon and total California girl!"

"Er... wow," I said. It was so weird that she sounded different! "Your English accent was brilliant, though. You really had me fooled."

"Thanks, Molly! I've been telling Jasper and Mom that I could make it as an actress! The only problem with it is staying out of the limelight, which I also wanted to do." She gestured towards her balcony. "But it's too late, I guess. And I bet I know who caused all this, whatever my moody twin thinks."

I bit my lip. "Has Jasper told you about me and Ameera? Er... sneaking in and..."

"Yes!" Jewel wagged a finger at me. "That was such a bad thing to do, Molly!"

"I'm really, really sorry," I mumbled.

She laughed. "I'll bet Ameera was behind it. Did you follow her to make sure she didn't do any damage?"

"Er... yes. Kind of," I said. But I decided I should be totally honest. "Plus I was bursting with curiosity."

"I'm not surprised," Jewel said. "I'd be the same. I was getting pretty sick of it all, to be honest. Jasper said it was about telling a few white lies to keep my life on the straight and narrow, but to me it was starting to feel a lot more like huge, outright whoppers. I was always worrying about what the people I cared about would think when they found out I hadn't been totally honest with them." She looked at me. "So mostly just you, then. And you've been so cool about it. Thanks."

I thanked her back, for being pretty cool herself. "So hiding was really all Jasper's idea?" I asked. I'd heard Jasper's account of this last week, but Jewel had been at school at the time.

"We came up with most of it together. I went a bit further than he did on most of it – like, the accent thing was my idea because I wanted to test myself, I guess." She took a sip of her latte. "But Jasper is *way* more scared than I am of being dragged into the limelight. He's not used to it – he didn't really grow up with it, and he stopped visiting Dad in the States years ago. Everyone just thinks he's the son of a single-parent music teacher. Which, of course, he is," she pondered.

I nodded.

"So, yeah, it started with me wanting a home – a real place to live, away from Dad's LA craziness. And Jasper had all these big plans for ways to protect me. But now I feel like *I'm* protecting *him* as much as the other way around. I had to do things like drag you out of that art exhibition we went to because *someone* had called the cameras in." She rolled her eyes.

"Art Boy? So it's true that he knows about you?"

She laughed. "I love the way you call him that. You sound so... *British*! Yes, of course he knows. I did *tell* him I was in hiding but it's like he's forgotten. He lives in a world of his own, that art guy. I think he's just a bit thoughtless, and kind of harmless. But Jasper actually seems to think he's *dangerous*." She sighed. "Then again, Jasper doesn't trust *anyone*."

I looked away, my heart sinking. I hated being high up on the list of people Jasper didn't trust. "So what's it like, pretending to be someone you're not?" I asked, partly to steer the conversation away from a subject that was making me feel so uncomfortable. I think we'd talked enough about Jasper.

She looked thoughtful. "It's been OK at school – I missed so much in my past that I actually *want* to learn, you know, so I like keeping my head down and hanging out in the library. But the rest of the time, it was becoming kind of a pain." She sighed. "And it's nearly the end of the school year. I couldn't have been Julie all summer just to keep Jasper happy!"

"Oh," I said. We seemed to have got back to Jasper again. "So you're really not angry with me about..."

Jewel shrugged. "If my brother's right that you spread the rumours – and I don't think he is – then you've probably done me a favour. All the fuss will die down when the press see I'm a regular girl. They'll get bored and find a real celebrity to bug. And I get to be myself again." She sighed. "So I'm definitely not angry with you, and I'm not going to stop being your friend, no matter what Jasper says. I'm sorry if this sounds harsh, but he'll just have to deal with it. I'm through with following his guidelines, and having him vet anyone who shows an interest in me."

I gave in and thought about Jasper. For the first time in a while, I managed to do it without being overcome with horrible, stomach-twisting feelings. Much. Wow, Jewel was so great to talk to. "But Jasper just wants what's best for you," I mumbled.

Jewel laughed. "Would *you* do everything your brother told you to do?"

"No. Definitely not. But Jamie's... not Jasper." And then some. So then my stomach did twist, and I took a huge swig of latte in the hope that it would help the ache. I also covered it up by telling Jewel everything that had happened last night with my friends.

"Go Molly!" she cheered. "Those guys don't seem so bad now I've got to know them, but I remember thinking they were kinda bullying you, back when I first met you. I'm so glad you're standing up to them."

"Really?" I said. Oh. "No, they're not bullies, they're just... them. Wendy's always been quick-tempered, and Ameera has this fierce loyalty."

"Well, you know them better than I do, Molly," she said. "But I'm still glad you told them how you feel."

We kept chatting. She told me all about her dad coming for the mural opening, and how worried she was about Jasper. "He hasn't seen him for years," she told me. "First he refused to travel, and then he refused to visit, even if Dad came here, which, admittedly, Dad didn't do often. He was pretty busy. But this accident has changed Dad's life, you know, and he wants to see his son." She sighed. "My brother can be so stubborn. He wouldn't even read Dad's letter, not for the longest time."

"But Jasper told me he needed to get on a plane," I told her, remembering. "Back when you were in LA, a few weeks ago. It was... kind of the reason Jasper and I started meeting up. I was helping him get over the panic attacks so that he could travel."

She looked shocked. "Seriously? Jasper was coming to LA? No way!"

I told her that was definitely how it had sounded.

She finished her latte and stood up. "Sorry, Molly, but I need to make a phone call. And then I have to spend some time with Mom."

"Oh, how is she?"

Jewel shrugged. "Still bad, but slightly brighter since you worked here. She's started to take the antidepressants now. I feel like I have a chance of getting my Mom back, you know? I think that effort she had to make when you were here really helped. So thanks for changing your placement. And from Jasper too. Whatever he thinks of you right now." She gave me a kind smile.

So then I left feeling miles better and tons worse at the same time. And also sort of glad to be Molly "Lilyford mall girl" Hart and not Jewel "California starlet" Stone.

Sunday, 3rd July

Just back from Dad's

Great day with Dad and Nan. Nobody mentioned romance or relationship troubles, unless you count the moment when Dad said he was going to offer Mum "a sum of money" for the new business she was starting.

Jamie gave me an "I told you so" glance and I looked back at him with a "she'll never accept it" eyebrow-raise.

When he did his "we'll see about that, but I'm not sorry anyway" smile, I called a truce and talked to Nan about biscuits instead.

Got home to find Mum watching the Wimbledon men's final and looking blissful. Again am happy to be a Hart... and can't stop thinking about Jasper. In a "sorry about his difficult family life" kind of way, I mean.

Among other ways.

Thursday, 7th July

Back from West Lilyford Community College

Dull dull dull week at school. What is the point of trooping into lessons when our brains have already checked out for the summer? And yet we do, for we are dutiful school sheep. Except Jewel who really seems to want to be there. Freaky. But fun.

I've spent every day so far with my freaky-but-fun friend and totally avoided Wendy and Ameera. It wasn't difficult at all because the whole school suddenly wanted to know Jewel, and we were constantly surrounded by people. Even super-cool sixth-formers, though not Liam, who was probably already in Spain. Oh, and we took a taxi into school – and back – because of the paparazzi hanging around. I suppose I can see how it might be annoying after a while and Jewel says fame's definitely not what it's cracked up to be, but right now... Freaky fun.

Monday was American Independence Day, which seemed like an appropriate day for Jewel to go public with her California accent. A couple of Year 9s told her she was doing an almost passable impression of an American, and one teacher told her off for being cheeky and sent her to the office, where they promised to inform all the teachers about Jewel's real identity. Apparently it's fairly common for teachers to live under rocks and have no idea what's going on in the news, the shops or the town they live in. I'm still surprised that loads of teachers didn't know that "Julie" was "Jewel" in the first place, but it turns out Jewel's mum arranged it all with the head teacher weeks ago, and he'd only told the admin staff. He's obviously better at keeping secrets than his super-loud voice would suggest.

I avoided all the texts I got from Wendy and Ameera, but I re-read the one from Liam a few times. And all the texts Jasper had ever sent me. Ouch. Cue the saddest Adele tracks I've ever downloaded.

And wallow.

Friday 8th July, evening
Taking action at The Lilies eco-mall, Lilyford, Part One

Jewel started it. The taxi dropped us off round the back of The Lilies after school and we wandered through the snapping photographers – I'd got used to it surprisingly quickly – and into the lift. It then took us three goes to remember the new code. Finally, the lift moved beyond the first floor. Through the glass doors, I noticed a black-clad figure on the stairs. He was carrying a large box, taking two steps at a time and easily beating our lift usage in terms of upwards progress.

Almost out of the blue – but not quite, when I realized that the figure disappearing up the stairs was Jasper – Jewel said, "He misses you, Molly."

I tried so hard to keep my voice casual. "Has he, er, said something?"

"No," Jewel admitted. "But I can tell by the music he's playing."

"Adele?" Odd how that sprang to mind.

Jewel shook her head. "His own tunes."

I tried to imagine Jasper playing songs called things like *"O My Molly, I Miss You So"*, but it didn't strike me as very likely. "But it's no good missing me if he still blames me for the whole..."

I gestured at the paps below. "...media circus. It's hopeless."

Jewel shrugged. "I don't know. I'm just saying he definitely misses you. Also, he's refusing to see Dad next week, even though Mom's saying it's OK with her, and her condition is an illness and nothing to do with Dad's new wife. It was unfortunate timing, maybe, with the stress of knowing our dad was in an accident. Plus Mom says she's a genuine fan of The Red Sardonyx and Jasper's wrong about her pining for Dad. Not that Jasper ever listens." She looked at me as the doors opened at my floor. "Except maybe to you. And he misses you and he's incredibly stubborn. Keep it in mind, OK? Have a great night, Molly!" Ooh. She totally sounded like a person from California.

Well. I decided I'd had enough of wallowing. I needed to prove to Jasper that I wasn't responsible for the paparazzi, at least. Even if he still never forgave me for the snooping thing, at least he'd know the truth.

This would mean locating Art Boy, I thought. I remembered that he hadn't been in his usual place last Friday and realized it was probably because the mural was finished and there was nothing to meet about. I couldn't believe I'd fully intended to take part and then never quite managed it. I suppose Art Boy was now just waiting for the great unveiling by Zircon next Friday. (Wow. Jasper and Jewel's dad.)

But how would I find Art Boy? I didn't fancy asking Jewel – I wanted to go it alone, really. I also knew Jasper was probably home, or at least running up and down the stairs with boxes, and I didn't want to see him. Not yet, anyway. Not until I had some evidence, or something. Hmm.

I thought of going to Mum's old work – they had all those Art Boy connections, didn't they? – but I decided that was a ridiculous idea. For a start, they'd sacked Mum. Also, I'd let them down at the last minute for a work placement. They wouldn't exactly welcome me with open arms. But thinking about that gave me the bright idea that there might be a clue near the mural itself – like contact details for the artist? I remembered the art thing I'd gone to at the law firm, and I thought I could picture a little container of business cards stuck near each painting there.

So I changed out of my school uniform and into stealthy spy clothes. (OK, dark jeans and my newest blue top.) And I headed to the ground floor.

The first thing that went wrong was that I bumped into Liam. He was standing outside a massive chain hardware shop close to Service Entrance D, looking at a stack of multi-coloured plastic buckets.

"Liam!" I said in shock. "You're not in Spain!"

"Molly, hey. Not yet! Mum's coming and going at the moment, packing and shopping for plastic stuff that she insists 'isn't the same' over there. We're leaving in a few days." He gave me such a natural, easy smile that I immediately wondered why I'd been obsessing about the way I'd hurt him last week. He was probably about to meet some hot Spanish girl called Carmelita, and he'd soon forget all about me. "At this rate, I think we'll be moving the entire mall to the Costa Brava."

"That would be cool," I said.

"It really would," he said, giving me a look that made Carmelita unlikely. Or jealous, maybe.

I gulped.

"I hope you didn't mind the text I sent, Molly," he said. "Just if you ever want to text, I'm keeping that phone for a bit and... Well, I wanted you to have my number, just in case."

"No, great. *Yes,* I mean. Thanks!" I looked around. The covered mural immediately caught my eye. And – jackpot! – standing underneath it, gazing upwards, was the unmistakeable arty hotness of Art Boy himself! "I've got to go now, Liam! I hope it all goes well! Thank you! Bye." I was so jumpy that I nearly sent my regards to Carmelita.

I bounded off in Art Boy's direction. Just as I was nearing him and wondering whether to call out to him – but what would I call? *"Hey, Art Boy?!"* – he unlocked a side door. I knew it was one of the mall's storerooms – there are a few of them by each service entrance, hidden behind partition walls, and they're mostly used by the mall's general support staff to store things like cleaning equipment. The security guards are always moaning about people trying to break into them. (*"What do they think is in there? It's all mops, not money."*) Anyway, Art Boy had obviously been given access to one for his project. Perfect! Now I could definitely speak to him alone. I didn't have a clue what I was going to say, mind you, but I'd figure that out later. I just hoped I'd understand him for a change, and also that I wouldn't accidentally attack him with any cheese canapés.

I slipped into the storeroom. It was brightly lit, windowless and smelled strongly of dust and paint stripper. Art Boy was in a far corner, heaving some paint cans around and talking animatedly into a phone. Oh no! Now I'd seem rude if I spoke to him. I hoped he'd finish his call quickly. I hid myself behind a large chair topped with a pile of clutter. I didn't want Art Boy to see me until he was off the phone. I mean, awkward or *what*!

I sensed someone next to me. I jumped and turned.

Black jeans, band t-shirt, Converse, pouty expression. It was Jasper!

"OMG, what are you doing here?" I hissed.

"I was coming down the stairs and I saw you walking in with him," he hissed back. "I decided to find out what exactly was going on with you two, and why you're so intent on wrecking Jewel's life." He glared at me before he added, "Why are we whispering?"

"What are you talking about? And I'm whispering because he doesn't know I'm –"

I froze. Art Boy was heading for the door, carrying a bunch of keys in one hand and what looked like a large sheet in the other. He was squashing the phone to his shoulder with his chin, fully focused on his conversation. "Found one! I knew I still had it. I'll get it all rigged up for you. Oh, and hey, don't worry about the twins – I'll make sure we get them where we want them!" His odd accent was making him sound almost... sinister. He didn't see me or Jasper as he continued. "So I'll come back and look for the other thing in a few minutes – I'll get this in the car first. What did you say you..." His voice faded out of earshot as he snapped off the lights and shut the storeroom door.

I heard a key turn in a lock.

A key. In a lock.

Art Boy had locked me into an airless, windowless storeroom.

With Jasper.

For a minute, neither of us spoke. It was seriously dark. I felt a bit scared.

"Now look what you've done!" I said to Jasper. "Is it like some kind of habit of yours? Getting us trapped in small spaces?"

"*Me*?" His indignant voice rang loudly from next to me. "I was following *you*! Every single time!"

"Well, this time it's definitely your fault! And that guy didn't know I was here – obviously! I wanted to see him to clear my name – because of you! You've been like this since the first day I met you, Jasper! Even after we... Why can't you trust me?"

"Oh, I don't know, let me think!" he shot back sarcastically. "Why did you sneak into my flat?"

"Why did you hide the truth about your family from me for so long?" I returned. "It was going to come out sooner or later, you know. And it's not exactly serious. Not like you're on the run from criminals or anything."

Or were they? What had Art Boy just said about *"the twins – I'll make sure we get them where we want them"*? Could he have been talking about Jewel and Jasper? Had Jasper heard that? And hadn't Jewel told me that he thought Art Boy was "dangerous"?

"It was serious to *us*," Jasper said. "Jewel was running from fame! You've ruined it now. I worked so hard to protect her."

"It wasn't me! And she seems fine, anyway. Have you asked her lately whether she *wants* protecting, Jasper?"

He didn't reply. I couldn't see his face but I knew he'd be pouting.

Or was he panicking? Oh no, I hoped he wasn't panicking.

I listened for his breathing but I couldn't hear anything. It had all gone quiet. I reached for his hand but there was nothing there. No one.

"Jasper? Are you OK?"

There was no answer. Eek! What if he'd fallen into some kind of evil lair created by Art Boy, or something? Or maybe he'd just passed out through fear? But he didn't do that... did he? Ooh, maybe he'd need the kiss of life! Could I do that in the dark? Wait – could I do that at *all*? And why was I even thinking about *that*?

I mentally shook myself. OK, I needed to find the light switch, and I needed to get us out of here quickly.

Unless Jasper was just sulking, in which case he could stay here, for all I cared, and I'd get out by myself.

Yeah! I'd had just about enough of Jasper and his attitude.

So that was the end of that.

Friday 8th July, evening

That was not the end of that

Oh, who am I kidding? Here's what I actually did next.

"Jasper!" I hissed urgently into the darkness.

There was still no reply. What *was* he playing at? Oh help, was he OK? My thoughts swung rapidly from annoyance to worry and back again.

I reached out with both hands until I felt the wall behind me. I traced its cold smoothness as I shuffled towards where I thought the door must be, feeling for a light switch as I went. Moving was hard because the ground was uneven with clutter and I kept tripping over who-knows-what, causing great crashing sounds as I went. I tried not to think about the mess I must be making and what Art Boy would think when he got back.

Or maybe I shouldn't care about that – not if Art Boy was some kind of terrible gangster type with dark intentions for Jasper and Jewel. Maybe he deserved to have me trashing his stuff. I stumbled over a hard object on the ground and gave it a big kick for good measure. Take that, mysterious and sinister Art Boy! I was so utterly kick-ass, me.

Eventually I reached what felt like a crack in the wall, and I detected the smallest streaks of light poking through, above and below what were probably door hinges. After that, it was only a matter of some concentrated groping around before I found a light switch. And – click! – the room lit up.

I instantly saw all the clutter that I'd noticed before, except that things looked twice as chaotic in the path I'd just taken. I'd clearly knocked over all sorts of things, including a big tin of paint, which was oozing from its lid and colouring the floor bright crimson. I glanced around the room and noticed that the back wall was completely covered by a huge sheet painted in stripes of the same red colour, so I figured it must be part of Art Boy's project. It was strange. And very messy.

There was still no sign of Jasper.

"Jasper, where *are* you?" I couldn't keep the note of panic out of my voice. I'd fully expected him to be sulking silently in some corner, but his total absence was just weird. There was no other way out of this room, surely? If there was, I would have heard the security guards complaining about it in the past.

I blinked a few times, partly because the light was dazzling and partly in the hope that it would make Jasper magically appear.

And then I heard a slight shuffling sound at the far end of the room, and I noticed that the large sheet covering the back wall was moving.

Maybe it wasn't right up against the wall after all. I looked up. The sheet was hanging from a long brass curtain pole, stuck to the side walls at either end. So maybe it had more room behind it? And Jasper, too? Having a very quiet panic attack?

In my rush to find out, I tripped over a chair leg, knocked the chair over and landed with a squelch right in the paint I'd spilled. Oh, great. My hands and knees dripped with sticky red liquid. I tried to shake the paint off but I only made things worse – I totally spattered my spy outfit with red, for a start. Then I accidentally put my head in my hands in despair, and after that my hair and face felt matted and wet, too.

Never mind that, though. Jasper was suffering! I tried to ignore the red trail I was leaving as I pushed the sheet aside and barrelled into the space behind it. Where Jasper was sitting! So I was right!

In my triumph, I tripped over a broom handle and dived right into Jasper.

"Ow!" he yelped, and I noticed straightaway that the paint had spread all over him, too. You couldn't tell with his dark clothes, but the way I'd landed on him left him with a red streak on his cheek. I brushed at it with my hand, which only added more smudgy redness to his face. It also made my heart race.

We were so close. Never mind the paint, I wanted... I wanted to kiss him. It was possibly inappropriate during this life-or-death situation, but there it was.

Jasper pulled away from me and I nearly said *"No, come back!"* out loud.

He yanked iPod-style wires from his ears. "Molly," he said. His voice was terse, like he was talking to a very annoying and foolish person. "What are you doing? And why are you covered in red stuff?"

I sat back, glaring at him. Had he been listening to music all this time? Is that why he hadn't heard me call to him? "I was worried about you!" I said. "Where did you go? *Why* did you go? Aren't you grateful to me for turning the lights on?"

"Oh, right. Thank you," he said in that same detached tone. "I just went and found my own space. Because I didn't want to hang around being insulted by you."

Oh, honestly! "I didn't *insult* you! I told you that Jewel didn't mind being outed as a famous person," I explained.

"You told me I didn't know what was best for my own sister!"

"That's not what I said and you know it! Anyway, maybe you *don't* know what's best for her." I tried to say it kindly. "It's not a crime. I'm sure you meant well, but maybe things just changed for Jewel." I considered the way I thought I knew my brother inside out, but he'd surprised me lately.

"Huh," Jasper said. He fiddled with his earpieces like he was dying to plug them back in.

Oh, what was the point of trying to be nice? "I can't believe you, Jasper! How did you sneak off without me hearing you?

How did you even know this space was here?"

Jasper pointed at the ground near where we'd originally been crouching. It was covered by piles of sheets, reaching all the way over to where he was now. I suppose the padding would have made his movements hard to detect. Plus when he'd sneaked off, I'd been busy focusing on how infuriating he was.

"I had a good look around before the lights went off," Jasper said. "And I saw the space behind this canvas. I had my eyes open, Molly."

"Oh yeah?" I yanked at his earphone wires. "Well, I had my *ears* open. I can't believe you were listening to *this* instead of me! I was so worried about you!" My voice wobbled. "I thought you might need my help." Or the kiss of life? Stop it, me! It was obvious he wanted nothing to do with me. "I thought you might be panicking!"

His expression softened. "Oh. Well, I nearly did," he admitted. "That's why I plugged into this. It calmed me down."

I tried not to think about the fact that *I* used to do that. I mean, good for Jasper, that he didn't need me anymore. No, *really*. I think. Yes. No, *really*. Wasn't it what we'd been working towards, when we first started meeting up? I couldn't exactly stay stuck to his side forever, just in case. Especially when he clearly didn't want me there.

"What were you listening to?" I asked, feeling slightly dazed.

He shifted a bit. "Just... a song I wrote and recorded last week," he said. "It's all keyboards so far, but I have lyrics for it in my head. I might get a friend from the music shop involved for the vocals."

"You have friends?" I asked without thinking. Well, I was busy squinting at what I could see of the display on his smartphone. It said: "Track 1: Molly".

"Of course I have – Oh." He followed my gaze and turned the phone over quickly, pressing buttons. "I wasn't listening to *that* track," he mumbled.

"Why does it say my name?" My voice came out extra-loud.

"It, er, doesn't." Jasper sniffed. "It says the name of the song I wrote."

"Called Molly?"

He looked away, his cheeks starting to turn the same colour as the paint streak on them. "Yes." He studied the ceiling. "Nothing to do with you, though," he added hurriedly.

"Oh. OK. What's it about, then?"

Jasper coughed. "Some random girl."

"Some random girl called Molly?"

"Er, yes."

I narrowed my eyes at him. "Can I listen to it?"

"No, you can't."

"Why not? What kind of song is it?"

His face flamed, outdoing the paint now. "It's a... kind of a..." His voice went so quiet that I could barely hear him anymore. "Like a ballad..."

Suddenly I didn't care whether or not I made a fool of myself. After all, it really sounded like Jasper had named a song after me, despite everything he blamed me for. "Is it a love song?" I asked.

Jasper looked horrified. "It's private," he said.

I rolled my eyes. "Like everything about you."

"What's that supposed to mean?"

"What do you *think* it means, Jasper?"

He glowered. "I think you've got some nerve, Molly, after what –"

"But you didn't let me explain the other day," I said. "You wouldn't listen to me!"

"So explain." He folded his arms. "I'm listening now."

Eek. I wasn't expecting that. I took a deep breath. "OK, so... I'm sorry I sneaked into your flat with Ameera – and I'd like to blame her and say that I was only trying to keep an eye on her, but really I was bursting with curiosity too. So I'm sorry. Really sorry." I looked right into his deep, long-lashed, fierce-looking eyes. "But I didn't read your letter. All we did was look at the walls. And I definitely didn't call anyone or tell anyone else!"

"That's no excuse. You shouldn't have –"

"I *know* I shouldn't have! I knew it at the time, I swear! It was just so... tempting." I sighed. "And I want you to know that it was after... that time we kissed. It honestly was. And I was... I was dying to find out more about you! Because I think about you." I gulped. "A lot. OK?" Well, there it was. I'd said it. Talk about laying my heart on the line. Was there anything more I could reveal?

"What about the other guy?" Jasper asked quietly, looking away and picking at a thread on his jeans. "The one you were on a date with... *that* night? The one whose party we went to?" He stared at the ground. "I heard you'd... got together. Since... us."

"Liam?"

Jasper nodded.

I swallowed. "Who told you that?"

"Those friends of yours. The one you sneaked into my flat with – Ameera, right? – and the one who locked us in the attic." He went back to picking at his jeans.

"Wendy?" OMG OMG. I would kill them. How much *more* could they ruin my life? I truly had the worst ex-friends in the world!

Jasper pulled a thread. "I saw them in the mall, and they ran over to talk to me. It sounded like they were trying to fix things between me and you, to be honest. At least at first." He smiled wryly at his jeans. "Ameera was trying to take all the blame for the snooping thing, and they were going on about how upset they were that we'd broken up." He cleared his throat and looked up. "And then they told me you were upset too. So much that you got together with this guy... Then they started having a go at each other for saying the wrong thing, and I left. They're not very tactful, are they?"

"No. They're really not." Oh no!

"So... is it true?"

I wanted to say, *"Do you care if it is?"* I also wanted to run away, possibly to find Wendy and Ameera and kill them. But I'd have to deal with them another time. Right now, I needed to be honest with Jasper, didn't I?

"Yeah, something did happen between me and Liam, kind of. But it's not... It's not..." How much worse could it be to admit this, after everything I'd already said? "It's not right with him. Like the way it is... with you." There. Now I really had told him everything. Argh!

Jasper was silent for ages. The red gloop on my hands was slowly forming globules. I pretended it was fascinating, as if I thought "watching paint dry" had been given a bad press in the past and I was gathering evidence, ready to reveal the truth in a worldwide exclusive.

After so long that I couldn't believe the paint was still wet, Jasper said quietly, "That means a lot to me, Molly. But... but it's still not OK."

"Oh," I said, utterly surprised that the room didn't fill with the sound of my heart breaking. "OK."

"No, Molly, listen." He turned to face me, taking both of my hands and totally ignoring the way he'd now coated his own hands in red paint. My pulse raced as he continued. "Because I have, you know, trust issues. That's what Jewel would say, only she'd say it in a wacky California accent." He smiled a tiny bit. "She's so happy she can be herself again. I suppose I know, deep down, that she's fine with the way things turned out for her."

"She is! She told me!"

"I know it. I do. She loves the limelight, despite the way she asked me to help her hide in Lilyford. I guess it's her true nature, or something." He sighed. "But it makes me scared of losing her again, Molly, you know? And when I get scared I... Well, you've seen me. I overreact. I don't deal well with fear. So I try to avoid it whenever I can." He looked at me as if he wasn't talking about Jewel anymore. As if he was talking about me. And he was scared of losing me.

I shuffled closer, nudging the canvas curtain out of the way as it swayed in our direction. "It'll be OK, Jasper. You'll see." I wanted to add, *"I'll help you through it,"* but I didn't want to push it. I was thinking it, though, and maybe he saw it when he looked at me, because he reached up and touched my face.

I mirrored his touch. This means that we were actually smearing red paint all over each other but I didn't care, and he didn't seem to either. He leaned towards me slightly. I sighed. He shut his eyes. I tilted my head...

And there was a huge crash. Out of the corner of my eye, I saw that the curtain rod which had been holding up the sheet had landed on a stack of paint cans, and they were rolling everywhere. And the canvas itself... was on top of Jasper. I scrabbled about, unfolding the cloth, unearthing him and covering everything in red paint in the process.

Meanwhile there came the unmistakeable sound of a key in the lock... followed by an ear-piercing scream. And the next thing I knew, Art Boy was standing over us, flapping crazily and looking like he was about to pass out with terror.

"Is that... BLOOD?" he yelled, eyes darting about like he wasn't sure whether to run, call the police, or both. He took a closer look. "Argh, I know you! You're Molly – Jewel Stone's friend? And... Jasper Stone?! Are you *murdering* him?"

"Jasper *Brady*," said Jasper, clearly the kind of corpse-to-be who likes to pay attention to detail.

"It's red paint," I told Art Boy, oddly cheered by the fact that he'd got me down as the perpetrator and not the victim here. He was obviously still traumatized by my cheese attack. And rightly so! I was so kick-ass. I remembered that I'd been suspicious of

Art Boy, but he didn't seem particularly scary right now.

"Red paint?" Art Boy looked even more horrified, which was slightly disturbing. "But that's my mural! It's due to be unveiled in a week's time! And now it's splashed with red emulsion and it's too late to do anything about it!" He narrowed his eyes at me. "Molly. You have ruined everything. Again!" His total wuss-out was highly reminiscent of the canapé incident.

"What do you mean, "again"? Actually, what do you mean *at all*? Isn't the mural behind the tarpaulin out there?" I asked.

"Part of it is already on the wall, yes – the part where we depicted all the garbage and detritus left behind by shoppers. The very essence of..." To be honest, I tuned out a bit at that point. I started listening again when Art Boy said, "But I was due to hang this over it! I was going to move it soon, but I've been busy arranging everything! So you see, Molly, *this* is – *was* – a crucial part of my mural. The result of weeks of hard work!"

I looked at the red-streaked canvas. "But it's almost completely blank. Apart from some red stripes and, er, the bits that me and Jasper added."

I looked at Jasper but he was just glowering at Art Boy.

Art Boy sighed. "Yes, it was mostly blank. It's a symbol of the emptiness and soullessness encountered within the commerciality of the mall. The red stripes are emblematic –"

I rolled my eyes. "Art Boy. What *are* you on about?" I was seriously starting to doubt that he was a criminal mastermind at all. "And while we're here..." – *and while you're a bit scared of me,* I didn't add – "...what exactly do you want with Jewel... and Jasper? What's been going on for the past few weeks, anyway?"

"What's been going on is that everything is conspiring against me! And everyone!" Art Boy ranted. "I'm only trying to make my way in the world and have the same advantages as... Oh!" He looked around the room and seemed to spot the additional chaos – all the paint cans I'd overturned and the chair I'd knocked over. "What's happened in here? What have you two done with my artistic materials?"

"You're the one who switched the light off and locked us in here," I said. Ooh, get *me*! I sounded so ultra-bold!

"I didn't know you were in here!"

"Well, we were. And I overheard you tell someone on the phone earlier that you'd *get the twins where you want them*. So what did you mean by that? Were you talking about Jasper and Jewel?"

He gave me a look. "Yes, of course I was. And I meant that I'd get them where we want them. Which is onstage with Zircon next Friday, making a media splash! Jewel's already told me she'll think about it. And if anyone can persuade Jasper, it's her."

Jasper's eyes widened. "No way," he said. "NO way am I doing that, I don't care what Jewel says. I'm not even talking to... *that man*, let alone appearing as his sidekick, posing for the paps, surrounded by his screaming fans. I won't play happy families when we're nothing of the sort!"

Art Boy kicked a paint can over. I thought about pointing out that he was now sabotaging *himself*, but I was too intrigued by what happened next.

Art Boy yelled, "You're so selfish, Jasper Stone!"

Of course, Jasper corrected him immediately. "Brady," he

announced. "My last name is Brady."

"It's Stone!" Art Boy insisted. "And that's *our father* you're talking about! So show some respect!"

Friday 8th July, evening
Taking action at The Lilies eco-mall, Lilyford, Part Two

I had to take a little break there because writing it out made me feel stunned all over again.

Art Boy was Jasper and Jewel's brother?!

???!!!!

Multiplied by a thousand!!!

"Jasper?" I said, but he'd stood up and was halfway to the door.

"I'm leaving," he said, stating the obvious. "I should never have come in here in the first place. I want nothing to do with him, Molly, and I'm... I'm so glad you're not involved with him after all."

I was just standing there like a lemon – except that I was painted red, so I was more like a tomato. My tomato face was probably showing signs of shock.

"But Wikipedia didn't say anything about an older brother," I mumbled, and immediately wished I hadn't.

Jasper stopped and glared at me. "Have you been cyber-stalking me? Honestly, Molly..." His shoulders drooped like he'd had enough. He shook his head, turned and walked away.

Out of my life. Again. With his smartphone containing the song he'd written about some random girl called Molly.

I wanted to run after him. I wanted to get back to that moment before the mural fell and Art Boy burst in. I was sure we'd been on the brink of kissing.

But I didn't move. I think... I think I was scared of the rejection. So maybe I wasn't quite so kick-ass after all.

Art Boy was watching me. "You and Jasper are a couple, huh?" he said. "I didn't realize." He sighed. "Can't you talk to him? Persuade him to go on for the gig? I promised Zircon." He pouted like a small boy.

Does it look to you like I can persuade Jasper to do anything? I thought, but I said, "I didn't realize you were Jasper and Jewel's brother."

Art Boy shrugged. He looked a bit sorry for himself. "Well, I wasn't when you first met me."

"What?" This was making less and less sense. "Surely you either are someone's brother or you're not?"

"Yes, usually. Unless your mother..." He hesitated. "Your semi-estranged mother is in a relationship with a rock star. And then the star has a horrible accident – which I was really sad about, of course, though I don't really know him. But then he proposed to her in hospital and they got secretly married." His eyes shone. "That's when Zircon became my dad."

"Your step-dad, surely?"

"If you like," Art Boy said. "Dad sounds much better for publicity. Except that it's all a big secret, which doesn't help at all with promotion. But I think I've persuaded them that it's OK to come clean about the secret marriage when he's over here. The press will love it. And I'll get the whole family onstage at the unveiling, and..." He went all dreamy. "It will guarantee me entry to the upper levels of the art world, I'm sure of it."

"Did Jewel really agree to this?"

"She seemed OK about it last time I spoke to her," he said. "I like Jewel, don't get me wrong – I mean, we'd met a few times before in California and Mexico, where my mother's from, as well as in Lilyford, where I live now." He paused and thought a bit. "But I was very disappointed that Jewel originally refused to help me publicize my art. I hired a camera crew to cover my private view before I was officially related to her, you know – I thought I could gather interest in the footage if someone famous was present. But Jewel was upset about the cameras, which I know was Jasper's fault, and then she did a runner, thanks to you."

I glared at Art Boy. "Jasper hates the thought of anyone exploiting his family for their own gain," I told him. I was starting to see what he meant, actually.

"But I'm not exploiting anyone!" Art Boy said, looking a bit shocked. "It's an opportunity, isn't it?" He sighed. "Jasper and Jewel have had this possibility all their life, but for me it's new. Surely it's only fair that I get to ride the wave of The Red Sardonyx fame a bit? And after all, I'm the artist in the family. I'm the one that arranged for Zircon to be here for the unveiling, and the one who told the paparazzi about Jewel..."

He'd admitted it! "But you knew Jewel didn't want that."

"Oh, I know she thought she wanted to hide, but she didn't really. Not deep down. Jewel's like me. She wants the fame. I did her a favour. I don't understand Jasper at all, though. Maybe you can make him see things from my point of view? I promised Zircon that I'd get him onstage and I don't want to let him down, now that he's agreed to get me all this publicity!" He glanced at me. "Don't look so shocked, Molly. I mean, I have to do what I can to stand out from the crowd, don't I?"

I'm not quite sure what got into me then. Maybe it was because he interrupted me and Jasper earlier, or because of all the heartache I'd had when Jasper thought I was the one who'd called the paps, when it was Art Boy all along and Rukshana was right. Come to think of it, it was Art Boy who'd got me snooping in Jasper's flat in the first place, albeit indirectly, with the unsubtle hints he'd been dropping to girls that he wanted to impress.

Or maybe it was just because Art Boy was standing in front of me looking smug and pretentious, and he was perfectly happy with the idea of using my friends. And he was even asking me to get involved.

I reached down behind me and picked up the half-spilled container of red emulsion – the paint that had now dried on me, and probably on Jasper, too. But there was plenty left in the tin, as I found out when I emptied it over Art Boy's head.

It ran in thick globs down his trendy Art Boy haircut as he opened his mouth in shock, promptly closing it again as the paint trickled down his face.

"How's that for standing out from the crowd?" I said.

I noticed there was still a little paint left in the tin, so I threw it at the precious mural. It landed in spatters that made Art Boy whimper.

"And leave Jasper and Jewel alone," I added before I walked out and went home for a wash.

So maybe I was fairly kick-ass after all.

Saturday 9th July

Family weirdness at the Hart residence, 5th floor, The Lilies eco-mall, Lilyford

Bumped into Jamie on his way to work this morning. He was looking a bit miserable, so I asked him what was wrong and he said, "It won't be any fun without Liam."

"But he's still here!" I said, and I couldn't believe I'd actually kind of forgotten that, after yesterday's excitement. Not that it made any difference. I knew for sure now that however I felt about Liam, it was nothing compared to my feelings for Jasper. And it probably never would be. Maybe Jasper and I would never manage to sort things out but that was OK. I wouldn't fall into Liam's arms just because I could. In fact, I could probably do with some time alone. I felt weirdly calm about it all and I smiled proudly to myself. Oh, if only Wendy and Ameera could hear my thoughts now – how far from an empty-headed mall girl was *I*?

"Uh, Measly?" Jamie was waving his hand in front of my face. "Have you heard a word I've said or have you been daydreaming about winning a gold medal in shopping or something?"

"In *shopping*? That sounds more like Ameera's chosen sport. Jamie, do you know me at all?"

"I know plenty! Too much!" He ruffled my hair and I had a sudden urge to throw paint at him, too, but there was none around. "What I was saying is that I know Liam's still in Lilyford right now, and I'm seeing him tonight. But I meant that I'll miss him at *work*. I was thinking of giving up that Saturday job, you know."

"Just because Liam's leaving?" I asked.

"Kind of," Jamie answered. "In the sense that I thought I'd get a summer job in Spain instead." He grinned. "You want to come with me, Molly? At least for a bit? The flights are really cheap and Dad will give us spending money, and Liam's family have loads of space. Don't worry about Liam – he knows you're just friends and he's OK with it."

"Oh, because of Carmelita?"

Jamie looked confused. "What?"

"Nothing. Yeah, I don't know. Maybe. I'll think about it. What does Mum say?"

"I haven't told her, but I think she'll be happy to have us out of her way for a bit. She has plans to take over the mall, or something. She was buzzing about it yesterday, saying that her previous project has fallen through, but she's met a definite new business partner now and it's all coming together."

I smiled. Wow, good for Mum.

"She says she just needs another injection of funds." Jamie gave me a look. "Which she could have if she stopped being stubborn and accepted Dad's offer. But I can't persuade her. Or not by myself, anyway." He looked at his phone. "Anyway, got to go, Measly! I think I'll hand in my notice today – can't wait!"

I swear he practically skipped out of the door.

I realized I truly was starting to *like* my brother. It was the weirdest feeling.

Sunday 10th July

After a day with Dad and Nan

Great day at Dad's. Am so proud of myself that I'm not moping about my lost relationship with Jasper, or my lost friendships with Wendy and Ameera. I am utterly calm and mature; I'm like a whole new Molly.

I let Nan make a big fuss of me and feed me extra biscuits, though, after she asked me, "How are things going with your mystery man?" I told her, very maturely and with just the smallest hint of a sob, that we'd mutually decided to go our separate ways.

"Young love," Nan said, sounding like an elderly person for once in her life. "There's a nice young couple in my tae kwon do class who remind me of you," she added, instantly knocking at least forty years off her previous age.

"Why? They like attacking people?" I asked, thinking about Art Boy and the paint. Well, Nan was talking about a martial arts class, after all.

"No. Well, yes, but I meant that they're scared of what it means to be together," Nan said. "They're always dancing around, breaking up and then making up every other lesson. It's sad to watch them hurt each other. I think they put themselves under too much pressure – they want everything to be perfect and happy-ever-after, and of course it isn't. But there's no law to say you can't commit just for a month or two. It's probably best to keep it short-term when you're in your teens."

"Nan!" I said. I swear I have the weirdest grandmother in the world. Isn't she supposed to wholeheartedly disapprove of anyone under the age of twenty doing anything? Let alone having short-term relationships with each other!

Besides, out of me and Jasper, I wasn't the one who was scared. Was I?

Dad took me aside after that and asked me whether I'd spoken to my mother about the offer he'd made, which she was stubbornly refusing.

"Me?" I asked. "Why would I speak to her about money, unless I'm asking her for a tenner?"

Dad sighed and said, "Never mind."

But I thought about it again when I got home and got the shock of my life. (Well, of my day.)

Mum was sitting in her usual Sunday afternoon position in front of the television. But next to her was Katie Brady, Jewel and Jasper's mum. She was smiling, sipping from a large mug of tea and looking loads better than she had the last time I'd seen her.

"Hello!" I said brightly, before I remembered that I might be unpopular in her house for various reasons.

She seemed all right with me, though. And after Mum had motioned to me to sit down, the two of them told me that they were planning on going into business together. Apparently they'd met at a beauty shop that Mum was checking out – Katie was trying to make an effort to do stuff for herself – and they'd got talking.

Mum had then totally abandoned her beauty shop idea – "I'm not sure I liked what they were selling, Molly" – and decided to go into partnership to start a proper Katie Brady Music School instead. They were both beaming about it. "There's a long way to go before we get it sorted – we're lacking funds, for a start, and my redundancy payment doesn't quite cover my share. But we both feel really good about the decision," Mum told me happily.

I had a niggling worry that Mum was doing this because of our neighbour's new-found fame and exposure. What if she was as bad as Art Boy? So I decided to ask her after Katie Brady had left.

She put my mind at rest instantly. "No way, Molly. Katie's not courting publicity, and she never has. She's hoping things will die down as soon as this Friday is over. She really has nothing to do with her ex. We have a lot in common." She laughed. "Like a lack of money and a refusal to let our exes help."

So then I remembered what Dad – and Jamie – had hinted at. They wanted me to persuade Mum to take the money, didn't they? But I didn't want to do that... Did I? I thought about Nan's words.

"Hey, Mum," I said. "Why don't you let Dad give you the money, but just short-term? Like, for a month or two? You don't have to take it forever, do you? I mean, you could pay him back when things take off, which I'm sure they will." I thought a bit. "And I could help you over the summer, if you like?" It might be awkward, working with Jasper's mum. But I was sure I could handle it.

Mum gave me a long look. "Goodness, Molly, you're growing up, aren't you?"

So then I had a long moan about what she'd cooked for dinner, just to prove that I hadn't changed *that* much.

Thursday, 14th July

After a day at West Lilyford Community College

School is getting more and more ridiculous as we get closer to the end of term. Even the *teachers* have mentally checked out now, and we've spent half of our lessons watching DVDs and doing word searches. Honestly, I don't know why they don't just give up and shut school a couple of weeks early. Though then I suppose all the messing about would just start earlier. So they could shorten the term a bit more? And so on... I'm just saying.

Anyway, the lack of schoolwork has meant an even greater focus on social lives and gossip. The biggest piece of news I heard was from Livvy, Tasha's friend, who was talking all excitedly to her friends because Tasha is now going out with a "hot artist" who has "celebrity connections". The guy definitely sounds a lot like Art Boy, which kind of makes me smile. They deserve each other. I'm so glad Jamie's mostly over Tasha.

I'm still ignoring Wendy and Ameera, but slightly more half-heartedly because I think they're desperate to try to make amends with me. Jewel put the idea in my head when I had a big moan to her about the way they'd told Jasper about Liam. I was halfway through telling her when I realized that I was talking about her brother and I should probably shut up, but she seemed to think it was all hilarious. Then she said, "OK, Molly, I'm starting to see what you mean about your friends. They're their own worst enemies most of the time, aren't they?" She laughed. "Listen, maybe you should give them another chance? But make sure they know you won't stand for any of that 'mall girl' nonsense ever again."

"Too right, I won't!" I said.

"And make sure Ameera stands up for herself too," Jewel added. "Your friend Wendy can be so forceful."

"She sure can," I agreed, trying not to think about the time Jasper and I had followed her into the attic at Liam's house.

"And one last thing. As your last remaining official friend, I should warn you that they're plotting something."

"What?"

"Wendy and Ameera. I overheard them in the restroom. They're planning to get you and Jasper back together. I'm not sure when or how. But Ameera asked me for Jasper's phone number and I gave it to her. You've been warned."

I groaned. A lot.

I also suddenly found myself missing Wendy and Ameera like mad. Even when Jewel invited me to spend part of the summer with her in Los Angeles.

"Seriously? California?" OMG – how fantastic would that be?

Jewel smiled. "Jasper might be coming too. Dad invited him in that letter, and I've spoken to him about it. He's not sure. But he didn't say no."

"Seriously? Jasper's actually considering... seeing his dad?" And going on a plane? Wow!

"I *know,* right? I have you to thank for this, Molly. I would never have tried to persuade him if you hadn't said he was thinking of coming to LA after the accident. But when I talked to him about it, he didn't bite my head off, even though he still has typical Jasper issues." She sighed. "This is huge."

"Huge," I echoed.

Thursday 14th July, later

Back from The Lilies eco-mall, Lilyford

It happened in the mall after school. Even though I'd been half expecting it, I was still surprised when I got a weird text from an unknown number. I wondered if it had come from Wendy's brother's phone, or one of Ameera's sisters'. The text said, "Meet @ 5 by Service Entrance B! URGENT – u must b there!"

Service Entrance B? That was only one of the mall's popular snogging spots. I shook my head at Wendy and Ameera's obviousness.

This didn't stop me turning up, though. Or my heart pounding as I waited. And waited. What if he didn't show up? I could imagine Wendy and Ameera trying to blag their way up to the flats to drag Jasper here themselves. I was kind of laughing inwardly to myself about it when he appeared beside me.

"Molly! It's you! Did you text me from a different phone?" Jasper said in an over-loud voice.

"No. Wendy and Ameera are trying to fix us up," I answered quietly. My heart sank at the way he wasn't meeting my eye. But then I noticed that he was looking towards a nearby pillar, where two figures were hiding (badly), giggling loudly and pulling at each other as they took it in turns to peer out at us.

Jasper moved closer. "I know," he whispered. "Jewel warned me."

Jewel told him! And he came anyway!

"She warned me too."

He gave a tiny smile, like maybe he was thinking what I'd just thought. "Look, Molly, about the other day..."

"I emptied a pot of red paint on Art Boy's head after you left," I told him.

His smile spread. "You're awesome." Then he straightened his face. "But Molly, I meant what I said."

"What did you say?"

"About you and me. How I didn't think it could... work out..."

"My nan says you don't have to commit," I told him in a big rush of words I hadn't thought through at all. "Or you do, but just for a month. Or something. You can just try it out! Money back guarantee!" I wasn't actually doing a very good job of representing what Nan had said at all.

He frowned. "You've been talking to your nan about me?"

"Yes. No. Not exactly." I took a deep breath. "The point is, don't worry. I think that was the point, anyway."

In the distance, the giggling grew louder.

"Listen, Jasper?" I moved closer and reached up to whisper in his ear. "Please will you pretend to kiss me so that they stop bugging us?"

"No," he said. "I won't."

I rolled my eyes. Honestly – he was the most stubborn boy in the world!

He'd also put his arms around me and was lowering his head towards mine, gazing right into my eyes. "I'll kiss you properly because I really, really want to."

And he did.

He was so stubborn. He was so gorgeous.

We were so back together.

For now.

Friday 15th July

Just back from West Lilyford Community College

I found Wendy and Ameera and gave them both a massive hug. When I told them about yesterday at the mall, they pretended that they didn't know what I was talking about for at least five minutes. Then it all burst out of them, especially Ameera who cannot keep a secret to save her life.

I let them think they were responsible for reuniting me with Jasper – well, in a weird way, they were – and then I told them both all the things I'd discussed with Jewel, about how I wasn't going to stand for that "mall girl" stuff anymore, not if we were going to stay friends.

"And besides, if I *am* a mall girl, then I'm proud of it," I told them. "I'm me, you know? I might live in a mall but I have a mind of my own."

They were falling over themselves to agree with me, and Wendy apologized like crazy for the Liam thing, and for everything. Then *I* squeaked in a small apology for the way I'd told Jamie about Wendy only being after his body, and Wendy didn't even get remotely upset at the memory. I have no idea how long all this peacetime will last.

Friends are great, but they're also weird. I'm not completely convinced that you choose them any more than you choose your family. You just deal with what you've got.

Later at the mall, my home, where I'm a mall girl and proud of it

There was a band playing in the mall – a tribute group for The Red Sardonynx – and I'd arranged to meet my friends there later. (Wendy! Ameera! BFFs again! Yay!)

First I was meeting Jasper, who'd texted asking me to meet him by Service Entrance D. It was a bit early yet for Zircon and the official mural unveiling, but then I didn't think Jasper wanted to go to that anyway. He'd made it pretty clear that he was going to avoid his dad, at least in the presence of the media.

"Molly! You have to see this," Jasper said as soon as I walked up to him. He gestured to a gap behind the tarpaulin. "We can squeeze in there. I checked."

"Oh, are you trying to get me alone in a confined space again?" I teased.

His eyes sparkled as he grinned shyly. "Maybe. But no, I wanted you to see this right now, first. Before everyone else starts going on about how fantastic it is. Besides, I don't want my dad to see I'm here."

I gave him a look.

"I know, I *know*. I'll talk to him, Molly, I promise. But on my own terms, and not tonight, OK? Even Jewel has decided not to do the stage thing. And I want to speak to Dad away from the cameras, and I don't want to give his so-called stepson the satisfaction of seeing us, you know?"

I nodded. I understood.

I let Jasper pull me behind the tarpaulin and we sat together on the mall floor, leaning into each other as we craned upwards at the mural. It was spectacular, but not exactly in a good way. It was a painting of a mound of chocolate wrappers, drinks containers from the food court, banana skins, orange peel, plastic bags and thousands of other things that regularly get thrown away in a typical day at The Lilies. It looked like a different person had painted every single piece, with weirdly mixed results. Hanging over half of it was the canvas that Jasper and I had ruined, splashed red and giving the whole thing an even odder effect.

"OMG," I said. "The mural is rubbish! Quite literally *rubbish*."

"Maybe that was the point," Jasper mused.

"He's definitely telling us something deep... about something," I agreed. "It's so bad that it's almost good, don't you think? You have to hand it to Art Boy."

Jasper looked at me. "*What* do you keep calling him?"

Oh. Oops. "Art..."

"Yes, yes. After that!"

"Boy?" I said tentatively.

"I thought that's what you said! I've heard you say it before. So why do you call him 'boy'?" he asked.

"Er... because he's male. And not that old," I explained. What was wrong with him? "You know. He's a boy? Who's into art? Like, you'd be Music Boy. Or Keyboard Boy." Or Gorgeous Boy, My Boyfriend Boy. I gripped his hand. Then I kissed him.

He was blushing when I pulled away, which was mega-cute. "Oh. I thought you'd just majorly misunderstood his last name."

"What do you mean, his last name? His first name's not Art, is it?" I laughed.

Jasper stared at me. "Er... yes."

"You have *got* to be kidding me! Art Boy's name is *Art*?"

"Art. Yes. Short for Arturo. His mum's from Mexico and it's a family name."

"No WAY!" I giggled. "Oh, please tell me his last name is Boy?" At this point, I may have snorted.

He shook his head at my laughter, but he was smiling. "No. Otherwise we wouldn't be having this conversation, would we?"

I just laughed in response.

"It's Guy. Art Guy."

"*No*! No, Art Boy cannot be called *Art Guy*! That's crazy."

"But you must have heard people say his name, Molly? You first met him a few weeks ago, didn't you? And I bet people have been talking about him."

I thought about it. "Rukshana called him "that art guy", I think." I thought a bit more. "And Jewel did."

"Well, there you go. Of course they did, because that's his name. He moved to Lilyford for the art school at Dad's suggestion – it was the college Mum used to go to. But Art himself has lived all over the place – a bit with his mum in Mexico, and some boarding schools. Jewel met him a few times through Dad, but I wanted nothing to do with him. I was horrified when Jewel told me she was actually hanging around with him, but I guess she didn't have many friends around here. Not then, anyway."

"You were right about him, though," I pointed out. "He tried to use Jewel, and he caused a lot of trouble."

"I know," Jasper said. "Though I suppose he's been... jealous of us, or something."

I nudged him. "You're getting way more forgiving, Jasper," I pointed out, only slightly teasing.

He looked thoughtful. "I guess so. Really, though, I've been thinking about how Art is the reason Dad knew about The Lilies in the first place, and the reason we moved here. Art recommended it to Dad." He rolled his eyes. "This mall is the most rock and roll place he could find for us without making me move schools."

It was so strange to hear Jasper talk freely about his life like this. "But your dad was the one who suggested Lilyford College to Art Boy," I pointed out. Then I giggled. "So Art Boy's name is really Art?" I couldn't seem to let it go.

"Yes. And I suppose if it wasn't for Art – and Dad – my family wouldn't have moved into the mall, and maybe we wouldn't be here right now. Me and you." He pulled me closer and looked deep into my eyes.

I was still laughing when I murmured, "Yay for Art."

Jasper drew me into a long, passionate kiss, which finally stopped my giggles. I needed all my energy for kissing him back.

I wasn't sure how much time passed before Zircon whipped off the tarpaulin to reveal Art Guy's mural (slightly mutilated by red splashes). I do know that Jasper and I just managed to scramble out and sneak away before the cameras took several shots of us totally meshed together by the newly decorated Service Entrance D. I imagined a headline inspired by Wendy. *"Mall Girl meets Mall Boy at The Lilies!"*

I held Jasper's hand tightly as we walked off into the sunset... under the mall's artificial lighting.

We walked around a bit to avoid the media frenzy, and then we headed for the centre of The Lilies, where a group of people had already abandoned the unveiling to listen to The Red

Sardonyx tribute band. They were dancing madly, and clearly having the best time. I spotted Mum and Katie doing a middle-aged shuffle at the side. They looked more like friends than business partners. Good for them. I realized that was probably what they needed – someone to talk to, someone who'd been divorced and was mothering ungrateful teenagers and who understood. As long as they didn't talk about me and Jasper too much. Cringe.

Nearer to the stage I spotted a blur of bouncing, happy people. I managed to pick out Jewel, Ameera and Wendy. And Jamie.

All my friends.

Jasper and I walked over to join them.

So I don't know what I'll do with my summer. Maybe I'll go with Jasper and Jewel to the States, or maybe I'll go with Jamie to Spain, just for fun. Or maybe I'll stay in Lilyford, help my mum and enjoy the mall – my home. I'm looking forward to deciding all by myself, because I might be a mall girl but I'm not remotely mindless, and whatever I do, I know it will be great.

I was way wrong at the start of this diary. My life is SO not over.

About the Author

Luisa Plaja has always loved stories, and began writing for magazines when she was a teenager. She is the author of many teen novels, including *Split by a Kiss* and *Kiss Date Love Hate*, and her books have been translated into several languages. As well as writing fiction, Luisa edits the teen website Chicklish and helps to run book clubs in libraries.

Luisa was born in Glasgow, grew up in Sicily and London, and now lives in Devon. She has two children and a house full of books.